WANDERLUST

A *Beautiful*
AMERICANS NOVEL

WANDERLUST

A *Beautiful* AMERICANS NOVEL

by lucy silag

razOr bill

AN IMPRINT OF PENGUIN GROUP (USA) Inc.

Wanderlust

RAZORBILL

Published by the Penguin Group
Penguin Young Readers Group
345 Hudson Street, New York, New York 10014, U.S.A.
Penguin Group (USA) Inc., 375 Hudson Street, New York, New York 10014, U.S.A.
Penguin Group (Canada), 90 Eglinton Avenue East, Suite 700, Toronto, Ontario, Canada
M4P 2Y3 (a division of Pearson Penguin Canada Inc.)
Penguin Books Ltd, 80 Strand, London WC2R 0RL, England
Penguin Ireland, 25 St Stephen's Green, Dublin 2, Ireland (a division of Penguin Books Ltd)
Penguin Group (Australia), 250 Camberwell Road, Camberwell, Victoria 3124,
Australia (a division of Pearson Australia Group Pty Ltd)
Penguin Books India Pvt Ltd, 11 Community Centre, Panchsheel Park, New Delhi—110
017, India
Penguin Group (NZ), 67 Apollo Drive, Rosedale, North Shore 0632, New Zealand
(a division of Pearson New Zealand Ltd.)
Penguin Books (South Africa) (Pty) Ltd, 24 Sturdee Avenue, Rosebank, Johannesburg 2196,
South Africa
Penguin Books Ltd, Registered Offices: 80 Strand, London WC2R 0RL, England

10 9 8 7 6 5 4 3 2 1

Razorbill hardcover ISBN: 9781595142238
Razorbill paperback ISBN: 9781595142870

Library of Congress Cataloging-in-Publication Data

Silag, Lucy.
Wanderlust : a Beautiful Americans novel / by Lucy Silag.
      p. cm.
Summary: Alex, Zack, Olivia, and Jay, four high school students on a study
abroad program in Paris, continue to enjoy their glamourous lifestyle while
trying to save their missing friend, PJ, before it is too late.
ISBN 978-1-59514-223-8 (alk. paper)
[1. Foreign study—Fiction. 2. Missing persons—Fiction. 3.
Secrets—Fiction. 4. Interpersonal relations—Fiction. 5. Paris
(France)—Fiction. 6. France—Fiction.] I. Title.
PZ7.S5793Wan 2009
[Fic]—dc22
                                    2009019040

Printed in the United States of America

For my mom

NOËL
Christmas

1. PJ

Wish You Were Here

ell, Annabel, I guess you got me to read this stupid book after all. I finally close my sister's dog-eared copy of *Madame Bovary*, the French classic by Gustave Flaubert. It was my sister's favorite. I lay it on my lap. I stare at the soft pastel rendering of the main character on its battered cover.

The book shakes. I can't stop my left leg, which is crossed on top of the right one, from twitching. My feet ache to move. To flee. This morning, tramping through the snow, staring straight ahead into the sparkling night streets of the seventeenth arrondissement—then the eighth, then the ninth, then finally the tenth—I felt *good*. I felt terrible, too, with my stomach roiling and every so often a tear melting the frost on my cheeks, but I felt myself getting farther away from Ternes, and closer, ever closer, to Annabel.

Annabel loved this book, but I can't really see why. Emma Bovary is a silly woman who creates her own downfall because she can't see how good she has it. She throws it all away for a little excitement in Rouen.

Is it possible? Could Annabel actually *admire* the character of Emma Bovary? Does she relate to her?

I pull my long hair from its ponytail, greasy from travel and the longest night of my life. Then I put my knit hat on. The periwinkle fibers of the handspun yarn my mom used are too bright, too cheery, for a day like today. My mom can't know where I am. She would be devastated if she knew I wasn't safe at home with my new French family. But if she *did*, I think it would comfort her to know this hat she made is keeping my head warm as I go to find my sister. I yank the ribbing down over my eyes. If only I could get warm again. If only I could shut the world out as easily as I pull my hat down over my face.

Fidgeting, I push my hat back up and hunt for my gloves. One minute I'm cold. The next minute I'm boiling hot, trying to shed my warm garments and finally feel some fresh air on my skin. Every laundry tag on my clothing irritates my dry, chapped skin. Every noise in the train car shakes me to my core. I'm thirsty. I spent three whole euros on a café noir at the Gare du Nord. I don't want to waste any more money on water until I get to Rouen. Which should have been hours ago.

I look again at *Madame Bovary*.

Maybe Annabel read Emma's famous line—"Oh, why, dear God, did I marry him?"—and got a sharp chill, wondering if, like Emma, she would come to regret her own marriage. Maybe *Madame Bovary* was the cautionary tale that sent my sister running out of town the day she was supposed to marry her longtime boyfriend, Dave.

Normandy, Gustave Flaubert's home province, slowly rolls by out the window next to me, gray and gloomy just the way he wrote it to be. Early this morning, as the fog lifted over the gently rolling hills of this coastal region, I read of Emma traipsing through similarly misty landscapes to meet her first lover. The train rolls slowly but smoothly north toward Rouen. This is where Emma went to meet Léon, her second lover. Rouen was where Emma got swept away by her desperate fantasy of another, more romantic life. I can't help but feel a sense of foreboding that Annabel, whatever her intentions in running away might have been, has been carried to Rouen to meet a similar fate. And now I'm running away to Rouen, too, because I saw that Annabel had circled the name of the town in her book. What good will meet me here, with the tragic *Madame Bovary* as my introduction to this strange, sleepy place?

The train lurches and thuds. It comes to a complete stop in a wide, snowy field many miles from any station. I stare out the window, willing the train to go on. *Please.*

The train still has not started moving again after a half hour.

The conductor makes a fuzzy announcement. We're delayed. We will not be in Rouen anytime soon. Rouen—a city that should only be an hour from Paris. An hour!

This train is too small, too narrow. I stumble over to the small, stinky lavatory just beyond the train compartment doorway. I read the French admonishment to only use the facilities when the train is in motion, but I *have* to go. Icy wind slips between the cracks in the window and under the flimsy bathroom door. It feels like the whole world has frozen.

Just as I zip up my jeans, the train rumbles forward, moving ahead and then to the right in an odd motion. I lose my balance for a moment. I imagine falling out of the bathroom, out the exit door of the train, and landing in a snowdrift. I'd walk for miles and never find anyone. I'd never find Annabel. I don't even have a cell phone. I imagine dying, cold and alone, and no one ever finding *me*. No one could even send my body back home to my parents to bury. And my parents wouldn't be able to bury me, anyhow, since they'll be in jail until they're too old to remember me. Alzheimer's runs in both of their families.

Only Annabel would remember me. She'd wonder why I never got her message. She'd wonder what ever happened to that book she gave me. She'd never know it was tucked into my jeans pocket. The pocket of a dead girl, frozen in the snow, who nobody ever identified.

I shake my head. These are the thoughts of a crazy person.

I can't see out of the cloudy brushed glass of the lavatory window. We are moving again—not quickly, but fairly steadily toward some place where I can get off this horrible train. I hurry to wash my hands under burningly cold sink water and return to my seat so I can find out what's going on. We are now moving east rather than north. The sun is behind us, about to set for the day.

I haven't eaten anything, nor have I slept since the night before last night. All of today got buried in *Madame Bovary*, in getting to Rouen. In forgetting the terrible events of last night.

Breathe, I coach myself. I can't let panic win. *Be strong. Breathe.*

When I close my eyes, sleep trying to overtake me, I find that I cannot think of anything but an old man's hands trying to grope at my body. I hear a woman's shriek and feel the sting of hot tea being thrown at me

11

in vicious anger. This was a Christmas Eve like no other. I had no choice but to run. I had to.

"Pardon?" Startled, agitated, I open my eyes to find a young, stocky guy in a baseball cap standing in the aisle. He's looking quizzically at me.

"Oui?" I respond. My hands go to the throat of my black wool coat. It feels tight, like it is trapping me.

"I think you are in my seat," he says, his English good but accented with a rich French inflection that's so familiar after living with the Marquets. I shake my head. I just want this guy to go away.

"It's not a problem," he continues with a smile. He gestures at the open seats all around us. "But the conductor might not like it. You know how the train personnel can be."

Seats on French trains are assigned, and the guy is right—the railway staff are sticklers for every passenger sitting in the correct seat. But I'm confused. I've been sitting here all morning. *Voiture* 25, *place* 61, just like it says on my ticket. Except . . .

Except that somehow I've ended up in *Voiture* 24, I infer as I look at the placard above the window. I must have gone in the wrong direction coming out of the bathroom.

"Oh!" I say, the word guttural and self-conscious. "I'm so sorry. I went to the wrong . . ."

"It's okay by me." The guy laughs. He has pale skin and large features, a different sort of aspect than most of the French guys at the Lycée. "No need to worry. It's not every day I come back from the snack car to find a beautiful American sitting in my seat. It makes this epic journey that much more bearable." For some reason, with his baseball cap and large build, he feels like an American to me, familiar like the guys from my program. Like Jay.

I warily smile back at him, despite my instinct not to trust him, not to trust anyone. *"Excusez-moi."* I rise to my feet, avoiding the guy's level eye contact.

"No, please, stay." He beckons for me to reseat myself. He sits down across the aisle from me. "Be my guest."

I look back toward the train car where I came from. I desperately want to go back to the silent solitude of my train ride before I sat in this guy's seat. But I can't be rude. I can't appear shifty. "Maybe for a moment," I say, keeping my voice light and airy so that it won't betray the thick layer of nervous sweat under my heavy wool cardigan. My dad's old sweater usually brings me so much comfort. Not today. Nothing could bring me comfort today except finding Annabel.

"So there's a strike? Is that what the problem is?" I switch over to speaking in French.

"Ah, oui," the guy answers. "You haven't really been to France if you haven't endured one of our train strikes. They always happen right when you need to get somewhere, and they usually last for weeks. I hope you are not in a hurry to be in Rouen."

Oh, but I am, I respond silently. I know not to vent to him. I can keep it inside until I get to Rouen. *Just let me get there.*

The power lines and rusty tracks outside the window indicate that we are approaching a station. The tattered sign hanging on the platform doesn't say Rouen, as I briefly hoped despite our changing direction. It says Forges-les-Eaux. I've never heard of this place. It looks small and desolate. Perhaps it would be palatable in the mild summer months. Now it's forgotten in the midst of a dark French winter.

All the train doors open. Last night, it snowed in Paris for the first time this winter, covering the city in an icy frosting. Here, it looks like it has been snowing for weeks. Some of the disconnected train cars sitting on the rails are buried in white.

The announcer comes back on the intercom. He orders all passengers to get off the train. The train will not be making any more stops. This train will terminate *ici*. The few people aboard grumble and poke around in their pockets for their cell phones.

"Quoi?" I gasp. I turn around to look back at the guy in the baseball cap to confirm that I've heard this right. He's gone. There's absolutely no trace that he was ever there at all.

In the frigid station, its cafés and bathrooms closed for the holidays, I scan a map of Normandy on the wall to see how far from Rouen I am. A few railway agents are wandering around the station, hurrying to close it down.

"Excusez-moi?" I stop one of them, a portly man in a dingy blue uniform. He's smoking a cigarette, ashing on the stained stone floor.

"We are on strike! *En grève!*" the man snaps at me. "*Pas de trains!* Consult the bus directory, *s'il vous plaît!*" He points at a map, old and brown at the edges, tacked on the opposite wall.

I anxiously scan the map. I bite my lip hard. I enjoy the pain in a weird way. I find Paris, then Rouen, then Forges-les-Eaux. I close my eyes. When I open them again, the map has not changed.

I'm horrified to see that it is like I suspected. The train I had been on had gone in the wrong direction. This set me off course by many kilometers. The bus desk, a small window with a sign reading L'AUTOBUS RÉGIONAL above it, is shuttered until the morning.

For the first time since I ran out of the Marquets' townhouse in the middle of the night, I regret my decision to leave Paris. Only an idiot would get herself marooned in this tiny village in Normandy on Christmas.

But no, I think when I remember how M. Marquet tried to slide his fat hands all over me in the dimly lit bedroom where I stayed in his swanky house in Ternes. The memory is blurred, patchy from lack of sleep, but I know, down to my rapidly freezing toes, that anywhere, even Forges-les-Eaux, is better than that miserable place I used to live.

Also stuck at the station is another girl about my age. Perhaps she's a little older. She's blond like me. My hair is long, unkempt, but her hair is cut short in a funky, artsy style that matches her bright outfit. She consults a pocket timetable near the entrance to the train station. Her face, all lines and angles like a print model, is dashed with worry as she pads a message into her cell phone.

The girl smiles widely when her phone beeps with a favorable text reply. She's about to open the heavy dark wooden door to the parking lot when she looks up and catches my eye. I can't help it. I'm staring at her plaintively. The blond girl shivers, looks at her watch, and again surveys the empty station around us.

She comes over to me, her light, almost invisible eyebrows furrowed together. "They are about to lock up the station," she tells me in French. "You can't stay here."

"I know," I say, my throat dry and crackling from the icy weather. "I need to get to Rouen. I *have* to get there."

"My brother lives in Gournay-en-Bray. It's not too far away," she says, hesitation flickering in her voice. "It's not Rouen . . . but you can get the commuter train from there. He's going to pick me up."

"Oh," I say. I'm not following.

"Do you want a ride?" she says. "You can't stay here," she says again. She obviously thinks I'm slow, a stupid American.

"Yes." I breathe gratefully. "But wait a second. Aren't all the trains on strike?"

"Just the intercity and international trains," the blond girl says. "The locals are going. I think there is one more to Rouen tonight. We'll have to hurry."

I follow her out to the curb, where she lights up a cigarette and offers one to me. I shake my head.

I wonder what Alex would do in this situation.

Alex wouldn't ever be in a jam like this. She'd have called a car service to pick her up as soon as she heard the word *grève*. Secondly, Alex would accept the cigarette with pleasure, if she didn't have one in her purple suede–gloved hand already.

That's just Alex. This far away from her, and I'm actually starting to miss her.

Who would have ever imagined? I think sadly.

I know I'll miss all of them—Alex, Zack, Olivia, Jay . . . everyone in the Programme Américain. *Especially* Jay. I thought of him as I read *Madame Bovary*, every time Flaubert described the heartsickness of the devoted Charles Bovary, and also in the descriptions of Léon and how he just wanted Emma to be happy. And I definitely thought of Jay when I looked up to see that French guy in the baseball cap standing over me, grinning at me as I realized my mistake. Jay often wears caps like that. Though I wonder if in this cold spell, he's replaced his Chicago Cubs hat with a beanie.

If I'd stayed in Paris, would I have found love with Jay? Would I have felt safe and secure and adored? When he finally kissed me, would his lips have felt as nice as they look? If I'd let him in, would he have figured out how to make me laugh, how to make me come out of my distracted, fearful shell? Would Jay have fixed me? Would my dream of a new life in Paris have worked?

It's a cold thought for a cold night. Despite my very best, very earnest efforts, I've made enemies of the Marquets. They are a powerful, hard-edged couple who want nothing to stand between them and political and social power. They are the kind of people who don't forgive, don't forget, and somehow know everything about you without you even knowing it.

In a few months I'll be eighteen. If I can find Annabel, hide out with her till then, I'll never have to go back to Vermont, and I'll never have to go back to Paris.

Annabel will know what to do. She's great at hiding.

The blond girl finishes her cigarette and stubs it out. She impatiently leans out on her platform boots to see if she can spot her brother's head-lights on the dark road leading up to the train station. I realize that I've been caught up in my thoughts for several quiet minutes as she smoked her cigarette.

"So you are from Paris?" I ask awkwardly.

"*Oui*. Well, I go to school there. At the École Nationale des Beaux-Arts. I'm a painter." I see then that paint is splattered in many places over her flared jeans. Her hands are also stained with charcoal and ink. Instantly I feel like I can talk to her, just from the slight layer of grit I see lining each of her fingernails. Just like mine when I'm working on a painting...

"I'm a painter, too!" I tell her. "It must be amazing to go to art school."

That had been one of my dreams, back when I had dreams like that.

"Where do you go to school?" she asks.

"At the Lycée de Monceau," I say without thinking. "I'm in the Programme Américain."

"Ah, the Lycée," she says. The Lycée is well known in Paris for being a strict French prep school with very stringent requirements for its students. Even non-Parisians often know of it. The Marquets' friends in the Dordogne were very impressed to hear that I went there. "And you are going to Rouen for Christmas?" the girl asks. "Do you have family there?"

"Um, well," I stall. "Um, yes. I think so."

"You don't know for sure?"

"No," I admit. "I think . . . I think my sister lives there." Speaking of Annabel makes her feel real and close. She has to be in Rouen. It might have taken me too long to figure it out, but it has to be true. I know it, deep down, as well as I knew she'd never marry Dave.

"I see," the girl says. Just then a car pulls up, a little silver Citroën with a hatchback. We pile into the car, squishing our backpacks and my canvas bag in on top of us. The girl and her brother have a short conversation that I can't quite make out. I assume the girl is filling him in that I'm hitching with them to Gournay-en-Bray. He nods at me.

I smile wanly. "Thanks for the ride," I say.

The lull of the smooth, empty road makes me nauseated and sleepy at the same time. The car is too warm to compensate for the bitter night. Within seconds I'm fast asleep. It seems like only a minute has gone by when I wake up in the harsh glare of another train station. This one is open, but barely.

I jump forward, pushing past the blond girl to get out of the car while wiping the crust of saliva from the corners of my mouth. I'm embarrassed that I was asleep with my mouth open. It has just been so long since I slept . . .

The Citroën hastily pulls away from the train station. As they drive off, I'm struck again by how much that girl resembled me. And an artist, too. In some other life, we could have been friends. But the girl and her brother are obviously eager to get home. I call good-bye to them. I feel the whoosh of the car exhaust warm on my ankles under my dirty socks. The cold air that replaces it travels under my jeans and up my legs to my shivering knees. Blinking, I stare toward the ticket desk.

My heart sinks as the timetable dangling from the roof of the station tells me that the last commuter train to Rouen just left the station. Glaringly empty under the harsh flourescent lights, Gournay-en-Bray's only transit hub glistens with years of hard use. Barely covering the smells of greased wheels and stale coffee from the shuttered café is a putrid ammonia stench. I'm filled with a horrible sense of doom.

It's going to be a long night.

2. ALEX

Somewhere Beautiful

"'ll strategize *much* better after a glass or two," I call to Jay, Olivia, and Zack as I pull a few bottles of Cabernet from the wine rack in Mme Rouille's kitchen.

"Are you sure it's okay?" I hear Zack ask Olivia.

"Would Alex care if it wasn't?" Olivia answers.

"I wouldn't drink your host family's wine if you told me not to!" I assure her, pulling open the kitchen drawers, looking for a corkscrew. "Besides, there are *dozens* of bottles in here. Who wants a glass?"

"Go right ahead," Olivia calls to me from the living room. "My parents sent a case from California to Mme Rouille right when I got here as a hostess gift. She won't touch the stuff since it's not French. She'll never know the difference if you drink it. But none for me, thanks."

"No thanks, Alex," Jay agrees.

I pour some of the thick red liquid into two large goblets, one for me and one for Zack. After taking a few sips, I top my glass back off and return to the living room, where my friends are stretched out in front of a large fire, where a platter of smoky cheeses, crusty slices of country bread, and rich charcuterie are placed on the floor next to Zack.

Zack is fiddling with the loose screw that holds his thick black glasses together. In the time that I've known Zack, I still don't know if those glasses are prescription or not. Something tells me they aren't. He shouldn't hide his gorgeous face, but I guess those glasses add to his hipster appeal.

Jay's dark eyes glow in the firelight, small and intense. Jay is one of those guys who looks strong and capable—the kind of guy you trust immediately. His parents are from somewhere in Central America. They passed onto him serious, straightforward features, a thick, stocky build, and an easy, affectionate nature that comes out in all his movements. People in our program gravitate gradually toward Jay. A few months ago, nobody knew who he was. Now he's someone everyone wants to be around. Especially Zack, who keeps shooting him furtive looks that are a mixture of open anguish and lovesick adoration.

Olivia sits cross-legged on the floor, perfectly still and rolled into a small, tight ball of muscle. She's teeny, but can sometimes surprise you by how easily she can fill up a room with energy. Her dark hair still has some streaks of California highlights left, but she's really transformed since I met her at the beginning of the semester. She used to wear flip-flops and warm-ups all the time—I mean, like, even out in public—but now she chooses classic sweaters and nice jeans and boots for everyday. I like to think that I can take a little credit for that change in her.

Olivia's parents, her little brother, Brian, and her boyfriend—excuse me, *ex*-boyfriend, Vince—have just returned to the Hilton on the Champs- Élysées after a traditional cozy Christmas: opening Christmas gifts, eating a honey-glazed roasted ham with mashed potatoes and wilted spinach, and just enjoying some time together. It would have been even nicer if we'd all really been as relaxed as we were acting. In truth, we were *dying* to ask each other a million questions.

As soon as Olivia's family and Vince left, we all started talking at once.

"What should we do about PJ?" Jay asked immediately. His wide shoulders were uncharacteristically tense.

"I can't believe you broke up with Vince!" I shouted at Olivia in shock. "He's adorable! And obviously totally brokenhearted!" I'd been so eager to meet Vince, Olivia's boyfriend of the past two-plus years, but Olivia hadn't seemed very interested in introducing him to her friends. When she mentioned this morning that she didn't think they were together anymore, I knew it couldn't be because he wasn't handsome or athletic. With a sun-brushed Roman nose and a perfectly square, even jaw, Vince is *smoking* hot. For four months, all Olivia could talk about was the day she'd finally be attending UCLA with Vince by her side. Until now. The bloom is apparently off the rose, and I'm *dying* to know why.

Meanwhile, Zack looked at me and demanded, "What was wrong with you this morning? Are you in some kind of trouble at school? Why were you acting so sick and depressed when Olivia, Jay, and I came over to tell you that PJ is missing?"

And Olivia buried her face in her hands. "I can't believe I'm really staying in Paris!" I knew she was happy, overjoyed even, but also freaked out at the semester ahead. Olivia was just accepted to a major Parisian dance company, the Paris Underground Ballet Theatre. Rehearsals, plus school at the Lycée, are going to take up every nanosecond of her time. "And I'm so worried about PJ! And you, Alex! Are you sure you're okay? Aren't you sad that your mom didn't come to Paris for Christmas?" She gave me a look of completely heartfelt distress.

Oh, Olivia. One day you are going to have to stop being such a worrywart.

"All right, everyone," I raised my voice above the din. "Everyone just slow down. For all of your information, I am doing just *fine* without my mom today." I felt a pang, knowing that wasn't *entirely* true. "I'm absolutely thrilled to be spending this holiday with you lovely people. Let's just get some wine and prioritize." That's when I darted into the Rouilles' kitchen to get myself a drink. PJ's disappearance couldn't have happened at a better time, if you ask me. I need *something* to distract me from the George fiasco. From the voice mail from my mother I still haven't checked. From that letter crunched in my pocket—from, well, everything.

Now that I'm curled up on the couch under a thick woven throw blanket, happily sipping my red wine, I'm ready to turn the conversation back to the biggest mystery of the day.

What the hell happened to PJ?

And as soon as these three fill me in on that funny business, I want to know how on earth Livvy justifies letting a guy as hot as Vince out of her front door without so much as a kiss. I saw it—Vince leaned in, Livvy leaned away, and the two former lovebirds shared a look that might as well have said it all. Livvy has moved on.

But *why*? And why don't I know about it yet?

And even though I never actually *told* any of them about my plans for me and George, I'm still kind of shocked that *no one* has asked me what happened with us.

I scrunch my argyle-stockinged feet under me, making more room for Zack to stretch out.

"So PJ is missing," I begin, taking another sip of luscious Cabernet. Mme Rouille should really try this stuff. It's not half bad, for a California vineyard.

Jay immediately pulls out the postcard with its self-portrait of a young Jean-Auguste-Dominique Ingres printed on one side, and PJ's messy scrawl on the other. He shows it to me again.

It reads:

> *Jay,*
>
> *I'll never forget you.*
>
> *One day, maybe we'll meet again and I can explain.*
>
> *I'll write when I'm ready to be found.*
>
> > *Love,*
> >
> > PJ

"And this was at your door this morning?" I ask Jay.

"Yup," Jay confirms, pacing the room like an inspector on TV. "I couldn't sleep after all the holiday festivities last night. I was too wired. So I went out to see if the newspaper had come yet, and it was tucked under the doormat. When I bent down to pick it up, I saw the Ingres postcard on the floor."

"Okay," I say. "And no one else got a postcard from her?"

Zack and Olivia shake their heads.

"What happened to her?" Olivia frets. "I wish she'd have come over, I wish she'd have explained!"

"If she'd come over, she'd have gotten an eyeful!" Zack teases. "She'd have run right back out!" Olivia's freckled face colors a deep red.

"What are you guys talking about?" I demand.

"Why don't I fill you in later?" Olivia says, avoiding my gaze but unconsciously letting her eyes wander to the hallway leading to the bedroom where she sleeps. Cluttered with expensive antiques, Olivia's homestay has a squeezed in feel to it, like the Rouilles moved all their belongings in here after living in a much larger house. Jay's pacing makes me nervous in the tight space.

There are pictures everywhere, mostly of Mme Rouille's son. His sweetly goofy mug is all over the living room where we are hanging out; Mme Rouille just *adores* her only son. She never wastes an opportunity to frame and hang another picture of him. Olivia catches me looking at one and blushes.

All of a sudden I wonder if perhaps there isn't a little something going on with Olivia and her host brother, Thomas, a handsomely nerdy medical student at the Sorbonne in Paris. That's got to be it! Olivia had been getting pretty friendly with Thomas before her family came to visit her for Christmas and brought Vince with them as a surprise. Oh, my God! How *scandalous*. I *love* it! I *have* been a good influence on that girl.

Told you so, Livvy. I knew she'd crack and find a new guy in Paris. Isn't that the whole point of coming here?

"Is it . . . ?" I ask. Zack and Olivia nod quickly. "Shut up!" I'm double glad I haven't told anyone about last night yet. How does Livvy get to have two boyfriends . . . when I have zero?

I love her, but what a little *brat!*

Olivia smiles nervously. She obviously doesn't want to discuss it in front of Jay, and I wouldn't either. Jay's one of the coolest, nicest guys in our program, but Olivia, Zack, and I aren't as close to him as we are with one another. But after spending all of Christmas Day with him, I feel a little bit more bonded to him. I mean, this morning when everyone came to tell me that PJ was missing, he saw me at my worst—unshowered and wearing sweats—not even cute ones!

I gaze over at Jay, feeling warm toward him, especially after this glass of wine. Then I smile back at Olivia. "Okay, just tell me later." I giggle. As jealous as I am of Olivia's ability to attract foxy men without even trying, she's too sweet to hold anything against her.

Olivia blushes with relief. Zack grins knowingly. How does *he* know the story with Thomas and Vince, and *I* don't? I move a little farther away from him, feeling less cozy.

"Here's the thing," I say, the wine giving me a little courage to say what's been on my mind all day. "PJ's a smart girl. A wackjob, yes; but intelligent all the same. I don't think she gave you this note as a cry for help Jay. She just wanted to say good-bye, and doesn't own a cell phone like a normal person so she couldn't just call you. That's why she left the postcard. She's gone."

"But I can't imagine what would have made her leave Paris. She loves it here—more than any of us," Olivia says. "I wonder if she had a fight with her host parents. I know this sounds mean, but the Marquets *are* kind of strange. I could see her being really weirded out over something goofy they did, like getting too drunk on Christmas Eve."

That would be just like PJ—finding it bizarre that her host parents drink. In her position, I'd be thrilled! Mine could stand to loosen up a bit.

Zack and Jay look at each other. "Jay called the Marquets," Zack tells us. "They aren't answering their phone. They must have gone to their château in the Dordogne without her."

"Maybe that's where she is, you guys. The Dordogne," I try and point out. It doesn't explain the card, but God knows if I had that option, I'd take a château in the south of France over Paris for Christmas any day. It's absolutely mortifying to be stuck in the city for the holidays. I'd have died if I ever had to do that back in New York.

"They never did seem too interested in getting to know her," Olivia comments without hearing me. "I wonder if they even know she's gone."

"We've got to find her," Jay says. "She's not with the Marquets. She wouldn't have written a postcard to me like that if she was just going to the Dordogne."

"But Jay," I say, trying to be reasonable. "Let's say she isn't at the Marquets' château, like you say. Then she could be *anywhere.* She might not even be in France anymore." I think back to the beginning of the semester, when a group of us almost got arrested after George (my so *ex*-crush) and I went into the back alley to smoke a joint. PJ saved the day by turning on some saucy charm we didn't even know she had. She flirted mercilessly with the cops, and they let us go. "I don't know where she learned it, but PJ's got street smarts. She probably managed to get herself a plane ticket back to the U.S." *Kind of how she got herself a plane ticket* to *France,* I think. *She didn't even have to ask me when I met her at the airport—I* offered *to help. Who says I'm the first sucker who fell for that routine?* I wonder, briefly, if any of us even knew PJ at all.

"She's in France," Jay says, determined. "I know she wouldn't leave France. You guys should have seen her at the Louvre—she almost fainted she was so happy to finally be inside that museum. We—we were *both* so happy."

Jay's voice catches then. His smooth, olive face is lined with pensive anxiety. I can tell by the way he keeps taking off his baseball cap and running his hand over his buzz-cut hair that the inaction of the day is getting to him. With Olivia's family around, he could grin and bear it, but now that we don't have to put on the show of happy teens studying abroad, he is not going to let this go until we find her.

"Okay," I say. I know how he feels. Until about twenty-four hours ago, I was head over heels in love myself. Love makes you do the wildest things.

I shudder at the memory of myself handing over an enormous wad of cash to pay for a suite at the Hôtel Le Meurice so that I could shack up all night with George before he went back to Boston for the holidays. Scratch that—*attempt* to shack up with him all night.

"So why don't we go to the cops? Or someone could call Mme Cuchon. It's not like we don't have her phone number."

Zack, Olivia, and I all look at Jay expectantly.

"She's right, Jay," Olivia says. "If she is in trouble, we need to get some help."

Jay shakes his head. "No adults. No cops. No Mme Cuchon. This is about something personal. Just give it a few days before we involve anyone else. Okay?"

Reluctantly, Olivia and Zack nod. I shrug. I'm in no hurry to have an involved conversation with Mme Cuchon about *anything*. If Jay doesn't want to sound the alarms, I think we're all better off.

I have this hunch that PJ *wants* us to come find her. If she really wanted to be left alone, she wouldn't have left that postcard for Jay. She'd have let us think she was in the Dordogne like she is supposed to be, enjoying some sort of classically roasted game pheasant for dinner and pretending the French aristocracy is as charming as they make themselves out to be.

I imagine that château like a design porn spread in *Vogue Living*—complete with behind-the-scenes crazy relatives, embarrassing affairs, and shoddy business deals. I mean, *I* could hang there, but PJ's not me, and I'm not PJ. Not by a long shot.

"Think back to your conversations with her, then. Where do you think she might be?" I ask Jay.

Jay furrows his brow. "Somewhere...somewhere beautiful."

I would laugh out loud at Jay's earnestness if the adorable concern on his face wasn't so touching.

We all sigh.

"Hey," Zack muses. "Who was that artist you and PJ did for the Louvre project?" Zack is bent over a large portrait atlas he's pulled from one of the many bookshelves banking either side of the Rouilles' fireplace, studying a map of France.

"Ingres!" Jay snaps his fingers, holding the postcard up again and waving it in Zack's face. "This guy!"

"Okay, okay." Zack rolls his eyes. "Sue me for not having your presentation memorized." I'm surprised at Zack's bitter tone. Usually he topples over himself like a schoolgirl to be nice to Jay. "But I do remember one thing from your report. PJ said that Ingres was from a small town in the Pyrenees. Isn't this it?" He points to a town just north of Toulouse called Montauban.

"Montauban! My dad owns a place in Montauban! He just bought a rugby team there!" I exclaim. Well, I *think* he did. Last time I spoke with my dad, he'd just offered a huge amount of money for a local team. He'd gone on and on about the sport, which he'd played at boarding school. He spent most of our short conversation on my birthday last year bragging about how much he could impress his business associates by taking them to games. That's how I remember the name, from googling the team after we got off the phone. Funny how that works—I can't wait to get off the phone with the man, but I'll spend hours on my laptop looking for details about his life. Of course, in the real estate pages of *Paris Match* online, there was a tidbit about how my dad had dropped a large sum on a penthouse in Montauban. Apparently the apartment is in a renovated medieval abbey.

"Really? Your dad has a house there?" Jay beams, resting for a moment on the arm of the couch next to me. He points to the map on the floor. "Look—Montauban is *so* close to Périgueux, where the Marquets have their country house. PJ loves it in the country. Man, I bet that's it! Maybe she just hopped on a train to spend some time in Ingres's stomping grounds, trying to get her bearings. This semester was tough on her. Alex, you're brilliant!"

I beam back. "Thanks!" I'm proud of myself. I didn't really do anything except have a ridiculously rich dad whom I never see, but if someone wants to tell me I'm brilliant, they can go right ahead.

Olivia pulls her white laptop out of her light blue backpack and does a quick online search. "You guys, we might be on to something. There's a whole museum dedicated to Ingres in Montauban, and *look*." She turns the screen so we can all see the photo of Montauban she's found. It shows a medieval bridge, all lit up at night over a glittering river. I remember the photo from my own Googling last year. "It looks *gorgeous* there."

I sigh in agreement, though the idea of my dad having a whole life there that I know nothing about makes me feel sick to my stomach.

Zack looks at Jay timidly, like he's our leader. "So we're going to Montauban? How are we going to get there?" The papers this morning were splashed with headlines about the train strike in France. All intercity train service has been canceled. The local lines are running, but they will only take you so far.

"We'll have to get a car," I say, imagining something sleek and luxurious with seat warmers and a nice stereo system. "Can we rent one?"

"I don't think we're old enough," Olivia says.

"No, we're old enough," Zack says, snapping the atlas shut. "It will just cost us a pretty penny."

Jay slides his hand into his pocket and pulls out a thick wad of euro bills. He tosses them onto the coffee table next to us. "You think this will cover it?"

"No, Jay!" Zack jumps to his feet. "Are you off your rocker? You can't do that! That's your scholarship money!"

"Why are you walking around town with all your scholarship money in your pocket?" I ask. The blue, pink, green, and orange bills remind me again of how much I spent last night at the Hôtel Le Meurice, and how I couldn't get it back if I tried.

"It's not *all* my scholarship money," Jay says. "The tuition and housing fees are paid directly to the Lycée. This is just the money I get for extra stuff, like my allowance. The Lycée gives me the whole semester's worth right at the beginning."

In my pocket, there's that letter from the Lycée. I've been carrying it around with me so that my nosy host mother, Marithe, doesn't find it when she's in my room looking for evidence that I've been smoking in there against her wishes. It's just not something I'm ready to deal with yet.

"Jay, this is insane," Zack says, shaking his head. He's still standing over us, his arms folded across his gray and red-striped skinny-fit sweater. His lip quivers when he's frustrated, the way it is doing now. He looks at Olivia to back him up.

"Zack's right, Jay," she says quietly. "What are you going to live on if you spend all this money on renting a car and going to Montauban? It's not just the car. We'll need to eat down there, and find a place to stay . . . and we don't even know for sure if PJ's really there."

"I *know* she's there, man," Jay says. "The postcard says it all. Ingres is the clue. Don't you get it? Why would she leave me this if she didn't want to be found? She wants me to go to where he was born, and how easy would it have been for her to get there when it is so close to Périgueux? That's where she's hiding. We'll find her."

And talk some sense into the girl! I think scornfully. What is PJ doing, sending us on a scavenger hunt around the south of France?

"We'll stay at my dad's," I offer, scrutinizing the pretty photograph on Olivia's computer again. "I'm sure his fridge will be stocked."

Suddenly, my doubts about whether or not PJ is there don't matter. I just want to go to Montauban and finally see where my dad lives.

"You *want* to stay with your dad?" Olivia asks me with suspicion. I most certainly *do not* want to stay with my dad, but that doesn't mean I don't want to stay at his condo. Rugby season is over, and besides, he spends his holidays in Vietnam at his family's ultra-luxe compound. Rugby is the only reason he has that condo, so I'm positive he won't even be there.

I've always wanted to go back to Vietnam with my dad, even though my mom told me that the time she spent there was among the most miserable of her life. Six months pregnant with me, recently married to my dad at the Hôtel de Ville in Paris, my mom was disapproved of by my dad's family on sight. But I've always thought that if they could see *me* again, they'd love me, and teach me to make pho, and show me the temples and the palaces of Vietnam. Who knows if they even eat pho? My impression is that the Nguyens are Francophiles through and through. I met them once, in Paris, as a small child. Just before my parents split up.

"Yup," I say simply. What they don't know won't hurt them.

"Well, that's easy enough," Jay says. He comes over and puts his hand on my shoulder gratefully. "I wasn't sure what I was going to tell my host family. If I say a group of us is going to visit your dad, they'll be fine with it."

"Perfect!" I say. I grin up at him. It's so *nice* to be appreciated for once. "What about you, Livvy? Zack?"

Zack shrugs. "I'm sure my host parents won't ask any questions. But I still think it's a terrible idea. We're going on the flimsiest of flimsy evidence." His eyes rest on Jay's hand, still on my shoulder.

"Well, we have to start somewhere," Olivia says. The go-getter in her likes that we have a plan, I can tell. Soon she'll be trying to organize us into committees and giving us each a schedule. "And I feel better about it, knowing Alex's dad will help us."

I almost snort, but catch myself just in time. All I know is that getting out of Dodge before Madame Cuchon gets ahold of my host mother—or my real mother, for that matter—sounds like music to my ears. I don't know yet what I'm going to do about that whole situation—the letter from school. The exam results. It's all simply too much to handle at the moment. I have to put it out of my head, or I'll go crazy.

Montauban. The name sounds rustic and provincial, peaceful. Quiet. The perfect place to hide out till I figure out how not to get sent back to New York. PJ just gave me the perfect place to stall for time.

Well done, Penelope Jane. Very well done. Despite myself, I actually want to *thank* PJ. Who knew it would come to this?

"So, shall we set off tomorrow morning?" I ask, setting my empty wineglass on the oak end table nearest to me.

"Definitely, man." Jay nods. He's pacing the room now. "Let's meet in front of the Gare Montparnasse tomorrow at seven. Then we can go check out the car rental agencies downstairs."

Seven seems just a *bit* too early after all this wine, but the others don't argue with it. Jay puts on his coat and heads out. He's got to catch the last métro to Montreuil before the line stops running for the night. He waves at all of us in a group farewell, but Zack won't even look at him.

I jump up off the couch, suddenly wired at the prospect of the task ahead, eager to leave Paris and my problems behind. I catch Jay as he's about to pull Livvy's front door closed behind him.

"We'll find her," I tell him in a low, encouraging voice. "Don't worry, okay? This is just some sort of weird mix-up."

Jay grimaces. "I can't *not* find her, Alex. You know?"

"I know." I touch his shoulder the way he touched mine. "I know."

3. OLIVIA

On the Top of the World

hey're finally gone. Finally! Two weeks of totally exhausting familial tension are over.

That's my first thought when I jump out of bed the morning after Christmas. My next thought is to wonder why the heck the phone is ringing at six A.M., the day after Christmas. I'm the only one home, since Thomas and Mme Rouille are still in the Alps.

I rush to answer it with a sharp sense of dread. Is it Alex with bad news about PJ? Is it my parents, deciding they can't give me their blessing to stay in Paris and dance with the Paris Underground Ballet Theatre after all?

"Olivia, it's Henri," a rough voice greets me over the line. Henri?

Oh, *Henri*. I've been so totally caught up worrying about PJ, my parents' emotional good-byes, the breakup with Vince, and much more deeply, the magical night with Thomas on Christmas Eve in my bedroom, I feel like I don't even know what's happening anymore!

"*Bonjour*," I say, pulling my sleepy self together to sound professional. Henri is the choreographer for the dance troupe where I just got a job. I'm the youngest dancer in the troupe. I don't want him to think he made a mistake asking me to join.

"Olivia, pardon me for calling so early," Henri says in rapid French. "I'm at the hospital—"

"Are you sick?" I burst out. Not *more* bad news.

"No, no, not me," Henri assures me. "It's Katica. She and André were rehearsing late last night and Katica woke up this morning with a terrible pain in her back. She has a pinched nerve. She can't—she can't dance."

Katica is a beautiful Hungarian principal dancer with the Underground. I visualize her expertly executed quadruple pirouette, and I can't believe she injured herself. But that's how ballet works—all of the sudden something happens, and you can't dance anymore.

"Oh, God," I say breathlessly. "You're kidding."

"Basically, Olivia, I'm screwed," he tells me. "I've called all the other principal dancers and all the experienced understudies. Everyone is on holiday outside Paris, except you."

I try to exhale inaudibly. I'd been too scared to call Henri and tell him that I wasn't coming back after the New Year to dance with the troupe. I had been going to slink away. Now I'm so glad that I hadn't.

"I can do it," I say right away, not even knowing yet what I am volunteering for. "*Bien sûr.*"

"*C'est parfait, ma chérie,*" Henri replies with a strong note of gratitude.

"Can you come to the rehearsal space today at ten A.M.? André will meet us there. We don't have much time to get you ready to perform."

I'm confused. The dancers are all on a break until after the New Year. What are we rehearsing?

Henri notices that I've missed a beat. "The New Year's Eve performance," he tells me. "I need you to dance at the *Revue Bohème*."

The Revue!

I forgot all about the duet for a benefit concert involving several of the more avant-garde companies around town. The dancers are going to be accompanied by a Moroccan woman singing folksongs in Arabic at a very slow speed. It is a rare chance for the Underground to perform for a wider audience, and despite the short performance time, Henri takes the choreography of any performance very seriously. I'd heard he'd decreased the tempo so that the dance itself was basically in slow motion and incredibly technically difficult. Henri's piece for the Revue includes a lot of floor movement with a modern, primal sensibility. I'll never be able to get up to speed in just a week.

"I'll be there at ten," I say, and then hang up the phone.

In the living room, as the sun starts to peek out over the horizon, I do some stretches to calm myself. When I've worked up the nerve, I call Alex.

"I can't go to Montauban today," I say, terrified of how she will react. "I'm dancing in the Revue Bohème on New Year's Eve. I have to start rehearsals this morning. Are you mad?"

"No, doll!" Alex chuckles. "Of course not! You do what you gotta do."

"They'll pay me to do it," I tell her. "I can still help pay for the rental car, and whatever you need to get PJ back to Paris. Plus, if I stay here, someone will be in Paris if she decides to come back."

"Liv, no need to make excuses," Alex says breezily. "You're right to stay in Paris. What's PJ's deal, anyway? I didn't want to say this in front of Jay, but it seems like every time I turn around, that girl's causing a big fuss over herself *again*. Remember when she, like, fled the orientation getting-to-know each-other circle? I mean, save the drama for your mama, right? It won't take more than a couple days to find her, I'm sure. We'll get her back in time for the Revue, and we'll all get to see you dance. Not to worry, Liv. I'm on it!"

"Thanks, Alex." She's surprisingly chipper, not to mention up very early for a change. "Are you guys all set?"

"Yup. Though," she says, muffling her voice a bit, "Zack is in a horrendous mood. Do you know what crawled up his ass?"

I hadn't digested how ardently in love with PJ that Jay was until everyone left my apartment last night. Watching Zack interact with Jay throughout the day, I'd noticed that Zack's eyes followed Jay everywhere. I bet my parents and Vince even noticed!

It must be hard for Zack to try to support the guy he himself has a major crush on, especially going off on a big road trip to find the girl Jay likes. But it feels too sad to casually speculate about it with Alex. "He's probably just worried about PJ. Be nice to him, Alex."

My voice sounds too harsh. "And thanks again for understanding about the Revue," I add more sweetly.

At nine I finish warming up and put on my coat to trek over to the rehearsal space near the Place d'Italie. The phone rings again, and again my mind fills with angst over what it might be *this* time.

"Olivia," a familiar voice greets me. Right away, I know who it is. My body immediately goes hot; a mental image of his bare torso above mine, falling into bed together, floods my brain.

"Thomas," I answer.

"I knew you would stay," he tells me. "I'm on my way back to Paris. I can't be away from you for another minute."

"But what about your trip? What about Mme Rouille?" Thomas and Mme Rouille went to the Alps for a vacation with their extended family as soon as Thomas finished his exams. They'd left before I announced that I wasn't going back to San Diego with my family after all.

"She will be okay. I will tell her I need to do some readings for next semester. *Maman* is busy with her sisters, besides." I giggle happily, relishing the funny way Thomas executes his carefully constructed English sentences. They are always just a teensy bit off, just like my French.

"Faites-vous du ski?" I ask. Thomas is an avid skier.

"Olivia, *tu connais Maman."* He laughs. *"Maman* is in the *salon de thé* all day, gossiping."

"Tell her I miss her already," I say fondly. I really, really do.

I'm cradling the phone between my ear and my shoulder. Thomas can't see me, so I beam like a goober around the empty kitchen. When he gets home, I'll act cool.

"So what will you do today?" Thomas asks me after a few quiet moments.

"Oh, jeez!" I shriek. "I have to go! I forgot to tell you—I mean, it just happened—I was cast in the Revue Bohème performance on New Year's Eve! I've got to get to rehearsal!"

I slam the phone down, too freaked to care if I have offended the new love of my life. But isn't that one of the things I totally like best about Thomas anyway? Artistic pursuits are a perfectly valid reason to hang up on someone. To Thomas, art is more important than manners.

I glance at a photo of Thomas on the front table, where Mme Rouille puts her keys and the mail. I almost kiss the glass protecting the picture. Almost. I'm not *that* much of a goober.

I warm up a little on the métro, which makes me look strange, but I want to stay loose so that I can handle the rehearsal today. I know it is going to be *majorly* intense. I'm doing slow pliés in between each of the stops on the number five line, releasing them only when the doors open at each station. The train takes forever, what with the post-Christmas slump and the wet, mucky weather. Stretching helps me relax and takes my mind off how late I might be.

Bursting frantically into the studio, I strip off my warm-ups and wiggle my arms and legs around. I'm plenty loose already, but I am also trying to hide my jitters. I've done a number of professional ensemble parts in the last year, but it's been a long time since I was a principal dancer in anything that wasn't being put on by my high school dance department back in San Diego. This piece has only *two* dancers—and I'm now one of them.

Henri arrives, with my dance partner, André, following behind him. Henri's Mohawk would make him stand out anywhere, but even among the hip dancers of the Underground, I knew he was the leader the moment I laid eyes on him. He's just one of those people everyone naturally looks up to. He never has to shush his dancers when we practice—everyone listens to every word he says with rapt attention.

Henri sees me stretching in the corner and presses his hands together and bows in my direction.

"Thank you for *ton dévouement* to the Underground, Olivia," he says. "Shall we get started?"

"Definitely," I nod. "Where do you want me?"

"You'll be here," Henri says. "And André is here." He points out our marks on the studio floor.

We move rapidly through the steps. André and I start low, our faces close to the ground, and we undulate upward, mirroring each other's motions as we face each other. The movements Henri has created are big and broad, and much more like modern dance than ballet.

"Don't take your eyes off him, Olivia," Henri instructs as he watches us practice. "Maintain eye contact no matter what."

One of the hardest sequences for me is an eight-count that requires André and me to hold our hands up toward each other as if we are leaning on the other's weight to stay upright, while each standing on the toe of one foot. Henri wants the leg holding each of us up to be bent, and our other leg stretched in an attitude so that our free foot is level with our heads. The positioning is awkward; it takes me some time to find my center. In the mirror opposite I can see my face flush with embarrassment and frustration. When I finally get it, Henri claps enthusiastically. I totally knew I could do it!

"Bon!" he shouts. "Now plié! Take your full eight counts. Keep it fluid and don't you dare let that leg drop."

I bend my knee so that I'm lowering, ever closer to the floor, at the same pace as André. He's got amazing strength in his legs. His face isn't showing how hard this is at all, nor are there nearly as many beads of sweat rolling down his dark face as there are on mine. "Now move through to a ball on the floor, get as tight as you can," Henri calls to us, keeping time by whacking his thigh loudly with the flat of his palm. "Tighter! Tighter!"

After hours of doing the routine with no music, just Henri keeping the beat, a striking woman in a long, brightly patterned dress and headscarf walks authoritatively through the door to the studio. She must be the accompanist.

"*Bonjour*, Kiki. Henri blows her a kiss. "Come in, come in."

I take the interruption as a chance to guzzle some water and pat myself dry with my hand towel.

"Dancers, let's start from the top," Henri beckons us. "This time with accompaniment."

When Kiki opens her mouth to sing, I can barely hold my pose. Her voice is low and cries out with aching and joy in every note. She sings in a slow, languid tempo. I'm used to light, quick steps, trying to be as weightless as possible. But here, the emotion of the choreography, especially when paired with this beautiful, haunting music, pulls at my limbs. It's as if I'm swimming through honey, trying to reach out and hold André but never getting close enough.

"*Oui!*" Henri yells. "*Oui*, Olivia!"

All through our final steps, the aching attitude and the sinking plié toward the floor, André and I have our eyes locked. Only at the end, when I know it's over, do I allow myself to curtsy, smiling into my knees with relief.

"*Et encore!*" Henri cries. So we do it again.

Henri is finally satiated after almost a full eight hours of rehearsal.

"Go home, Olivia," he says. My concentration is waning, my thoughts rushing ahead to seeing Thomas again.

"Fantastic job today, Olivia," André says to me in English as he walks with me to the métro. André is British-Jamaican, just a few years older than me. He's leaps and bounds more talented, though. I'm shocked he's even talking to me.

"Thank you." I blush.

"So what are you up to tonight? Homework?"

I can tell that André is just joking, but it still stings that he, and likely the other dancers at the Underground, finds it funny that I'm still in high school.

"My—my boyfriend is coming home from the Alps tonight," I say. It slips out. I wonder what Thomas would say if he heard me call him my boyfriend—already!

"Hot date then?" André teases. We've arrived back at the Place d'Italie métro station. "Don't let me keep you. I'm going to visit Katica. She'll be just *horrified* to hear how good you were today, Olivia."

I don't know what to say. "Tell her hello for me," I finally mumble.

"Olivia! That's bollocks. If you want to dance with the Underground, you're going to have to lighten up," André tells me, the humor dancing around the corners of his eyes. "Katica will be so relieved that you can cover for her this week. And seriously, you were bloody amazing just now. Watching your face as we danced together was a trip. It was like you were in another realm. Dancing is a true escape for you, huh?"

I think about that, an *escape*.

That word recalls PJ, hustling out of town in the wee hours of Christmas morning, escaping Paris, the Marquets, the Lycée, *us*. There's been a lump in my throat for the last twenty-four hours, whenever I think about PJ. She must be scared, all alone out there, trying to *escape* some mystery demon—some secret she couldn't confide in me. Since I found out that she's missing, I've felt like such a failure as a friend. I cross my fingers that Alex and the others find her soon and bring her back to Paris for good.

"Dancing's not an *escape* for me," I tell André. "It's more like it's the only place where I really feel at home."

I race up the stairs to the apartment. Thomas has the door opened before I even get to it, and his angular, handsome face catches the light. His cool blue eyes immediately light up when he sees me. I fall into his arms without another word. The soft, worn corduroy of his scholarly blazer is perfectly inviting after the sting of the winter night. I climb up his long torso so that my legs are wrapped firmly around his thin hips. He carries me toward the bedroom, kissing me deeply on the mouth the whole way.

4. ZACK

Behind the Wheel

"You're joking," I spit out when Alex blithely informs me that Olivia isn't coming to Montauban with us.

"Nope," Alex says, slipping her BlackBerry back into the huge camel-colored tote bag she always has with her. "She sends her love, though."

I stare at the rental-car clerk, a young, pert Asian woman who's going over the rental-car agreement with Jay a few feet in front of us. I should be listening, since it's my parents' credit card she swiped for the insurance and incidentals should anything happen to us on the way, but all I can think about it is how Olivia totally just abandoned me.

"Did she give a reason?" I say, sounding more wounded than I want to.

"Of course she did, silly," Alex responds. "She's dancing in a show on

New Year's Eve, the Revue Bohème. It's a huge deal, actually. I can't wait to see her in it."

"Ready to go, guys?" Jay says, jangling the keys in front of us, his breath visible in the winter air. "The car's in the lot outside."

"Definitely!" Alex cries, popping her spearmint gum. "I can't wait!"

I plod along after them. Jay was here at the Gare Montparnasse when Alex and I arrived a little after seven this morning. He looked restless, an empty cup of coffee next to him on the bench where he was sitting.

"Well, ain't you up early," I remarked in a friendly tone when he spotted us approaching the plaza in front of the darkened train station. "Been waitin' long?"

"I didn't sleep," Jay said without smiling. The shortness of his tone stung. "Let's go. I checked the rates online; Eurauto is the cheapest one for drivers under eighteen."

Once the paperwork is done, we follow Jay down the escalator to the basement, where the rental-car desks are. He's got an olive green hooded sweater on under a nice black wool coat, and he's wearing charcoal gray chinos with his Chuck Taylors. He is more dressed up than usual, and I wonder if he chose his clothes carefully this morning, imagining that he wanted to look good when he came barreling into Montauban to rescue his true love.

"New sweater?" I ask him.

"Yup," he says distractedly, scanning the large empty basement hall for the budget rental agency, Eurauto, to pick up the keys. "My mom sent it over as a Christmas gift."

"Oooooh," Alex says. "I *like*. Go, Mom." She fingers the soft wool of the hood. "Nice coat, too. I love it when a man travels in style!"

Jay finally cracks a smile. "You'll laugh when you see the car then." He chuckles. "Just wait."

I know Jay asked for the cheapest possible four-seater, but I never imagined how bad it could be. When we go to the back of the train station, Jay points to the space with our rental parked in it.

"Oh, man," he says under his breath. Alex howls in response.

The car is an old model of a make I've never heard of in my life, likely one that's long stopped manufacturing cars. Painted teal green and upholstered in a complementary purple fabric, the little sedan has a cheesy pink stripe running along either side of it.

"That ain't a car!" I screech. "That there's a straight-up *jalopy*. Jay, you've done rented the ugliest car in the whole lot!" I'm hoping he'll loosen up if we give him a hard time.

Alex giggles. Jay doesn't.

Jay opens the trunk with a loud clank and throws his backpack inside. "Ready to hit the road?" He doesn't wait for us to answer. Instead he unlocks the driver's-side door and jumps in the car.

"This is *so* exciting!" Alex drags her Louis Vuitton duffel bag up to the back of the car and waits for me to hoist it into the trunk for her. She motions as if she is going to help, but she can't really see over the fuzzy hot pink angora scarf covering her face.

"Watch it!" she gripes when I almost drop it. "There's important stuff in there."

Alex had been full of confidence at Olivia's last night that we'd be able to find PJ in a matter of a couple days, but she has packed as if she'll be gone all month. I know not to read into it, though—Alex packed the same way on the class trip to Lyon last month.

"God almighty, that's heavy," I say. "I hope I don't have to be your porter boy for the whole trip."

"Maybe Jay can carry it if you can't."

As I arrange her suitcase next to Jay's backpack so that there will be enough room for my backpack in the densely packed trunk, Alex rushes around and grabs the front seat. I hear her giggle in delight at something Jay says, and I start to absorb the fact that Alex actually thinks this is *fun*. How twisted can she get? Our friend is *missing*, for crying out loud!

Jay's got the car warmed up when I get into the backseat, the cushion sagged from years of use. The car smells like stale cigarette smoke, vanilla air freshener, and bleach. I gag and crack a window, letting in crisp, frozen air.

"Thanks, doll!" Alex says to me. *Doll* is a new thing she's doing lately. Everyone is a *doll*. Except French people. Alex won't actually go so far as to call a French person *poupée*.

Once we're out of the lot, Jay hands Alex a big foldout road map of France. "Get me out of the city, okay?"

"No problem," Alex chirps. "What street are we on?"

We drive around in circles around the fourteenth arrondissement for several minutes until I can't take it anymore. "Jeez, Alex, give me that!" I snatch the map away from her and lay it out over my lap.

"Jay, hang a right," I instruct. "Then another right, then a left. We have to turn back around. The highway entrance is behind us."

"Whoa there, killer," Alex says. "Take it easy." She tries to make her voice as sunny as it was when we got into the car, but I sense the edge beneath. I scowl and get us onto the highway with as few terse words as possible.

Alex falls asleep about fifteen minutes outside of Paris, curled into a pink silk pillow she's brought with her. She likes to sleep on satin or silk because her glossy black hair stays smooth against the slippery fabric. In the side-view mirror, I can see her lips are pursed sweetly, and I feel bad. Why did I blow up at her? She's just being herself.

"Thanks, man," Jay says quietly. "I thought we were never going to get out of Paris." His gratitude lifts my spirits.

"Alex is a genius in many ways," I whisper ever so softly, "but don't ever rely on her for directions again."

"Understood, my friend," Jay says with a quick grin toward me in the backseat. Now that we're on the road, headed toward PJ at a hundred kilometers per hour, Jay's letting himself relax. I take a deep breath and wonder if this trip might not be kind of fun after all. Once we find PJ, Jay will be happy. And if Jay's happy, I'll be happy. Even if Jay and I aren't meant to be, I still want him to . . . I still want him to get what he wants. I want to help him see things through.

I send Pierson, my best friend from Memphis who is studying abroad in Amsterdam this year, a text.

WHAT R U DOIN RIGHT NOW? U'LL NVR GUESS WHAT I'M DOIN.

Pierson loves—*loves*, I'm telling you—to hear about all the people I've met in the Programme Américain. He calls PJ Beautiful Princess Penelope and always asks if we can use her as a surrogate if we end up thirty and alone and want to have a baby together. He's seen her picture on my Facebook page.

"I keep lookin' at this, I might just go straight again," he commented under it. PJ doesn't have a Facebook page. I'm not sure what she'd think of what he wrote.

I'll never forget the first time I saw PJ. She looked like a linebacker, walking with Alex toward the rest of our group at Charles de Gaulle Airport, with a big brown backpack strapped onto her lithe frame. It was still practically summer then, and all the girls were tan but PJ. Her skin was as pale then as it was the last time I saw her, on the last day of the semester before we were all dismissed for winter break. Even in the few months since we'd all started at the Lycée, PJ's white blonde hair had grown at least an inch or two, and she'd had it fanned around her shoulders like a glowing hood. PJ's haunted eyes were more tired than usual, but I chalked it up to sleepless nights preparing for the big Final Comp exam at the end of the semester. The test was the hardest I'd ever taken, and I scraped by with a B. PJ, for all her spaciness, is a stellar student. I'm sure she couldn't have gotten less than an A+, so that can't be the reason she ran away. What was she hiding behind that heavy expression the last time I saw her? When we find her, are we really going to be able to help her at all?

"Whatcha thinking about?" Jay asks me, breaking into my daydream. He catches my eye in the rearview mirror. His tone is so sweet and solicitous that I can *almost* imagine he has a crush on me, the way I spent most of last semester fantasizing about him doing. My chest hurts and my cheeks burn, thinking about the confession I made to him only a couple of days ago. The way he looked at me with utter confusion. How he explained, so gently, that he didn't feel the same way.

My phone beeps.

WHAT? Pierson has texted back.

I shake my head and drop my phone into my pocket, turning my attention back to Jay. I lean forward between the two front seats. "Just thinkin' about PJ," I say. "You think we're really gonna find her in this random little town?"

"I'm not sure," Jay says after a minute, real doubt in his voice. The sun is starting to peep out behind the murky morning clouds, and the car is finally warming up. Apparently, the heater in this time machine is a little out of sorts. After a few more miles of highway have passed, he sighs and says, "We have to, man."

Outside of Orléans, Jay pulls over at a gas station off the A10 highway. His eyes are bleary when he turns to face me. "I'm starting to fade," he admits. "Will you drive?" He looks chagrined. I'd been dozing off in the backseat, and I wonder how long he's been struggling to stay awake. He must have been serious about his not sleeping last night.

"Sure will," I say.

Alex shifts in her seat, roused from her heavy midmorning slumber. "Are we eating?" she asks loudly, mid-yawn. "I'm absolutely starved."

"No, we're just switching drivers," I say.

"Oh." Alex takes off her sunglasses and rubs her eyes. "I'll drive."

"You want to?" Jay asks. She looks pretty comfortable curled up into the passenger seat. I think it's safe to say that neither of us expected Alex to volunteer to drive on this little road trip of ours.

"Yeah," she says. "I'm a really good driver. My cousin Emily in Westchester lets me use her car all the time."

"Well, okay." Jay opens the driver's-side door and gets out while Alex slides over the bench seat to take Jay's place behind the wheel. I guess that means I'm still in the back for a while. I pick up my phone to send Pierson another text.

"Sweet!" Alex flips the sunshade down and checks herself in the little mirror, fluffing her wavy black hair and making a kissy face at her own reflection. "I love driving!"

I raise my eyebrows at her, but she's not looking. Once Jay is buckled in, she turns the ignition over and pumps the gas. "Montauban, here we come!" With a startling jerk, we squeal our way out of the gas station and pull back onto the A10, burning rubber all the way.

"Alex, watch the *heck* out!" I scream as she nearly barrels into a semi-rig truck and trailer going at least half our speed. "Did you eat crazy beans for breakfast? Dang, child!"

Alex lets out a shrill giggle. "I didn't see that guy. Sorry, people."

Jay loosens his grip on the dashboard. "Easy there, lead foot," he says. "We get into an accident and not only do we not get to PJ, we also get kicked out of the program."

"Oh, Jay, stop," Alex protests. "We aren't going to get into an 'accident.'" We tense as she lifts both hands off the wheel to accent "accident" with air quotations. "This car just drives differently from my cousin's Acura. I'm getting used to it, that's all." She looks over at him, grinning, but she's got her eyes off the road for too long. Jay doesn't smile back.

"Seriously, Alex, watch the road," I scold her before Jay loses it. "Jay's right. We'll get kicked out of the program for sure if we get caught leaving Paris unsupervised."

"No one is getting into an accident, and no one is going to find out we left," Alex says. "Zack, chill!"

"I will chill as soon as you promise not to kill us!" I look to Jay for support. He's looking out the window.

"What is your problem, anyway, Zack?" Alex asks, her voiced heated.

"Why did you even come? You're just bringing everybody down."

I suck my breath in sharply. *Don't go there, Alex, just do not go there.* She knows why I came on this trip: because if Jay asks me for help, there is no way I can say no. I want to get over him, God knows I do, but I haven't yet. Until then, the old habit of putting him first dies pretty hard.

Just then, a large piece of cardboard flies off the top of the trailer in front of us. It bounces crazily around the highway, heading straight for our windshield. Alex's reaction is to slam heavily on the brakes, cars whooshing by on either side of us, making our wheels screech and slide in either direction.

I hear Alex's throaty, shrill scream as I close my eyes and wait for the impact from behind, or in front, whichever might come first. All I can hope is that in the afterlife I'll get a chance to tell her what a tremendously *terrible* driver she is.

Somehow Jay coaches Alex off the highway. Tears are pouring out from under her big Gucci sunglasses when I open my eyes again. The car comes to a halt on a lonely service road. Our only company is parked rigs like the one Alex almost just hit a few seconds ago. She fumbles for the door handle and steps shakily out of the car. Jay puts his head in his hands but stays put in the front seat. "*Dios mio,*" he whispers. "*Jesucristo.*" I can see him cross his crumpled chest and take out a small gold cross on a chain around his neck. He's really, really shaken up. I resist the aching urge to climb over the center consul and comfort him in my arms.

All of the sudden, red hot anger comes over me. I jump out of the car. Over my shoulder the A10 is busy and loud, and I shout to make myself heard.

"I thought you were a good driver!" I march up in front of her face. Alex is tying and retying her pink scarf, her hands shaking. "What was that? My seven-year-old sister could drive better than that! My *dog* could drive better than that. I'd like a word with the shit-for-brains who gave you your license. Is that what they call driving in New York? Getting your friends killed while you see how long you can go without paying attention?"

I'm horrified to find myself braying like a baby, too. I'm so relieved to be alive that my harsh words are coming out accompanied by a river of honest-to-God *sobs*.

Please don't let Jay see, I think while I try my hardest to make them stop.

"Tell me, Alex," I say more calmly a few moments later, the rumbling trucks passing on the highway directly behind us. "Just how long have you had your license?"

Alex puffs out her cheeks, thinking. She takes a long time to answer, and when she does, I can't hear what she mumbles.

"What?" I yell.

"I said I don't have it yet!" Alex bursts out. "Okay? Are you happy? I don't have my license yet."

"Sweet Jesus, Alex!" I can't believe it. I honestly can't believe it. She can't be this stupid. It is literally not possible.

"Don't tell Jay," she begs. "He'll be so pissed. And I *am* a good driver. Emily *does* let me drive all the time."

"Your cousin lets you drive her *Acura* without a license?" I'm still in shock.

"It's just a 2005." She sniffles.

Jay opens the passenger-side door and shouts at us that we need to get back on the road.

"Okay, get in front, Zack," Jay commands. "Alex, you're not driving again."

Well, I should think *not*. After that near-death experience, I'd say Alex should not only be revoked of any road-trip driving privileges but also be apprehended by the French Department of Transportation for reckless endangerment of American study-abroad students (and perhaps a few French truck drivers as well!). Is she freakin' *joking* with this stunt this morning?

When my hands stop shaking, I text Pierson back.

SRSLY CONSIDERING THE IDEA THAT TOO MANY SPA TREATMENTS INDUCE SOCIOPATHY IN 17-YR-OLD GIRLS. ALEX JUST ALMOST KILLED US ALL. BUT HER HAIR STILL LOOKS FAB. WILL EXPLAIN LATER.

For a few hours, we drive in silence. Finally the signs start foretelling that Montauban is not far off. About 120 kilometers away, Jay pulls into a truck stop. We eat prewrapped tuna sandwiches quickly, without talking. Once we get back on the A10, I reach over my shoulder and extend my hand to Alex. She holds it all the way to Montauban. I press my forgiveness back into her grip.

5. PJ

Sisters in the Night

always knew the hour before the sun starts to rise is the very coldest part of the night, but I'd never really thought about it until now. Hunkered down into a little corner of the Gournay-en-Bray station, my white breath rising from my mouth and into the moonlit empty space in front of me, I think I know why. This is the hour of the day when the earth has been without the sun's rays the longest. The ground is losing its heat. The structures atop it are bracing with chill by now. I remind myself that in a few hours the railway staff will have to come and open this place back up. They'll turn the heat and all the lights back on. Then I can just jump on a train to Rouen—any train—and leave my long, lonely, freezing night in Gournay-en-Bray behind me. Forever.

When I close my eyes, I see *her.*

Annabel runs toward me. Her skin is glowing despite the lack of light in here. Her dark hair is speckled with amber, the way it always is in the summer. She's got a quilt in her arms. It's one that my mom made from all of our baby clothes. My mom made two of them, actually. The one that she gave me is lying on the bed in the room where I was staying in the Marquets' town house in Paris. I didn't have time to grab it before I ran out of their house. But when I see Annabel, somewhere in that hazy space between sleep and reality, she is bringing it to me. She's going to wrap me in it and guide me back to somewhere warm. Her smile alone could melt the ice off the roof of this place.

But then I see M. Marquet, too. He's sitting on my quilt, his hefty body splayed comfortably on my bed. He's breathing hard, and the whiskey on his breath sends a million little prickles up the back of my neck. He's reaching for me. In the corner of the train station, I know I can't get away. I'm trapped. Unless Annabel gets here first, he'll get me. He'll hurt me. And behind that immediate threat is the nagging sickness over the fact that he and his wife know my secret. They won't protect me from it. They know my parents are in jail and they might stay there for a long time.

I shake myself awake every few minutes. It must be almost daylight. When that happens, I'll need to go back into the bathroom until the train station opens. I can't let the guards see me, see that I've slept here. Then I'll come out of the bathroom doors, as soon as I can sense that there are enough people in here that I'll blend back into the crowd. I'll get on the commuter train to Rouen. Even if it takes another day, another week, I'll get there. *I can do this.*

My eyes close again, their lids so heavy, it's a relief. I dream of the Claude Monet room at the Louvre museum. This time, Jay and I are holding hands as we look at all the paintings. He turns to me, beaming, and maybe we'll kiss now, if I just tilt my head a tiny bit forward . . .

"Mademoiselle!" When I wake up a train station agent is shaking me violently. *"Réveillez-vous! Qu'est-ce qui se passe?"* The waiting area where I'd spent the night is awash in bright sunlight. It must be at least seven o'clock. There are even a few passengers milling about.

I swallow hard and look at the figures standing above me.

"Je suis très desolée," I mumble. I've never been good at going without sleep.

Everyone who works at this train station at this miserable hour is gathered around me. One of them has her cell phone out, obviously calling the police. They think I'm a transient, a dirty runaway that needs to be sent home. Instinctively, I hug my jacket to my chest.

"Stay right there," one of the male agents barks at me when I try to get to my feet. "You're in big trouble."

I bite my lip and widen my eyes. I wonder if he might take pity on me if I look as innocent as possible.

"Je dois aller aux toilettes," I explain meekly.

The agent shakes his head. "We are waiting for the authorities to arrive."

Another agent, a woman, clucks her tongue. She speaks to him quietly in French. *"Et si elle a ses règles?"*

"Oui, oui," I say, thinking fast. I look down as if I'm terribly embarrassed, which I am, but not because she thinks I might have my period. The agents look away from me, too.

The female agent pulls me off the floor with a firm grasp. She leads me to the bathroom. From my stall, I can see her standing up against the doorway. She's making sure I can't get away from her. I'm grateful for her compassion, helping me get away like that, but I don't think that compassion will extend to helping me sneak out a window.

As I pee, I shuffle around in my coat so that it sounds like I am digging out a tampon. What I'm really doing is taking any forms of ID out of my pockets—my Vermont driver's license, my Lycée ID, my social security card—and placing them noiselessly into the toilet bowl, hoping they'll flush without bouncing back up to the surface. I can't toss my passport. That I might need down the line.

With a deep breath, I wrap my passport in toilet paper. Sliding my underwear and jeans back on, I bundle it in between my legs. If it comes down to a strip search, the authorities will certainly find it. But how often does it come down to a strip search? I'm willing to take my chances. And, hey—this is better than trying to wrap it up in plastic and swallow it whole, which I did, in fact, consider as the agent led me toward the grimy station bathroom.

"Ça va bien?" she asks me when I come out of the stall.

"Oui, merci," I say. I give her a feeble smile. She doesn't smile back.

There are two cops and a social worker standing with the other agents when we get back. I can tell that she's a social worker because she's wearing a suit instead of a uniform. The female agent grips me as if I was a wily puppy making an aim for the door.

"Quel âge avez-vous?" the social worker says. She's young and pretty, with a crown of curly brown hair and dimples in her cheeks and one in her chin. Her voice is the kindest of any I've heard this morning.

"*Dix-huit*," I lie immediately. Eighteen.

"What's your name?" she asks me. "We'd like to talk to you about why you had to sleep in the train station last night."

"Emma," I say, careful to keep my French as accentless as possible. "*Je m'appelle* Emma Léon."

"Emma, *je m'appelle* Binet Nagou." The social worker offers her hand. "Tell me, are you in school?"

"*Oui,*" I tell Binet. "A L'Ecole Nationale des Beaux-Arts. *Je suis peintre.*" I remember the angular face of the girl who helped me last night. I remember how eagerly she waited for her brother, and how quickly they sped away once they dropped me off.

"My brother lives here in Gournay-en-Bray," I tell the group in French. "I thought I'd come surprise him for a Christmas visit. *Bien sûr,* all the trains are messed up because of the strike. When I called his mobile to come pick me up, it went straight to voice mail. I called my mom. She told me my brother went to Grenoble with his friends. She told me to come right back to Paris. By that time, none of the trains were running. So I slept here."

"Can we see your ID?" one of the cops asks.

I open my wallet. "Oh!" I cry out in fake surprise. "Where is it?" I dig around my back pocket, the whole time uncomfortably aware of my passport between my legs.

"I must have left it at the dorm," I lie.

"And your train ticket?" asks one of the station agents.

"I threw it away when I got off the train last night," I say smoothly.

"*Alors,*" a cop says, peering at me strangely.

"I'm really, really sorry," I say, lowering my voice. "Can I just go try and find my way back to Paris? I promise I won't ever do anything like this again."

All the adults look at each other, then me. I can tell the agents want to have me thrown out of the station. In truth, it is *their* staff that should have made sure the place was clear last night. If I'd been a criminal causing trouble, their necks would be on the block right now. And I can tell the cops want to give me a ticket, just to have something to do.

But Binet wants to have a chat with me, and she calls off the dogs before anything more can happen. "Let's just sit for a moment, Emma."

I follow her to a wooden bench. Trains are pulling onto the tracks outside the big picture windows facing the back of the train station. Small-town French people, wearing work boots, heavy winter coats, scarves tied under their chins, are starting to mill about. The cops and the agents watch us from a distance.

"Emma, I want you to know that I am here to help," Binet implores. "It is for that reason, and not out of any disrespect, that I want to ask you the following question. Tell me, Emma, are you . . . have you been working as a prostitute?"

My mouth drops open. *"Non!"* I practically shout. *"Qu'est-ce que vous dites?"*

"Emma, in Normandy there are shelters for women like you."

"Oh, my God." I shake my head slowly back and forth for emphasis. "Never. I would *never.*"

In disgust I inch away from her, horrified at what she's just suggested. For a moment her sweet face transforms into the jowly visage of M. Marquet, and just like when his face was so close to mine on Christmas Eve, I can't breathe. I can't see. All I can do is keep myself from screaming.

"I can help you," Binet is insisting. But I just shake my head.

"I'm not a . . . prostitute. I'm a student. I don't need your help, I just need to get back to Paris. Am I free to go?" I can't look at her.

"Yes, Emma, I suppose." She hands me a small business card, her name and number printed on it. "If you ever get into trouble like this again, just call me. Please don't sleep in a train station again."

"Fine," I say. I fixate toward the timetable and reel away from her, from all of them, the agents in their navy uniforms and the cops with their heavy boots and rigid batons tucked into their belts. I can't get to the Rouen-bound train briskly enough. It's sitting on the very last platform. Let them wonder about my route. Let Binet worry about whether or not I will be okay. All I know is that I have to get to Annabel. She's the only one who understands the situation. I don't know if she's really in Rouen. I have no idea. All I know is that searching for her is better than knowing I'm truly all alone.

I have to find her, I repeat to myself, burning tears weighing at the corners of my eyes.

Prostitutes . . . hands . . . the concrete floor of the Gournay-en-Bray station, the way I could feel it through my coat and my jeans and eventually the soles of my shoes. All the way to Rouen I slip in and out of dreams about the past few days. I dream of the cute guy in the baseball cap and the train surrounded by barren, snowy fields. I imagine the cops deciding I was a streetwalker, a poor, destitute student in need of a shelter home. When the train screeches into Rouen station, I rub my eyes and swallow the anger and fear that have been following me as long as I have been on this journey.

I step off the train. I find myself in a city very unlike what I had pictured as I read *Madame Bovary* yesterday. I was expecting a small backwater town. In fact, Rouen is quite bustling. Probably even more bustling than it was in Flaubert's day.

St. Joan of Arc was martyred in this town, in a market square not far from this very train station. I learn this from the "*BIENVENUE À ROUEN*" billboard in the lobby, where I recharge with a vending-machine espresso. When I finish my drink, I push open the doors and make my way down the Rue de Jeanne d'Arc, my mind flashing with the image of the young girl roped to a pillar and set aflame. I feel like I can hear her screams as I get closer to the place where she died in agony—or maybe that's just exhaustion.

At the Rue du Gros-Horloge, I make a right, following the Rouen tourist route down the long pedestrianized street leading to something— a square, perhaps a church—at its end. All around me rise brightly colored half-timbered houses, adding to the quaint and slightly spooky flavor of the place. I imagine knights and castles, peasants and townspeople with dirty clothes and bad teeth. The tourists here are soaking it up. It's not even midmorning and yet the cobblestones are filled every which way with people, storefronts lined with little Joan of Arc figurines.

When I see the Gothic cathedral at the end of the street, it shocks me. It's enormous—bigger than Notre Dame, bigger than any of the many magnificent churches in Paris. The crowded street gives way to a clear view of the carved stone masterpiece, which it overwhelms everything around it.

I feel like I have seen it before. I remember, then, why Rouen was a name that sounded familiar to me when I saw it circled in Annabel's book.

Claude Monet made a series of paintings of the *Cathédrale Notre-Dame de Rouen*, and though I've never been a huge fan of the Impressionists, I'd been struck when I saw them by how Monet managed to capture all this grandeur with his blurry strokes. While the rest of his work seems so hazy, and steeped in memory, this series I'd been fond of because it was striking and evocative and different.

I remember my dream early this morning—Jay and I were in the Monet room at the Louvre. Monet. Monet! I must have known on some level.

"Oh, wow," I say breathlessly. Tourists, many of them English-speaking, smile at me in agreement.

In *Madame Bovary*, Emma arranged to meet her lover Léon here. Here, where she prayed for divine intervention.

I creep into the cathedral, holding my breath. *Annabel, I know you are close to me,* I try to tell her silently. *Please let my instincts be right.*

I take a lap around the cathedral. I visit each little chapel, hoping there Annabel might be. At the last one, I rest my weary body on one of the small chairs inside it. I rest my chin on my chest and close my eyes, my hair draping either side of my face.

I'm not sure how much time passes, but after a long period of silence, I feel someone behind me. I can't turn around for the hope I feel swelling in my chest.

Could it be Annabel? Could she have known to meet me here? The way Emma met Léon at this church?

Behind me stands not Annabel but a priest. "It's time to go, *mon enfant*. The church is closing."

Back in the rapidly emptying cathedral square, my stomach aches with hollow hunger. I need to eat something.

There's a café nearby, with coffee, sandwiches, and, I notice, Internet service. I chew on bread, butter, and jam. It doesn't taste like anything.

I haven't found Annabel yet. I'm scared.

I ask to use a computer. It takes me a long time to figure out what exactly I want to type into an email.

Jay,

I'm so confused. Exhausted.

I didn't think this would be so hard. I don't know what I thought...

Please. Whatever you do, don't call the cops or Mme Cuchon. You have to promise me you won't.

Tell me you'll help me if I need you to. I can get through this if you just write me back and tell me that one thing.

PJ

I push SEND before I can think twice. Then I click on the email I just sent and read it again, over and over, until it doesn't even make sense anymore.

It isn't often you are forced to make a split-second decision that could alter your life for good, and then have an eternity to think about whether or not it was the right one.

All I could think about as I fled the house on the Place des Ternes was that I had to get away from the Marquets. No matter what they know about me, I am better off away from them. In my mind's eye I could see Annabel's swash of dark hair dashing by, teasing me to follow. Her favorite book happened to be sitting on my desk next to where I'd laid down my coat. I grabbed everything my hands could carry. I ran through the falling snow as fast as I could, all the while imagining a long dark ponytail swinging in the distance ahead of me. I followed the vision all the way to Rouen. And now I've got nowhere else to go.

The computer terminal beeps to warn me that my time is nearly through. I log off.

Out the window of the café, I can see a falafel cart set up on the curb. It's turning a heavy business selling pitas stuffed with hummus, tomato, pickles, cabbage, and fried balls of ground chickpeas. Each sandwich is smothered in tahini and hot sauce, and the locals take theirs in with two hands, devouring them as they walk away.

A young woman dressed in a plaid swing coat from the fifties walks up to the stand. She points at the ingredients she wants. I can hear her comfortable, unself-conscious laugh, sharp and clear. She avoids speaking in French.

Annabel loves France, but she can't speak the language. She's awful at it.

My heart stops beating.

"Annabel . . . Annabel!"

I knew it. And yet I can't believe it. I must be seriously losing my mind, thinking too much about the past. I rub my eyes. There she is, still—about to turn away now. I leap from my chair like I've been struck by lightning. The chair clatters to the floor as I rush toward the window. Her blue eyes are splotchy and puffy with fatigue, but those eyes are unmistakable.

I race through the café, out the door, and onto the street, not caring who I have to shove out of my way. I'm shaking as I fling myself at her.

I wouldn't have trusted my own judgment, not after the last two days I've had, but when I smell that woodsy scent, sweet like apples . . .

It's her.

6. OLIVIA

Life is for Living

"*L*et's stay here forever," Thomas whispers into my ear, his face buried against the cotton pillowcase. In the dimmed candlelight of the bedroom Thomas grew up in, which I'm inhabiting for the year, I can just make out the three little moles near Thomas's perfect pink ear. His skin is like a baby's—soft and smooth.

I got back from rehearsal a few hours ago. Thomas was waiting for me, making a big show of brewing lemon tea and begging to let him get in the shower with me.

"*Absolument!*" I insisted, but I hurried to wash the dance-studio grime off of me so I could get back to him. Once I was scrubbed down and wrapped up in my robe, I got into the little twin bed with him, the one where we've been sleeping every night since he got back from the Alps.

Mme Rouille is, mercifully, still there, vacationing with her sisters, totally oblivious.

"Aren't you hungry?" I giggle. It's after eight. "I'm starving."

"There is a *bûche de Noël* left in the *frigo*," Thomas suggests. "Bring it in here. I will feed it to you."

I snort. "Thomas, no! I need real food, not sweets . . ." I gently rub his flat stomach. "So do you. Let's go get something to eat."

"And leave this perfect place?" Thomas throws a slender arm over me. "I do not dream of it."

"Hmm." I roll over so that my face is against his smooth chest. "Doesn't a nice bowl of French onion soup sound good right now?" I lick my lips noisily.

"But it's so cold out there," Thomas says. "And you'd really rather have soup than me?"

"I'd like to have both," I tell him. "Let's go down to Café Dumont. Please? I'll buy."

Thomas jumps out of bed. "It is my responsibility to make sure you do the best of Paris. If it is soup that you want to eat, then I will take you to the best French onion soup in the entire city."

"Really?" I squeal. Thomas stands in his boxers in front of me, and it is all I can do not to pull him back under the blankets with me. But I really am hungry. I jump out of bed and pull some jeans on and a big sweater. The candles make a pleasant birthdaylike smell as I blow them out.

"*On y va!*" I call from the front hallway, fluffing my wet hair in front of the entryway mirror. "You ready?"

Thomas checks his phone as he slips his coat on. "Well, as long as we are going out . . ."

"*Oui?*"

"Can I invite some friends to meet us? It has been a long time since I have seen them," Thomas says.

"*Bien sûr,*" I say. "I'd love to get to know your friends." I keep my voice tempered, but inside, I'd be thrilled to see that part of Thomas's life—the life he leads outside this apartment.

Thomas sends a quick text to his friends. We lock the door behind us, taking a moment to share a breathless kiss before going downstairs.

Thomas leads me down the Avenue des Ternes and makes a right on Avenue Niel. I've never walked up this way before.

"I'm taking you to one of the best bistros in Paris. You will adore it," Thomas promises. "My friends, they are already here."

I rush down the street alongside Thomas, my mittened hands shoved deep into the pockets of my wool peacoat.

Thomas pulls the door open to a large, hazy bar-restaurant on the corner of Avenue Niel and Rue Laugier. It's chock-full of people, most of them drinking tall glasses of beer and eating peanuts. A group of people I vaguely recognize is sitting around a table near the bar.

I remember Inés, Xavier, and Rémy from the night of PJ's party earlier this fall. They are Thomas's "crew" from the Sorbonne. Well, really, the group has known each other since they went to the Lycée de Monceau together before college. They all grew up in Ternes.

Unlike Thomas, his friends don't want to be doctors.

Inés has funky, choppy hair and the coolest bohemian clothes. She told me the night I met her that she wants to be a writer, maybe a poet. Xavier makes beautiful sculptures and is studying to be an architect. It's funny that he's so adept with his hands, despite being a kind of stocky, awkward guy. He looks way old, but Thomas told me he's twenty. Rémy is into art history—he can tell you the year any one of the paintings in the Louvre was painted and why each one is so important. He's also lanky like Thomas, and slightly arrogant. He seems like he could be a player—but nothing like the players I knew back at my high school.

Inés leaps from her chair the moment she sees Thomas and me walk in. Since I last saw her, she's dyed her light brown hair a deep shade of purple, and tonight she's wearing skinny gray jeans, a bright flowy top that hangs off her thin clavicle, and an old-looking army jacket with a crazy silk scarf trailing her neck. "Oleeeeeevia!" she shrieks, smacking two very wet kisses on my cheeks and pulling my hat off my head. "It eez so wonderful to see your beautiful face!"

Xavier and Rémy pull me down to their seated level to kiss me hello as well. Xavier, a rotund character who is way prematurely balding in the front, pounds the empty seat next to him with his big fist. Rémy grins at me sexily, revealing some crooked teeth as he smoothly grabs an extra chair from a nearby table for Thomas.

"Seet! Seet!" Inés is shouting as Xavier announces, "Let us get more beers!"

"No, no, it's okay," I say, but Thomas and his friends will have none of it. Finally, I just accept a pint of 1664 with a smile. If we're going out, I guess that means we're going *out*.

Thomas orders French onion soup, *moules frites*, several more pints of beer. The waiter-slash-bartender brings us an enormous basket of bread. I dig in heartily, avoiding the mussels but savoring each salty fry and creamy bite of soup. It's been ages since I ate this indulgently, maybe not since Alex's birthday dinner, right around the time I was accepted to the Underground.

"Practicing for the Revue has turned me into a total heifer!" I cry, gesturing at what a large portion of my food is gone after only about five minutes. "I swear, I usually don't eat like this."

"Life is for living," Inés tells me, her voice full of sage wisdom. She rips off another chunk of bread and sops up the last of her soup with it. "How can you live without good food?" Alex would say the same thing.

"I just hope I can keep up with André tomorrow!" I laugh, patting my full stomach.

"Olivia is dancing in the Revue Bohème," Thomas tells his friends proudly. "She's been cast in a duet."

"*Sacre bleu, c'est fantastique!*" Xavier shouts. "You are not joking?" I shake my head, smiling. "No, he's not joking."

Inés grabs my hands and kisses them. "That is spectacular!"

"You really are a ballerina, aren't you?" Rémy looks at me, impressed.

"Well, yes, I guess I am." I laugh.

"Well, we must celebrate, then," Inés says. She gets up and gets more beers from the bar.

Thomas's friends are unlike any that I've ever had before. Xavier rents a large funky warehouse in Clichy where he does his art and also lives most of the time. According to Thomas, he barely ever goes to his classes. He smokes hand-rolled cigarettes and loves to complain about the ugly modern buildings that crowd around the Boulevard Périphérique, the ring road that separates Paris proper from the city's high-rise suburbs. Xavier is a classicist. But his sculptures, funnily enough, are weird and wacky and totally new.

Inés, like Thomas, always has a notebook with her to jot down everything she finds interesting about Paris. She's a dedicated literature student and often bursts into recitations of obscure French poetry that even Thomas doesn't know. Rémy and Inés are not a couple, but after several rounds of drinks, they start to act like one—passionately kissing right in front of everyone.

Meanwhile, Rémy is totally one of those guys girls' mothers warn them about—disastrously handsome, tall, and hopelessly immature. Already, Inés was the one to unfold his napkin and put it in his lap. She wiped the *moules* juice off his wrist as it ran toward the folded-up cuff of his wrinkled white shirt. When he was considering having a brandy, she reminded him that drinking brandy upsets his stomach.

They are just so adorable together, though it confuses me why they aren't officially a couple. I wonder briefly whether they also date other people, and the idea makes my head spin a little. They're all so different from my friends at home.

By midnight, the bistro has fairly emptied out. Inés and Thomas are fiercely debating philosophy, their arguments peppered with witty asides from Rémy, who plays the trumpet in an Afro-Caribbean jazz trio with a bunch of sixty-year-old men he met when he was doing the Civil Service for a year working in an old folks' home.

I'm resting my chin on my hand, leaning over the beer-splattered table. I could listen to them for hours. They're like *no one* I've ever known. I can't remember Vince's friends ever getting so worked up about the relationship between music and sexuality, for instance, which is what they are now debating.

Thomas takes a hundred-euro bill out of his wallet and places it on our table. "Shall we, *mes amis*?"

"I don't want to leave until I get to see our star ballerina in action," Inés says. "Dance for us! Give us a preview of the show."

"*Oui!*" Thomas, Rémy, and Xavier agree. "*Faiscca!*"

I laugh. "I'm *so* not sober enough to do that right now."

Inés and Xavier push some tables out of the way. "Olivia! We are not letting you leave until you dance a solo for us—"

"Think of it as your payment for dinner!" Thomas tells me.

"So I have to dance for my soup, do I?" I stand up, feeling giddy, and straighten my spine. I know I'm wasted because I am actually going to do it. "Fine then!"

Instead of the routine that we are doing for the Revue Bohème, I decide to wow my new friends with some of my best tricks. Spotting the wall, I whip around into a series of pirouettes that I know will leave them speechless. After about eighteen times around on the tip of my UGG boot and pliéing only when I absolutely have to, I finally curtsy to my audience. The group bursts out with cheers.

"Brava! Brava!" Rémy yells.

I can't help giggling as the hairy old bartender scowls at us. "Time to go, kids!" he warns us. "No more funny business."

I squeal when Thomas picks me up and slings me over his shoulder. "I remember the time you last danced and drank. You ended up in crutches, *non?*"

I am laughing too hard to answer.

"To bed!" Thomas shouts, and he carries me home like that, singing and laughing all the way back to the apartment.

LA SAINT -SYLVESTRE
New Year's Eve

7. ALEX

New Year's Resolutions

t doesn't take long for us to find my dad's digs in Montauban. In a town this small, all the rich people tend to live in one area. Google Maps takes care of the rest. We're all eager to get out of the car and stretch, especially Jay, who received an email from PJ on his phone just before we arrived into town. He's convinced she really needs us and has been rushing Zack to get us here as quickly as possible so he can officially begin his search.

When we find the address I knew to be my dad's from reading the international real estate news, it's dark out and I'm uneasy, but I don't want Jay and Zack to know that. I tell them to wait in the car, and I'll go check out the apartment. I take a deep breath and walk right up to the concierge with a big smile.

"Je m'appelle Alex Nguyen, la fille de M. Nguyen. Le Monsieur Nguyen du Montauban National?" I inform him.

"Ah! Mademoiselle Nguyen!" The concierge is an elderly little man with crinkly eyes and a sweet smile. *"Bonsoir!"*

"Mon père n'est pas ici, n'est-ce pas? Il va au Vietnam, oui?"

"Oui, oui, bien sûr," the concierge replies. I sigh in relief. My dad's in Vietnam, as I had assumed. Far, far from here.

Already my French is stretched beyond its limits, but I jump ahead before the concierge starts to think anything fishy is going on. "My father said you could let my friends and me into the apartment," I say as smoothly as possible. "We're going to be staying here for a couple of days."

"Comment? C'est vrai?" he asks. I want to go pluck Zack from the car because I can't understand the rest of what the concierge says. I just have such a hard time with listening comprehension. Go figure, right?

Finally, the concierge offers me his hand and motions toward the elevator and up the stairs. He says something about his faulty memory, and I can't believe our good luck. This poor guy probably feels terrible that he didn't remember I was coming.

I might not know much about my dad, but one thing I definitely know for sure is that he loves the "old school" aspect of France. He doesn't do modern or sleek. It doesn't surprise me that he's bought an apartment in a renovated medieval monastery not far from the town square. But to judge by the lobby, I can tell that this place is going to be over-the-top nice.

I'm suddenly nervous to see it—my father's *home*. Well, one of his homes. I run back out to the parked car, grab Jay and Zack and pull them and our luggage inside.

Once we're assembled, the concierge introduces himself as Monsieur Garty. He regards us all with pleasant looks. We cram into the little elevator that takes us up to the top level. France's buildings, especially in little cities like Montauban, are built low because they are so old. A penthouse in France is hardly what it is in New York. All the same, this penthouse is one of the most impressive homes I have ever seen. And, mind you, I have seen a lot of *very* impressive places. I mean, I went to school at Brooklyn Prep. That's the best school in Brooklyn, some say in all of New York. My classmates are the children of VIPs. We get around, you know?

M. Garty unlocks the carved front doors using a high-tech access card. He punches in a security code to disable the alarm and flips on row after row of tasteful, rosy lights that line the arched ceiling of the space. The furnishings in my dad's place are spare, with large open spaces dividing the rooms instead of walls. Everything is sort of old-fashioned and oversized, like the huge, polished wood table in the kitchen in place of a counter. I see that the appliances and the entertainment systems are top of the line, but everything is discreet and classy. And true to form, my dad has invested in a few massively expensive pieces of antique art: one very ornate large portrait of a group of French cavalry riding off to war and one of those tapestries you see in museums sometimes, with the unicorns and the maidens on them. They have a couple at the Met in New York.

"*Mon Dieu,*" Zack gapes. "The Marquets have nothing on this place." PJ's host parents are notorious at the Lycée for having what was by far the most lavish homestay of any of the participating families.

"You've got that right," Jay agrees. "Check out that TV!" He points to a Samsung TV mounted on the wall across from the kitchen. It's so big you could watch it easily from anywhere you were standing in the apartment.

M. Garty takes us to a staircase tucked away behind the bathroom, and when we climb it, we find a master bedroom, another bathroom, and a little guest room at the top.

"*C'était le clocher,*" M. Garty explains. I glance at Zack.

"The former bell tower," Zack explains.

Oh, how absolutely *divine.*

Pushing back the curtains in the master bedroom, I can see the whole town spread out before me in the dark: the bridge, the town square, all the dimly lit bistros starting to serve dinner.

"*C'est très agréable. Merci beaucoup.*" I signal at M. Garty. He hands me a spare set of access cards (one for me and one I hand to Jay) with all the trust in the world. Along with each card is a small piece of paper with the security code for the alarm system scrawled on to it. When he shows himself out, I catch Zack and Jay grinning foolishly at each other, obviously stoked to find their accommodations so posh. I turn away from them. They have no idea what I've just pulled off, that my dad has no clue we're even here. That he could be less than pleased if he finds out.

Later that night, as I tuck into the master bed beside Zack, who is already completely out, I gaze at the blue face of my BlackBerry. I'll have to call my mother back eventually. Who knows if she's gotten wind yet of my not-so-pleasant status (or lack thereof) at the Lycée. But what will I tell her? Besides, she is *so* not one to worry about me and my happiness. She made that much clear to me this past semester by totally taking away my funds and leaving me completely on my own. And then not showing up on Christmas? If she doesn't want to give me the time of day, *fine*. It's mutual.

I hit DELETE without even listening to the voice mail, shut off my phone, and tuck it under my pillow. Then I settle into the fluffy down comforter, gaze out the dark window at the tiny, dime-sized moon, and wait for sleep to come.

From the moment we wake up the next morning, Jay goes out hunting for PJ. Zack and I are sleeping in the bed in the master bedroom together. Jay took the smaller guest room. I hear Jay leave before I have even gotten out of bed. I roll over and face Zack, who has slept through the noise in the apartment beneath us.

Zack is so beautiful. He's one of those boys that you'd call pretty, especially once you found out he was gay. He tends to get his hair cut in different ways—when I first met him in September, his hair was long, like the seventies. Now it's cut shorter, but still longish in the front. His dark-framed glasses are folded up on the bedside table next to him, and without them, he looks younger, more boyish than ever. I feel a rush of affection for him and can't resist hugging him, even though I know it will wake him up.

"Ugh, Alex, no," Zack mumbles sleepily. "Get off!" He tries to roll away but I won't let him.

"Come on, Zack," I whine. "I need a hug."

Zack rubs his eyes and reaches for his glasses. "What's wrong?"

I sit up in bed, pulling the white sheet up to my chin. "I'm not sure."

Zack sits up, too, his hair rumpled and out of place. "You want to talk?"

I consider for a moment. What to say? Where to start?

"Alex, what's up?" Zack prods. "We still haven't talked about why we found you in such a slovenly state on Christmas morning. It's so unlike you. Did something happen with your host family?"

I can tell from the way he asks that he knows that there is absolutely nothing wrong between my host family, the Pomeroys, and me. My host parents, Marîthe and Alain, barely register in my day-to-day life in Paris. They mean well, but they are like, nonentities. I know Zack gets how I feel about them because his host family is exactly the same, except with one more sibling. Apart from periodically being totally grossed out by my little ten-year-old host brother, Sebastien, and his grimy little friends, I feel totally ambivalent about them.

"No," I say.

"Are you in trouble with your mom?" Zack asks. "How come she didn't come to Paris for Christmas?"

"She made other plans," I say stonily.

"What about the test? Did you do okay on the Final Comp?"

I roll my eyes. "Of *course* I did." I don't know why I just can't bear to tell him. I don't want him to think I'm a failure, I guess.

"And George? Did you get a chance to say good-bye to him before the break?"

I don't know what to say to *that*.

"Is that what's wrong, Alex?" Zack knows he's onto something.

I put my head on Zack's shoulder. He smells like detergent. His clothes, even what he sleeps in, are always perfectly laundered and pressed. It's comforting.

After a few minutes of Zack waiting expectantly for me to answer him, and my own thoughts wandering away from this depressing conversation that, to tell the truth, I don't find to be any of Zack's business, anyway, I decide to get up. Why dwell on something that clearly wasn't meant to be? My heart hurts a little. But dredging up all the gory details would only make it worse.

"I'm going to take a shower, doll. Then let's go get some breakfast."

Jay's note, left on the kitchen table, simply says he's out looking and will be back tonight. Zack thinks he and I better go check out the Ingres Museum in the meantime, so after we eat, we head over to it.

The Ingres Museum is a small collection housed in a totally gorgeous mansion overlooking the banks of the Garonne River. The paintings are to die for! I wish I could buy one.

But oh, that's right . . . I'm broke. Thanks, Mom.

We have to work up our nerve, but eventually we ask all the clerks and the tour guides if they've seen a tall American girl with long white blond hair, most likely wearing a ratty brown grandfather cardigan with elbow patches and jeans with holes in them. We describe her periwinkle hat, her canvas bag she carries notebooks and sketch pads around in. But no one at the Ingres Museum has any recollection of seeing a girl like that wandering through their galleries.

Defeated, we email Olivia from my BlackBerry.

Any sign of PJ? Nothing in Montauban yet.

I light a cigarette and smoke it in the gravel garden outside the museum entrance while we wait. After a while, the device beeps with a response.

You're kidding. I haven't heard from her either. I'm getting really worried.

Zack and I don't have anything to write back. We're getting worried, too.

In front of the Evêché Church that night, we see some punky street kids with a skinny dog trying to collect money in a little cardboard box. The box only has a few coins in it, and the dog is chewing hungrily on a stick. I elbow Zack. He empties his pockets and gives the kids all the change he has.

One of them, a guy, lifts his black puffy hat in a salutation to us. His eyes are blank, but I can feel him watching us as we rush away from him.

That night, I wake up around one A.M. to hear Jay punching in the code to activate the alarm. M. Garty must have helped him get back into the building. I grab my BlackBerry and text Jay in the next room.

Find anything?

Nothing. Somehow I can feel his desperation through the screen of my BlackBerry. I want to text him back something inspiring, something that will get him through the night. I want to reassure him that we didn't make a mistake coming here.

Well, it's not my fault that he totally latched onto Zack's suggestion about the birthplace of Ingres, I reason in the dark. Still, I wish we'd found her today. I'd had this idea in my head that we'd just find her in the galleries of the museum, gazing thoughtfully at some painting, and she'd be thrilled to see us. And for once in my life, I would know what it was like to come through for someone. And have my dad (or even just my dad's ritzy real estate holdings) come through for *me.* I flip over on the big bed, uncomfortably.

There's always the chance we could find her tomorrow, or even the next day, I decide. Even though Zack is sleeping soundly next to me, I can almost hear him guffaw in response.

Yeah, right.

★ ★ ★

It doesn't take long to get the lay of Montauban. In the last two days, our little trifecta has fallen into a sad routine: Zack and I sleep late, get breakfast once we've showered and gotten dressed, and then wander around town. Jay disappears long before we get up, and returns to the apartment sullen and dejected every night.

Unable to get Jay to commit to a time when we might be able to return to Paris, I email Olivia from my BlackBerry the news I know she's dreading getting.

Livvy,

We're still looking for PJ in Montauban. We can't come back to Paris just yet. U cool with us missing your show?

xx Alex

In true Olivia form, the message I get a few minutes later is profusely generous:

Alex,

Please just do whatever you can to find her. I wish I could be there. Give a bise to Zack and to Jay for me. I love you all.

Hearts,

Liv

The morning of New Year's Eve, I wake up before the sun comes up. We aren't supposed to be here still. Olivia's been emailing us from Paris, urgently asking if we've found PJ yet. Needless to say, we haven't.

I can't fall back asleep. I keep thinking of PJ, of the creepy and sort of sexy way that she's always fidgeting with her clothes. The way her jeans are too loose around her hips, and the pale sliver of skin between the bottom of her shirt and the belt of her jeans when she leans over. The boys at the Lycée were mad for her. You could tell every time she moved that their eyes were following her. It drove me crazy the way she drove them crazy. And now it's driving me crazy to think of all the skeezy old freaks out there, seeing her and wanting her, too. It's weird to actually feel—what, protective?—over PJ, but now that she's gone, I kind of do. The world can be a disgusting place and most men are jerks. I've learned that the hard way.

Silently, I slip out from under the duvet I am sharing with Zack and dig around in the kitchen until I find a canister of preground Illy coffee beans. There is an espresso machine on the counter, pushed against the corner under the cupboards. I fiddle with it for a while. It can't be that hard to make a cup of coffee.

"Having a little trouble there?" Jay's tenor in the silent apartment bellows like a megaphone. My bare feet bounce off the wooden floor, causing yet another capful of wet espresso grounds to go flying over my shirt, leaving a big damp spot.

"Oh, God, Jay, you scared me!" I paw at the brown mess I made on my chest. "Do you know how to use these things?" I gesture at the espresso machine.

Jay shakes his closely shaved head. He doesn't have a shirt on, just gym shorts riding low around the waistband of his plaid boxers. His chest is mostly hairless and naturally tan, though I can see a tan line on his impressive upper arm, where his soccer shirt probably hits. What is it about guys' arms? They are incredible. "Your dad doesn't have a regular coffeemaker?" he asks sleepily.

"Um," I say. I feel a tad underdressed. My pajama shorts aren't really shorts so much as bloomers, and the ruffles of lace around the hem give them a very lingerie look. So cute, right? I love them. I'm also not wearing a bra, and half of my white tank top is soaked! I guess it's Jay's lucky day, if he ever stops worrying about PJ long enough to notice.

"I bet he does." Jay looks around, and ends up finding one above the sink.

"There isn't any milk," I tell him. Despite how I promised my friends that my dad's fridge would be stocked, I knew it wouldn't be, and I was right. He never eats at home. For him it's five stars for every meal.

"That's okay," Jay answers. "You got any sugar?"

There's a sugar bowl in the middle of the wooden kitchen table, and we load our coffee cups with the raw crystals.

"Sorry about the milk," I apologize for want of anything else to say. I toss my hair out of my eyes and watch Jay's bare back as he walks across the room. He takes his coffee over to the couch.

I never realized that just sipping coffee could be so *hot*. I follow him and sit down on the couch, too.

"That's okay," he says. "This is how I like my coffee, anyway."

"Really?" I squint at him. "I like mine with *lots* of milk."

"You would."

I flick him in the bicep. "Shut up."

We drink our coffee in silence, just one little lamp hanging above us in the predawn darkness. The sun rises late this time of year. All of Montauban is still asleep.

"What does that mean, anyway? 'You would,'" I ask Jay.

Jay laughs. "Ha. Nothing. I just like giving you shit."

"Oh," I reply. "Well. I can think of about two hundred better things to make fun of me for than how I like my coffee."

"Oh, man," Jay groans. "Don't say that."

I can't help giggling. "Why not?"

Jay grins, his brown eyes crinkling at the corners. "I know better than to give *you* the upper hand. Girls like you, man. They bat their eyelashes and work their way into your sympathies, and then, bam! You're changing the oil in their cars, watching their kid brother while they go shopping, driving them to go to the prom with some dirtbag older guy."

Ha! Just when you think Jay is a humorless, lovesick puppy, you remember his hidden sarcastic side. When he teases me, it makes me feel cute—desirable.

I catch a scent of his musky deodorant and shiver. For a moment, I imagine Zack isn't here. I think of what would happen if I scooted closer to Jay and kissed his sleepy, scratchy cheek. Would he pull me under his muscular arm and hold me tight and forget about PJ? Would he keep teasing me in that sexy way as he took me upstairs to his room?

What would it be like to have a boyfriend like Jay—smart, sensible, and strong, and yet funny, mellow, and down-to-earth? Jay's the kind of guy you're best friends with for years, and then one day, you realize he's a damn *fox*. The whole shirtless thing doesn't hurt either.

Jay downs the rest of his coffee. "All right, *chica*. I'm out of here."

"Where do you go all day?" I really have been wondering. Jay leaves Zack and me on our own to try to find PJ and absorbs himself in his own missions, not ever revealing what he may or may not have discovered when he is by himself all day. Montauban is not that big of a town.

I wonder, sometimes, if he isn't just waiting in some special spot, hoping that she will eventually appear. That's why I don't ask; the mental image is too sad, too pathetic. I don't want that to be true.

"I look for my girl," Jay answers me, shrugging. There's a sincerity in his eyes that causes me to choke on my coffee.

His girl. I look down at the last of my dregs. *His girl* ran away. *His girl* didn't appreciate him like she should have. Much as I feel for ole PJ, I can't help thinking this is all backwards. It's not fair. She *chose* to run away. But I chose to be right here.

Jay goes upstairs to take a shower. I take our mugs back to the kitchen and leave them in the sink, pondering.

I want to be his girl.

I *need* to be his girl.

The best-friend boyfriend. The guy you know you can trust because he already knows everything about you and he loves you anyway. Like Zack ... but straight. You help him out, make it so he can't imagine you not being there—and *voilà*!

He's madly in love with you and no one else.

8.ZACK

Counting Down

can't decide whether I find Alex's singing in the shower annoying or amusing. On the one hand, I was never one to silence a heartfelt rendition of "Total Eclipse of the Heart." On the other, Alex's warbling sounds like a cat being barbequed for Sunday lunch.

I pound on the door and yell, "Pipe down, little sparrow! You're wakin' the neighbors."

"We'd only be making it right . . ." she sings on. What put her in such a good mood?

Pierson sent me some texts while he was out last night:

U HAF TO COME HERE. SRSLY MEGACOOL.

HANNES N ME R OUT RIGHT NOW. HOT GUYS EVERYWHERE. HOP A TRAIN GUY!

U MUST BE SLEEPIN. LOOOOOOOOOSER. TALK L8R.

Around lunchtime, Jay bursts into Alex's dad's living room. Alex is still upstairs getting dressed. I'm cleaning up the kitchen—for some reason, there are stinky espresso grounds everywhere. I didn't expect to see Jay at all today. The past few days, I've been avoiding him—letting him get up and get ready to leave without any interference. It's hard, but good for me, to get him out of my sight.

He still does it to me; I still stop whatever I'm doing when he walks into a room. He's a magnet for my undivided attention.

"Man, you'll never believe this!"

"What?" I set down the sponge I was using and wipe my hands on a clean linen dishcloth. "Did you find PJ?"

"She Gchatted me!"

"WHAT?" I shriek. "She done what?"

Alex pounds down the stairs in a swinging fringe miniskirt, brown tights and boots, and a white bouclé sweater belted around the waist. Her hair is still wet and only one of her eyes is made up yet. I notice Jay, despite his franticness, appreciates her formfitting outfit.

"What did I miss?" The eyeliner pencil is still in her hand.

"PJ," Jay pants. "She Gchatted me. You know how on Gchat you can be invisible? She was invisible. I . . ." He stops and gets his bearings. "I went to the library to look up some stuff about the area. I was reading about all the different artists on their Web archive and had my Gmail open. Then suddenly it dings that someone was chatting me. It was PJ!"

"Oh, my God!" I say. That's shocking. It's also shocking that the library was open on New Year's Eve day. The French are great believers in closing for public holidays. I find this tradition charming, though it annoys many Americans, like Alex who believes in a twenty-four-hour-lifestyle despite her hereditary Francophilia.

In my view, life only offers you so many chances to spend a day in complete relaxation—why refuse the opportunity? "Where is she?" I ask.

Jay shakes his head. "She wouldn't tell me!"

"What did she say?" Alex demands. "Jay, tell us what she said!"

Jay pulls off his hat. The color creeps back into his face. He hasn't shaved in a few days, and his stubble is dark and thick. I've never seen him come to the Lycée being anything but absolutely smooth. He must be really losing it.

"Okay," Jay says. "So she types, 'Jay, you there?' and I type, 'PJ! I'm here. Where are you? What can I do?'"

As much as I want to find our girl and bring her back to Paris, this is mildly revolting. Even for me. And I have a pretty high tolerance for schmaltz.

"She doesn't type anything back, but I have this feeling she's still there. And then Gchat says she entered text, so I am just sitting there, waiting and waiting. It keeps saying, 'Penelope is typing . . .' but it is taking forever. So, the article I was looking at online, right before that happened, it was about this guy named Toulouse-Lautrec, from Toulouse, you know, not far from here—you know him?"

I shake my head. Alex nods knowledgeably. She's hanging on to every breathless word, just like me. But in my case, there's more than one kind of torture going on.

"So I was like, looking at the title of the article in the minimized browser window, and I'm like, 'Toulouse! Are you in Toulouse?' I mean, I typed that to PJ."

"And?" Alex and I say at the same time.

"And she writes back, 'I wish you were here, too.'"

I look at Jay, then Alex, then back to Jay. "What does that mean? Where is she?"

"She's in Toulouse!" Alex cries.

"I asked her again, 'Are you in Toulouse?' but then it said, 'Penelope is offline. Chats will be sent via email.' And she didn't come back on."

"What?" I'm horribly confused.

Alex is, too. "So does that mean she's in Toulouse or not?" I can hardly believe it, but there is real terror in Alex's eyes. This is the most concerned I've seen her get over PJ—ever.

"I don't know! Because I don't know if she typed that before or after I asked her about Toulouse! And then she got off so fast."

"Heck, I'll go to Toulouse," I say. "What have we got *to lose*?" I laugh at my pun.

Jay and Alex don't laugh. "This is serious, Zack," Alex says.

"I'm being serious!" I say. "Let's go there. Tonight. If she's in Toulouse on New Year's Eve, don't you think we'll see her? Isn't that the best night of the year to see someone randomly on the street?"

Alex nods. "It would be fun to go out in Toulouse . . ." I can see the little wheels in her mind turning, but I can't figure out what on earth she's got up her sleeve.

"Who knows if she's hiding or if she'll be out. But Toulouse is only an hour away, and some of the articles I was reading at the library were saying that Toulouse is a really young, hip city—the kind of place where artists have been hanging out for centuries. It seems like the kind of place PJ might be drawn to," Jay says. "You guys are right. Why don't we go tonight?"

Alex beams. "Perfect! I can't wait!"

I look back at Jay, expecting him to look disgusted at her cheerfulness. He beams right back at her.

Alex grabs my hand and pulls me back upstairs and into the bathroom.

"Tonight is going to be fabulous! Thank *God* we are upgrading our New Year's Eve plans," Alex says. She gets to work lining her other eye. "Oh, my God, Zack! I have to find something to wear. Will you help? What are *you* going to wear?"

I close the lid to the toilet and sit down on it.

"How come you are so stoked about going to Toulouse? I mean, I know it's worth a shot, but I feel like it's a *long* shot," I say to her. "Don't you?"

"We don't have anything better to do," Alex says.

"I know," I say. "But it's not like we can really celebrate tonight. Jay's a mess, and I—I'm not feeling that festive myself."

Oh, to rewind my life just a week, before I deluded myself into believing Jay might like me, too. Letting go of my crush on him is way harder than I expected. I can't help wondering if he's already put my confession out of his head completely. I hope so. And yet . . . I don't.

"Zack." Alex sets down her eyeliner and turns to me. "It is precisely because you two are so down in the dumps that I want to go to Toulouse. Jay needs to stay busy, and you, honey—you can't go on like this. You keep moping around this apartment waiting for the front door to open and Jay to take you in his arms and tell you he really is gay for you after all and I'm afraid you're gonna be waiting a thousand years. Don't you want to get dressed up and get down tonight?"

I giggle and grab her eyeliner. I slick some on, something I've never done before. "So we're not just going to spend the whole night looking for PJ?" I feel a pang of guilt, but we both know the truth. The chances of us just randomly running into her—in the fourth largest city in France—are slim to *totally nonexistent*. And we're still not completely sure if she even wants or needs our help, anyway. I feel bad, doubting Jay's whole purpose for being here. But I do wonder if his concern isn't a bit extreme.

"Ha!" Alex says. "No, we aren't. But don't tell Jay that. This project gives him *such* hope."

GUESS WHAT? NEW YEAR'S SHAPIN UP 2 B COOLER THAN I THOUGHT! I text Pierson later. GOING CLUBBIN IN TOULOUSE.

Sending that text to Pierson feels so good. For once, I've got something exciting to report from France.

Jay volunteers to drive, and Alex grabs the front seat before I have a chance to. *Bien sûr.* What else could be expected?

Yesterday Alex found the most fabulous furry Dr. Zhivago style hat in a closet at her dad's condo while we were bumming around doing nothing. "Wear the hat tonight! You'll be Julie Christie! You'll be freakin' fabulous!" I urged her when she was prancing around in her New Year's Eve outfit of a black flapper dress and her red high heels.

I wish I hadn't been so effusively enthusiastic about the hat—she doesn't fit in the front seat when she wears it! She has to lean her seat way back into a reclining position so that she won't have to take it off to fit in the car.

"What's with St. Petersburg?" Jay asks her as she situates herself. "Isn't your head sweating under there?"

Alex just laughs. "Don't make fun of my hat! Zack told me it was super cute. She flips down the passenger-side visor mirror and admires herself. "It *is* cute!"

It's dusk by the time we find ourselves in the *centre ville*, and Jay is all business. He locates a parking lot where we can pay twenty euros to keep the car all night—a bargain on New Year's Eve. Once we park, Jay bundles up in his nice black coat and wraps a scarf around his neck. He'd changed before he left, back into the dressier clothes he was wearing on the first day of the trip.

Jay just makes you want to cry sometimes. He's so sincere!

"Hey, Jay," I say as he locks the car. "It's good we're doin' this. You know that, right?"

He just sighs. "You guys have my cell?"

Alex and I nod.

"All right, well I'm going to take this photo into a couple hotels and restaurants and just start asking people if they've seen her. I'll call you when it's time to meet back up and get the car."

"Jay!" I exclaim. "Don't you want to be together on New Year's Eve?" I wonder if he can sense how excited Alex and I were about tonight for reasons not having anything to do with PJ.

"Oh," Jay says. "I guess I do. I just thought we'd have better chances if we split up. Cover more ground. But maybe I will have found PJ by then. And we can all ring in the New Year together."

"Perfect. So you'll call us?" I ask. Jay grimaces, and then turns away to melt into a crowd of tourists trolling the pink city.

Alex looks stricken.

"We'll be okay without him," I tell her. *I will be okay without him,* I repeat to myself. *I will!* "Want to go for tapas?" Toulouse's cuisine is said to strongly influence Spain, only a short distance south of us.

Alex adjusts her hat while looking in the direction Jay went. "Come to think of it, I would love to."

After several courses of crusty toast drizzled in peppery cheese and layered with ham, along with roasted tomatoes and olives, not to mention a few bottles of the house red wine, I'm dizzy with pleasure to be in Toulouse. The streets are starting to fill with revelers setting off noisemakers in preemptive celebration of a new year, a new beginning. My pulse quickens with excitement.

Alex is a bit quiet, but as usual, she tears into her food—and guzzles her wine—without reserve.

"Did you ever think that this is where you'd be ringing in the New Year?" I ask her.

"Ha, no," Alex says. "I assumed I'd be kissing George under the Eiffel Tower when the clock strikes, if not announcing our engagement."

"Are you ever going to tell me what really happened with you guys?"

Alex shrugs. "Nothing. That's the whole problem." I wonder if she is finally going to spill. "I guess he's into Patty now." That George was interested in Patty had been apparent for some time. That had not deterred Alex's ambition before.

"So it's over? For real? You aren't going to make another play for him?"

"Nope," Alex says, soaking her bread in olive oil and covering it with sea salt and chili pepper flakes. "I'm over him."

I don't know what to say.

"What about you? You still like Jay?"

"No," I lie, because I'm not going to let it be a lie for too much longer. "I'm ready to meet some new guys. Like tonight!"

"Where?" Alex laughs.

"I found a place we could go . . ." Earlier I'd done a Web search for Toulouse on some gay travel sights. "Maybe tonight's the night. Like, when everyone is kissing at midnight . . ."

"Say no more," Alex says. "Onward!"

Toulouse's classiest gay club is called Suggestion, and it's fairly demure, especially for New Year's Eve. From the outside, it looks like a chic restaurant with dimmed lights, a few nice oak bars, and some sweet, comfy couches. I've never been to a gay club before, but I'm disconcerted to realize that I'd been expecting dudes dancing in cages and waiters in leather underwear.

The club's cover is reasonable and we tip a (fully and nicely dressed) guy near the entrance to store our coats together so that we'll be unencumbered out there.

The dance floor is beginning to fill up with young, attractive guys, and despite the fact that they don't go for her kind, Alex heads straight for the center. The DJ spinning tonight is phenomenal, mixing funky salsa beats into hit pop songs and hip-hop hooks. I fetch us some vodka tonics from the bar and join Alex.

I feel freer, looser than I've been in a long while. I feel like a dork, dancing with a girl in a gay club, but I can't stop laughing just the same. I'm not a super great dancer, but what I lack in ability or technique I make up for in charm. I can do the robot, the lawnmower, throw out some jazz hands here and there. What I love about this place is that maybe for the first time in my life, I feel totally fine about being such a dork.

Within an hour of drinks and dancing, my gray T-shirt looks black from being soaked with so much sweat. I'm sparkly, too, because Alex likes to do this move where she rubs up on me which makes her shimmer powder rub off onto my clothes and skin. I can see guys watching us, maybe wondering if she's my girlfriend, then getting a closer look at me and deciding that I'm gay, too. I wonder if it is obvious to people, despite how I try to keep it to myself as much as possible. Is it obvious to my teachers, my parents, strangers, people in a club? If it's as obvious as it feels, then why do I spend so much time hiding it?

LUVIN TOULOUSE, I text Pierson. DANCING W/ THE HOTTEST GUYS EVER!

UR A STUD, Pierson texts back right away. 2NITES THE NITE! MAKE OUT!

Just then, the buzzer of Alex's BlackBerry goes off and I see Jay's text to meet up at a bar down the street, near the Place Saint-Sernin. I'm sort of disappointed—we've been having such a great time.

"Should I tell Jay to come here instead?" Alex shouts over the music to me.

"Nooooooooooo." I shake my head. "I don't want him here. He'll be too weirded out."

"Well, are you ready to go, then?" she asks.

"You go on without me." I wave her away. "I'll text you guys later."

"Really? You're really okay with me just going right now?"

"Sure. Have fun! See ya." I dash back onto the dance floor.

The music leaps and dives in energetic, frantic spurts, drawing more and more guys onto the dance floor.

On to me!

I don't even need any more drinks. I just want to keep dancing, not just tonight but forever. Everyone's pushing and grinding against each other, hot and sweaty and eager to be touched and twirled around. Everyone is smiling, closing their eyes, feeling the music, feeling good to be alive.

One guy, standing near the bar, looks at me and gives me a shy smile. He's not dancing, and in my dance-induced euphoria, I almost mistake him for Jay. Maybe Alex brought him back here, I think for a split second, terrified Jay will have seen me dancing like I'm on drugs. But when I realize it's someone I don't even know, I feel keen disappointment that it isn't Jay after all.

I stop dancing and turn away from the smiling guy.

My guts twist. Jay. If only Jay would just have been gay like me! Why did I get all those signals, all those good feelings, all throughout the fall, when he has been straight all along?

I grab my coat and head for the door. The doorman stops me, laughs in my face. *"Attendez! Il est minuit!"*

"Dix, neuf, huit . . ." I can hear everyone start to count down the seconds until midnight, at the top of their lungs. I run out of the club into the crisp cold night.

In a few seconds, it'll be a whole new year. But I wonder if anything is ever really going to change.

9. OLIVIA

The Writing on the Wall

From the wings of the ornate 1890s-era theatre in Montmartre, I can see Katica in the audience, but not Thomas. I guess that's a good thing . . . I might not be able to concentrate if I knew where in the crowd he was sitting.

"Go!" Henri hisses at me when the curtain closes on the risqué cabaret-style act right before ours. In the pitch black, I find my position, and when the curtain rises again, it's just me and André facing one another, each of us bathed in the bright glow of our own spotlight.

Kiki starts off low, her voice echoing along the floor of the auditorium as we dance slowly in time to the gradual crescendo of her song. Everybody in the whole place seems to be holding their breath. Kiki's voice could move mountains.

I've been practicing this routine for ten hours a day for almost a whole week now. It's almost effortless. Instead of thinking in steps and eight-counts, I move along with André as if this routine is as natural to us as walking. I barely even sweat. At one point, when I meet André's gaze, I even smile a bit.

The applause when we finish is incredible. Through some fluke, we're the final act of the night, and in a half hour all the people who bought tickets to the performance will gather in the ballroom for a late night New Year's Eve benefit with drinks and two long buffet tables full of shrimp cocktail and other decadent, festive foods. It's the most chi-chi party I've ever been invited to. I'm so excited, in spite of the fact that my friends aren't back yet. In spite of the fact that PJ is not back yet.

I run offstage after our final ovation, grasping André's hand and running straight into Henri's arms. Henri bounces like a child, holding us all in a three-way embrace. *"Vous étiez fantastiques!"* he cries. *"Très, très joli!"*

I scream with pleasure as I'm lifted off the ground in a swift motion that pulls me away from André and Henri and firmly into the arms of the person with whom I most want to share this wonderful moment.

Thomas is overcome with feeling. "Olivia," he says with that gorgeous accent of his. "That was . . . truthfully . . . out of the worlds."

I know what he's getting at. *"Merci beaucoup, mon ami,"* I flirt. "I'm glad you liked it."

Henri and then André come over and introduce themselves to Thomas, and then Kiki kisses me twice on each cheek and tells me I did her proud. I've never felt so accomplished, so good at what I do, so unde-niably *happy*, in all of my sixteen years. And to be accepted so lovingly by a French audience, a *Parisian* audience . . . some ballerinas wait for this for their entire careers.

I only wish my parents, and Brian, could have seen it. Then they'd really get why I'd stayed here in Paris. And, with a pang, I realize that I really did want my friends to be here, too, so that they'd get to see this side of me.

I'd asked for four tickets to the Revue Bohème performance and New Year's Eve party, back when I thought Jay, Zack, Alex, and hopefully PJ, would be here for it. When Alex told me they were going to stay in Montauban, I'd given the passes to Thomas and told him to invite Inés, Rémy, and Xavier to the performance.

Thomas pops open a bottle of Brut and holds the fizzing bottle up in the air above us. "To Olivia!" he declares. "Tonight, we celebrate you."

I quickly change into a red jersey scoop neck dress with some black tights and some simple black flat shoes that don't do anything for my height but are very comfortable after being on the points of my toes for so many hours this week. When I find Thomas and his group again in the ballroom, taking full advantage of the free-flowing wine and whiskey from the bar, they embrace me with as much excitement as I know my own friends would have.

"Olivia, when I was watching you dance," Inés tells me, "I had to open my notebook and write it all down. You looked so beautiful, so elegant, so poised."

"The choreography was absolutely transcendent!" Xavier crows, rubbing his half-bald head. "I thought I had died and gone to ballet heaven."

I chuckle. "Shush!" I say, so happy to know that they are being sincere.

Thomas slips his arms around my waist. "You are the best. *La meilleure!*"

Nearly a foot and a half taller than me, Rémy bends down to kiss my hand. "Too beautiful for words. Amazing job!"

"Olivia, can I pour you some champagne?" Thomas asks me with a kiss.

"Just a small glass, I think," I agree. I feel like celebrating!

The Revue Bohème party is an odd mix of Parisians, from grand dames to young gay dandies to models on the arms of older businessmen in sharkskin suits. There are trannies working the dance floor, some little people performing a circus on a stage at the front of the room. The music is old-fashioned. It seems like the entire heart and soul of Montmartre has come out to celebrate all that is wonderful about life and new beginnings, and, of course, art.

Thomas and I dance, not dancing the way I would at a normal party, but the old-fashioned way, with his hands placed gently around my waist and him leading me in waltzes around the room. The full skirt of my dress swings buoyantly around me. I can't keep myself from imbibing many more glasses of champagne. When the clock strikes twelve, Thomas dips me low, toward the ground, and kisses me so ardently that several onlookers cheer.

We dance for hours, stopping only to refill our glasses. By the time the party is over, at four A.M., Inés and Rémy have relocated to Inés's apartment above a shoe repair shop in the sixth, and Xavier has long since started the long walk back to his studio.

Thomas and I emerge from the theatre to find Montmartre's streets slowly emptying of New Year's Eve revelers, only a few firecrackers going off in the distance every couple of minutes.

"Ah, Olivia, my love," Thomas says. I blush fervently, unable to hide my ridiculous happiness. All of the rehearsing, all of the time spent working through those same four minutes of routine, listening to Kiki's low, slow singing until I could have sung the melody right along with her, has paid off. And now I have so much to show for it: new friends like Inés, and André, and the favor of Henri. André even told me earlier that with my hair swept up in the bun and all the stage makeup still on my face, I am quite the *belle du jour*.

A ringlet of Thomas's sandy, curly hair falls forward toward his nose, and I reach up with my gloved hand to push it aside.

Thomas pulls something out of his pocket. It's a kids' pack of light blue chalk. How odd. "Thomas, why do you have that?" Thomas can be so goofy sometimes.

Thomas laughs. "Oh, it is just a project the others and I did on New Year's Eve last year. We wrote in chalk all over the whole of Paris. It was amazing!"

"What do you mean?" I ask, confused.

"It works like this," Thomas explains. He bends down and writes something on the pavement with one of the pieces of chalk. When he stands up, I can see that it's a call to arms, of a sort.

L'ART AU-DESSUS DE TOUT.

"Thomas!" I scold him laughingly. "You shouldn't vandalize."

"It's not vandalism, Olivia," he says. "It's children's chalk. Why shouldn't I get to play the same games I played in the street as a child?"

"I guess you're right," I say. "Give me one."

I write in large, swirling cursive: *BALLET, C'EST LA VIE.*

"*Oui! C'est parfait!*" Thomas runs down the center of the street to a bare brick wall. On it, he writes, *OLIVIA JE T'AIME.*

Thomas turns around to see what I think of it. I can't stop blushing. The champagne all night made me feel light and airy, and seeing what he's written makes me feel that I really could just float away.

On the street, a few yards down, I respond in kind. *THOMAS, JE T'ADORE.*

"Do you, Olivia?" Thomas asks me.

"Maybe." I giggle. "Maybe not!"

Thomas's blue eyes widen and suddenly he's chasing me down the Rue Caulaincourt, shrieking and laughing and begging me, in his funny half-English half-French, to say that it's true, that I do love him.

I run faster and faster, laughing so hard I could double over, but loving the way the cold night air feels against my face. When Thomas catches up with me, we draw a large mural of symbols and words on the bare street. There's a peace sign, flowers, a paintbrush, and, of course, the words *"BEAUT'E"* and *"A LA FRANCE!"* and more pronouncements that yes, Thomas and I do love each other.

Standing back and looking at our masterpiece as the first lights of morning peeks around the tall Montmartre hill, I whisper it in Thomas's ear. "I love you, Thomas."

"The fates align to bring us together," Thomas replies and bends his head toward mine for a lingering kiss that melts my sore toes. "You are everything."

A light rain starts to fall as we float through the seventeenth to Ternes. By the time we get to the apartment, the skies have opened and it is pouring. Knowing that this is our last day in the apartment alone without Mme Rouille, we dry off and close the curtains, sleeping in each other's satisfied arms until the late afternoon.

10. PJ

Now That We're Together

Annabel lives in a fourth-floor walk-up apartment squeezed into the dormer of an old building. It's a one-bedroom apartment. It has a utility kitchen, a tiny bathroom, and lots of windows looking out over her street corner. From one you can see all the way to a lit-up church on a hillside. "That's the Abbatiale Saint-Ouen," Annabel tells me when she catches me gazing out her window toward it one morning. Her accent is terrible. She'd kill me if I try to correct her, though.

There's a loft above the living room, but I sleep next to Annabel.

"Took you long enough, Peej," she says to me as we fall asleep.

"I never read *Madame Bovary* till yesterday," I admit. "I didn't know you'd been trying to tell me where to find you."

"Yeah, right." Annabel's voice is packed with hurt, and I know she doesn't believe me.

"I was so happy in Paris. . . ," I tell her.

"You were?"

Oh, God. Yes. Jay, and Olivia, and the Louvre, and the Lycée. The art room, where I spent hours perfecting the portrait I was painting to turn in with our project about Ingres. The travel plans I would spend hours making using the Internet in the computer lab. The rolling fields of the Dordogne. It hasn't been all bad this semester. Not at all.

"Yup."

"So it was working?" Annabel asks.

"What do you mean?"

"Your escape plan. You found a new life?"

I think about that for a moment. "I tried to. It didn't work as well as I'd hoped."

"I didn't think it would." Annabel's tone is cold, and I hate her, instantly.

How does she *do* that, size me up and take me down in one fell swoop? It's always been like that. Just when I think I'm doing something right, she's there to tell me I am wrong.

"You weren't *there*, Annabel," I mutter. "What was I supposed to *do*?"

Annabel is silent.

"You have no idea how screwed up everything got," I tell her, pulling the quilt up to my chin. Her apartment is cold, badly insulated, and very drafty. "Mom was a mess about where you were. Dad, too. And Dave—I don't know if he'll ever recover. We went out looking for you—all the way up to Canada. Did you know that? Did you know they risked everything so that they could try to find you? And that's when they got caught?"

It had been a terrible night. Mom, Dad, Dave, and I had ridden up north. We stopped so I could pee and the cops cornered my parents in a gas station parking lot. A few days later, after I'd already left for France, DEA agents raided my house and took my parents to jail. They'd been illegally selling prescription drugs smuggled over the border.

"Please don't tell me that you want me to apologize for Paris," I say. "I won't do it. Not after the way you left." I'm surprised at my own conviction. I didn't realize that underneath missing her, I was so angry at her, too.

"It must have been awful," Annabel says.

I sigh in response. I feel guilty, too. It's not like I stuck around to see the fallout. We both bailed. Annabel just got out sooner than I did.

"Why did you just leave like that? How come you didn't tell me where you were going? I could have come with you. Everything could have been different . . . "

"I just had to get away," Annabel says. "Like, that very moment. I had to!"

I don't understand, but that's Annabel for you.

A few moments later, Annabel rolls her body close to mine, wrapping her arms around the quilt. I can feel her long brown hair intertwining with my blond hair, and when she pushes the quilt back away from my face and lays her head down on mine, the tears on our wet cheeks intermingle.

"I'm so glad you found me," she whispers.

I reached up to touch her cheek. "I didn't know what else to do. Suddenly I just needed you so badly I couldn't stand it another minute."

A few minutes later, Annabel rolls back over and falls asleep. Just like she always has, she sleeps heavily but with a lot of movement.

I lie awake for a long time, unable to make sense of anything. Just as I'm drifting off, Annabel kicks violently at the bedclothes and lets out a wretched moan, like a baby left on a doorstep: haunted and terrified of not making it through the night.

"Shhhh," I try to comfort her sleeping form. "It's okay now that we're together. We'll be okay."

The next morning I wake up, stand up, and immediately come crashing down to the floor next to Annabel's bed. My head knocks into the wall and makes such a loud noise that it sends Annabel reeling out from under the covers, her hair a dark cloud around her scant shoulders.

"Oh, my God, PJ, are you okay? What happened?" She looms over me, her eyes bleary from crying in her sleep.

I can't answer her.

"It's okay, Penny Lane," Annabel says, feeling my forehead. "I think you've just caught a fever. Let's get you back into bed."

I lie back down and sleep for nearly four straight days.

I can hear Annabel coming and going as if in a dream. She sings to me in my sleep, campfire songs she loves to sing outside in the summer. She simmers a chicken on the stove in the little kitchen and brings me the broth, which she feeds to me herself. I see her, through the raging headaches and nauseous dizzy waves of the flu, enjoying this chance to care for me, to play big sister again. She's always loved to do that.

Several times I wake up not knowing where I am. Annabel pops up in bed when she feels me stir, and asks me if I need something. Even if I don't, she'll sometimes go out to the kitchen and futz around for a while, clanking dishes and cupboard doors and bringing me back tea or ice water. A few times, I think I hear her talking to someone, but then I realize I'm just having another nightmare.

I lurch toward the kitchen the morning of New Year's Eve, aiming for coffee, or just a glass of water. It's quiet. Annabel is not in the loft, nor the little bathroom.

An antique-looking brown clock on the end table next to the couch tells me it's eleven A.M. I wonder if the thing even works—the light coming through the window is dim.

I take a seat in a small chair nearest to the corner window, which looks out over all of Rouen, all the way down the Rue de la République to the Seine. A part of me cannot believe, especially considering my long train journey, that this is the same Seine that cuts a line through Paris, separating the French capital into two distinct halves.

I wait for Annabel to return from wherever she is, contemplating the street scene below. In the bathroom, as I brush my teeth, I wonder (again) if I am the first guest Annabel has ever brought back to this little apartment. There are short dark hairs rimming the bathtub, and a sweaty, crumpled T-shirt hides behind the door in there, making it impossible to keep the entryway open so the damp room can air out. It's been hard to piece together very much about Annabel's life since I last saw her. I'd been so focused on finding her that I hadn't stopped to think what she might be doing in the day to day.

"Bonjour?" her voice calls as the latch clicks and the creaky door to her apartment opens. "PJ?"

"I'm in here," I call, flushing the toilet and scrubbing my hands with the bar of cheap soap on the counter.

"I brought cheese," she calls back to me. "And croissants!"

When I open the bathroom door to join her in the kitchen, I see that Annabel has gone all out. There are several kinds of cheese spread out onto the counter, and the croissants she bought are so flaky and crumbling under the weight of their butter content that I have to grab for one right away.

"I got some apples, too," she says, placing three small green apples next to the cheese.

"I love apples," I say, my mouth still full of croissant.

"I know you do, silly," Annabel says, turning away to stuff some bottles of wine in the fridge. "I'm your sister. I know everything about you."

"Okay, so I need to talk to you," she tells me after she eats. "Now that you are all settled in and feeling better, I have someone I've been dying for you to meet!"

I don't say anything.

"PJ? Are you okay? Do you need to go back to bed?"

"Uh-huh," I say with a nod, and then go back to bed.

I dream that Jay likes Olivia, and not me, and that I return to the Lycée to find out they are getting married. "No, please!" I beg Olivia. "I never got to know him! What about Vince?"

Olivia laughs at me. Her snickering face turns into the hard, ugly feature of Adele Marquet, my former host mother. "You don't know anything about cruelty!" she screams.

I jump out of bed and run to the bathroom, where the apples, cheese, and croissants come bubbling up in three giant heaves. "Annabel?" I croak out. "Are you here?"

Silence.

I wash my face off and open the door, shivering in Annabel's short nightgown.

"Happy New Year," a low, grumbly voice says, and I look out to find a dark, hairy man dressed in a billowy white shirt and black pants stretched out on Annabel's sofa. Annabel is nowhere in sight.

The man raises a bottle of wine in my direction. "Happy fucking New Year."

11. ALEX

Confessions

---

trek up the street through the dark city of Toulouse, hugging my coat around me. I hear people cheering and laughing in all the restaurants and bars I pass. Jay's sitting alone at a fairly empty pub, no PJ in sight.

"No luck?" I ask sympathetically as I hop onto the heavy wooden stool next to him. The bartender comes over and gets me a Kronenbourg. It's refreshing after all that dancing.

"Nope. What about you guys?"

"Um," I say. Of course, Zack and I hadn't asked a single person if they'd seen a tall blond girl in Toulouse on the run from the Lycée de Monceau. We'd been having too much fun. One look at Jay's face, and you can tell he's been having anything but fun.

"Didn't think so," he says before I can answer. "*Dios mio*, this is a mess."

"Jay," I interject. I'm ready to be there for him.

"You guys just don't get it. I've never felt this way about anyone before," Jay says.

I catch my breath. Turning Jay's feelings from PJ to me is not going to be easy. But I can see that this is what I must do. PJ is making him miserable.

"I mean, don't get me wrong. I'm so grateful to you, Alex. It's really solid of you to bring us down here, to your dad's place, and I know you guys are ready to go back to Paris. But I could never, ever live with myself if I didn't at least make sure she knows I'm looking. I keep writing to her, telling her where we are. I sent her an email saying we'd be in Toulouse tonight. I gave her your dad's address, everything. She doesn't *want* to be found. She doesn't want *me*. I can't believe how crazy I'm letting this make me!"

"Jay, it's not about *you*. PJ is obviously just going through something right now. She needs time to work it out. And your instincts are good. You probably know PJ's wants and needs better than anyone at the Lycée. If you think she's in Toulouse, she's probably in Toulouse. And if she's here . . . and she *is* checking her email . . . well, then maybe you're providing her with just the safe space she needs by being here. She obviously doesn't want to be Paris. But she needs us. So let's just be patient. She'll email you, and we can meet her down here—or wherever she wants us to meet her—rather than making her go back to Paris where she obviously doesn't want to be right now. Okay?"

I hate, hate, *hate* being the one to prop up his devotion to PJ like this, but as his self-designated new best friend, I realize the importance of supporting him. I know this is how best to win Jay over. Soon he'll realize that he's over PJ—I mean, she's giving him absolutely nothing to work with—but he'll always remember how I stuck by him.

"Besides," I go on. "I don't have any desire to be in Paris right now." At least that much is true.

Jay looks up at the TV above the bar. On the screen, there are about a million people in the Champ de Mars, gathering under the Eiffel Tower, waiting for the clock to strike midnight, and for the fireworks over the Seine.

"You're really something," he mumbles without looking at me.

"What?"

"You *do* get it, huh?" Jay turns to me and gives me the most sincerely thankful expression. "I always thought a rich girl like you wouldn't really have her head on straight. But you're totally right."

"Well, it's not like I've never been in love before." I laugh. I look at him bashfully, as if I'm embarrassed, but really I'm glad to have an opportunity to unload a little onto him. It can only strengthen our growing bond as the very best of friends.

"You? Unrequited love?" Jay mocks me. "Why do I find that hard to believe?"

"Ever met a guy named George, Jay?" I say. "Trust me, I *know* what unrequited love feels like. I know what it feels like when the person you're in love with toys with your heart for four months and then leaves you high and dry in a suite at the Hôtel Le Meurice in the middle of the night on Christmas Eve, wanting you to celebrate his new love for a certain Texan tartlet named Patty."

My voice comes out more rough than I'd meant for it to. I'd only been using this to endear myself to Jay, but it feels good to be honest about how that little shit-eater broke my heart. Really good.

"Alex, are you serious?" Jay gapes at me. "George likes *Patty?*"

"Yup." I didn't mean to go into quite this much detail, but I can't help it; I'm kind of on a roll. "And he's not the first one to break my heart. You should have seen me this time last year. My French teacher asked me to tutor this new kid in our class from California, Jeremy. Every Saturday afternoon he came over and I helped him get up to speed with our class. After a while, our study sessions turned into make-out sessions and what do you know I've suddenly lost my virginity to the kid. As soon as we did the deed, he told our French teacher that he felt good enough about his French to discontinue the tutoring, and she agreed. Then he didn't speak to me for like three months, so I started skipping out on French class to avoid him, like, every day, since it was my last period of the day. Spring Break last year I saw him on a flight back from Miami—my mom and I had been in St. Barts for the week, and he'd been in Puerto Rico with his family—and the whole business started up again. I thought he was finally going to ask me to be his girlfriend, for real, when he asked me to come to a couple of his shows. He's in this indie band; they're actually really good. But then one night I went backstage and saw him making out with this freshman *skank* named Marissa. I never went back to French class at Brooklyn Prep again. I had to take an incomplete for the second semester." I don't mention that my mom had to basically promise her magazine's sponsorship of the Brooklyn Prep Charity Gala to get them not to rescind my Programme Américain acceptance. Fat lot of good that does me now, though.

Jay is quiet for some time after that, sipping a soda. Maybe that was a little too much information. Did I actually just tell him the entire Jeremy situation, including the virginity part?

"Whoa, Alex." Jay flags down the bartender for another pint of Kronenbourg for me, and another Coca-Cola for him. I've guzzled mine and he's nearly done. One strange thing about France—and there are a lot of strange things here along with the wonderful—is that it is perfectly socially acceptable to go up to a bar, even on New Year's Eve, and drink soda all night. The French don't value drunkenness so much as they value the fine practice of fashionably hanging out. "That's intense."

"So don't go around saying I always get what I want," I mumble, wishing I could take some of that back. I suck down half of my fresh beer in one gulp, my face turning red. I've probably ruined things with Jay before they even started.

"I won't," Jay replies. "I most definitely will never say that about you." He looks at me again. "But can I just tell you . . ."

"Say it." What have I got to lose?

"I don't know the other guy, but George is a tool. He's an idiot to go for Patty over you, and he's an idiot about almost everything else as well. You are so much better off without him."

I start laughing. "You think?"

"Definitely. Man, that kid wouldn't stand a chance in my neighborhood back in Minneapolis. The shoes alone would get his ass beat."

"You'd beat up George for his shoes?" I giggle. I adore imagining that scene.

"Not me personally. I believe in nonviolence, all the way. But I'm just saying . . ."

The few other patrons of the bar are rustling around a bit, and suddenly start counting down. It must be almost midnight!

"Dix, neuf, huit . . ." the bar shouts.

"Oh, my God!" I squeal. "Oh, no, where's Zack?"

All at once the bar erupts, and Jay and I hug. I feel profoundly frightened that I've scared him away. He's such an amazing hugger. I feel so safe in his arms.

"It'll be a good year," Jay says with a deep breath. "I'm starting to get the feeling."

"Looks like I missed the big moment," I hear Zack say from behind us, and when I turn around, there he is as bedraggled and exhausted as I have ever seen him. He looks like he's been absolutely *ravished* by dancers.

"There you are!" I exclaim. *"Bonne année!"* I kiss him on the cheek. "How was it?" I ask more quietly. "Did you have a New Year's Eve kiss?"

"Mission aborted," he admits. "I can't do it like this, in a club, on New Year's Eve. Too shady."

"Gotcha," I say. I finish my beer and set the glass down on the bar. I still feel awkward about what I just told Jay. "Want to get out of here?"

Jay and Zack nod. We snake through the crowds in the streets and silently walk back to the parking lot where we left the car.

Zack takes the front seat. I pull off my hat and set it next to me on the backseat, wondering how dumb I must have looked in it.

After a few minutes on the highway toward Montauban, I hear a strange noise coming from the front of the car. I realize Zack is passed out, his head bobbing forward and a low groan escaping his throat with every breath. He's snoring like an old grandpa!

"Man, Alex, is that you?" Jay asks.

I smack his seat. "You know that is not me! I never snore!"

"You think you don't," Jay says. "But the prettiest girls always do. Fact of life."

I smack the seat again, but in the back, my face is stretched so far into a maniacally happy grin that my teeth are actually getting cold.

The prettiest girls.

Maybe this will work out better than I thought.

LE JOUR DE L'AN
New Year's Day

12. ZACK

Love Triangle

*W*ell, ain't that the worst part of waking up after painting the town red. I'm still wearing my New Year's Eve outfit this morning, the gray T-shirt stinky with smoke, booze, and yes, vomit.

All I remember from the ride home to Montauban was asking Jay to pull over, opening the door so I could puke on the street, and then passing out in the backseat. Alex and Jay must have pulled me up to bed.

Alex isn't in bed next to me, so I assume I was too disgusting to sleep with.

Could she have slept with Jay?

Oh, Lord, here comes that vodka coming back to say howdy.

I lurch into the bathroom and hover around the toilet for a while, but after heaving a little and nothing coming up, I feel the acuteness pass and I decide the best thing would be a shower and several tumblers of water.

Alex's dad's bathroom is covered in dark black, very bacheloresque tiles. The shower itself doesn't have curtains but instead these low tiled walls that keep the shower separate from the rest of the bathroom, and a little tiled step that you can sit on while you wash yourself. I sit here on the step for a long while, letting the heavy pressure of the shower water beat down on me. It feels damn good to be clean again.

Now about that hammer poundin' down on my every thought. I've got a headache like a screamin' freight train. I guzzle at least eight cups of water and rummage around in Alex's sparkly turquoise dop kit to find whatever hangover remedies she might have brought with her. There's loads of makeup, perfumes, jewelry, even a small polished stone engraved with the word *Calm*. But no ibuprofen or even aspirin.

Jay's case is zipped up and tucked away on the black shelf over the toilet. It's one thing for me to hunt through Alex's junk, but to go through Jay's? What would he think?

However, the effort it would take to yell down the stairs to Jay and Alex, not to mention the loud noise I would have to suffer of them yelling their response at me, all tinged with my choking embarrassment of getting way too drunk last night, feels impossible to undergo. I decide it's worth the invasion of Jay's privacy.

In his travel case there is no Advil, but there are some other interesting items . . . especially the *condoms* I see slid into the side pocket!

As if it was a diseased rat, I drop the case, barely avoiding splashing the whole thing right into the toilet.

Lord-a-mercy!

I feel like my dry, dehydrated eyes are going to pop right out of my skull.

"Oh. My God." Just as fast as I can, I close up Jay's case and shove it back up onto the shelf. "Who were *those* for?"

My cell phone beeps. I swear I wouldn't make it another day on this trip if not for Pierson's and my running text convo.

HOW'S MEDUSA? ☺ WILD NIGHT? WHAT TROUBLE SHE GET UP IN NOW?

I laugh out loud.

Alex's reputation as a party girl hasn't escaped Pierson, despite the fact they have never had the pleasure of making each other's acquaintance. She became the subject of so many of my emails to Pierson last semester—kind of like Hannes was the main focus of Pierson's emails. Once, I sent Pierson a photo of me and my "teen queen" (again, his words, not mine) and he took to calling Alex "Medusa," after the mythical legend about the goddess with snakes growing out of her head. He thought it fitting because in the picture, Alex had curled and teased out her hair so big that she added at least three inches to her height.

NO TROUBLE 4 HER. I'M HURTING, THO, BC I DRANK WAY TOO MANY VODKA TONICS LAST NITE, I text back. I THRU UP.

SHUT YOUR MOUTH.

TRUE STORY.

THAT'S MY BOY. COWBOY UP!

YEE HAW. HOW'S AMSTERDAM?

PRETTY EFFIN RAD. YOU GOTTA COME HERE, GUY. LAST NIGHT I HAD TEN HOT DUDES ALL OVER ME AND HANNES HAD TO FIGHT THEM OFF!!!!

My throat gets tight at the mention of Hannes.

SO COOL, I write.

SRSLY. COME 4 A VISIT.

HA! It's too ridiculous to even entertain the thought.

Y NOT?

STUCK IN MONTAUBAN, LOOKING 4 THE LUV OF JAY'S LIFE.

U FOUND BPP YET? BPP=Beautiful Princess Penelope.

NOPE.

SOUNDS LIKE IT'S ABOUT TIME TO BLOW THAT POPSTAND.

Alex is making pancakes when I get downstairs.

"Since when do you know how to cook?" I ask her.

"Pancakes are Jay's favorite." She smiles sweetly at Jay. "He asked me to make them."

"Well, ain't that sweet of you," I mumble. "Feel like making me some?"

"Sure, of course, I was just about to ask," Alex says. She melts a pat of butter in the frying pan. "How many do you want?"

Eating anything doesn't really sound that good right now, but I know it will make me feel less like a zombie if I do.

"Can I start with two?" I ask.

"*Bien sûr, mon chéri,*" Alex says. "You want fruit? Jay found a market that was open this morning. I said that I would go, but he beat me to it!" Again, Alex fixes an overly excited smile on Jay. Her bizarre behavior is not helping my nausea.

I accept my pancakes and turn all my efforts to keeping them down.

ULL NVR BLIEVE THIS, I text Pierson on the sly. MEDUSA IS COOKING.

NAW. DON'T BELIEVE IT.

I SWEAR! I snap a photo of Alex flipping a pancake. SEE?

WHAT'S THE MOTIVE? Pierson asks.

WHAT DO U MEAN?

WHAT'S SHE TRYING TO GET? GIRL'S NOT GONNA COOK 4 U 2 UNLESS SHE GOT SOMETHING UP HER DRIES VAN NOTEN SLEEVE.

"Can I get you another pancake, Jay?" Alex asks. Suddenly, I register that Alex is showered and coiffed, something that usually does not happen until much later in the morning. What's more, her outfit is simple: jeans, sturdy running shoes, and a tight-fitting hoodie. "More syrup? We're going to need our strength today."

"For what?" I ask. "Strength for what?"

Alex and Jay exchange a look. Jay hands her his plate so that she'll put another pancake on it.

"We think PJ gave us a clue this morning," Alex says. "Right, Jay?"

"It might be a clue," Jay tells me. "It might not." He reaches in his pocket and produces his phone. "Check this out."

I read the email message on the screen.

I think I've gone and ruined everything. Truly, Jay, my life is in ruins. I wish I could tell you more.

Bonne année.

PJ

"What does that mean?" I ask. "Where's the clue?"

"Ruins. Her life is in ruins," Alex explains.

"Alex thinks she's trying to tell me—us—that she's hiding near or in some ruins. What do you think?" Jay looks honestly interested in my opinion. I bite my lip. I'm not sure what to say.

"Well, she did use the word twice," I say.

"I know, right?" Alex says. "That *has* to be a clue."

"What ruins, though?" I ask. I chew on my pancakes quietly. They're slightly burned but very buttery and sweet. Who knew Alex had it in her? "There are tons of ruins in France."

"Well, Jay told her we're in Montauban. And that we went to Toulouse. And now she's saying she's in ruins—"

"Her life is in ruins," Jay interjects. "Not necessarily her."

"Yes, yes, I know, but I think that's it!" Alex says. "Because there are some ruins so close to here. And I was thinking we could go there, and maybe she's like camping in them. I mean, PJ's the type who would camp, and like, think it was fun. You know?"

"What ruins were you thinking?" I clear my throat. Alex jumps up to get us each a glass of orange juice. "Thanks," I say. "You got this juice today, too?"

"Um-hmm," Alex says, nodding at Jay. "We were starved for a good breakfast this morning. Last night was *so* disappointing."

I remember Alex butt bumping a guy in a tight T-shirt in the club last night, then pounding a beer when I came in to find her with Jay at the pub. She didn't seem too disappointed then.

"What ruins?" I ask again.

"Montségur," Jay and Alex say at the same time. "We're just about to leave."

"I hope you weren't planning on going without me," I say, all innocence. "I'm just sick at the thought of going another day without PJ. I'm worried to *death* about her."

Jay puts his dishes in the sink. "Let's go, then."

Alex jumps up and follows him out the door. Damn straight, I'm worried about something. And wouldn't you know it, it ain't PJ. God bless her.

★ ★ ★

We pass through Toulouse on the way to Montségur. I look longingly at the pink city, remembering all the guys I danced with last night.
All around us on the road after that are trees, trees, and more trees. The
branches of the forests in these hills are bare and brown, but I imagine
that in summer they are thick with shady leaves. The forest surroundings
make me feel like we are here hunting down a witch, or going on a long,
arduous trek into unknown territory. It's giving me the creeps.

Alex connects to a tourist-info site about Montségur on her BlackBerry
and reads all about it to us on the last hour of our drive to the little village.

"Montségur was a fortified settlement of the Cathars," Alex tells us.
"The Cathars were early Christians—Rome called them heretics and
waged war on them during the Crusades. The ruins are situated at the
top of a mountain, which is why the Cathars were able to hold out for so
long. They called it Safe Mountain."

"We're *so* close to Spain right now," I say dreamily, noting a road sign
for the border station. "Let's just drive all the way to Bar*the*lona. How
fabulous would *that* be?" Barcelona sounds cosmopolitan and exotic.
Montségur sounds barren and remote. The kind of place where you don't
come back the same. I don't share those thoughts with my friends. They'll
probably just think I have a wicked hangover. Which I do.

"I don't think PJ is in Barcelona," Alex says, pursing her lips. "I don't
think Jay wants to go there."

"I *know*, Alex," I say. "I was just kidding."

"Oh," she replies. Apparently, Alex has entirely lost her sense of humor,
if not her sense of adventure and taste for harebrained ideas leading us to
the middle of nowhere. I haven't seen a gas station—or any buildings at

all, for that matter, for several kilometers. "I bet we find her in Montségur. Don't you think it was a good idea to go there, Jay?"

"Um, I guess so," Jay says, grimacing out the front windshield as he looks for the turnoff to Montségur. "Man, I don't know what to do anymore."

"Safe Mountain. It's perfect! I could not have written it better myself." Alex claps in appreciation of her own genius.

I feel a little better as we drive through a couple villages on the windy road to Montsegur. There aren't many hotels or bistros, but I do see lit up houses in between all the other buildings, boarded up for the winter, or perhaps forever. Jay handles the road well, but it is slow going as we creep higher up the hill to the castle site. The air is wetter, heavier up here. Jay has to slow down to just a few kilometers per hour to avoid driving into the steep ditches lining the road.

"Alex, this is a major tourist site, right?" Jay asks, looking a little skeptical as he pulls into a narrow parking lot at the foot of a steep hill. When we get out of the car, a black mountain looms over us, a fortress in ruins at its peak. There is no one around, just a sign pointing toward the trailhead. He was probably imagining something more akin to the tourist sites we visited as a class last semester with Mme Cuchon—crowds everywhere, with booths selling water and beer, and plenty of tough-looking security people around.

"Yup," Alex says, her tone blithe. "The French Ministry of Culture says that parts of the castle at the top of the mountain date from 1244. People from all over the world come here to hike this trail."

We get out of the car. My stomach growls unhappily, not liking the pancakes it's trying to digest or the uphill hike laid out in front of us.

"Let's do this," Jay says, and we set out up the hill to the castle.

Alex has packed water bottles and even peanut butter sandwiches. She brings them out as we catch our breath on the side of the path. The incline is sharp, and the hike is more rigorous than any of us expected. I have half a mind to turn around and go back. My lungs are burning. But if Alex the Chimney can do it, there is no way I can give up now.

"My dad loves peanut butter." Alex giggles. "I knew he'd have a stash of Skippy hidden in the condo somewhere!"

Jay laughs, having relaxed a bit as we make progress up the well-marked path. "Thanks, Alex. You really thought of everything."

"Your dad has a thing for Skippy?" I ask incredulously. "That doesn't sound very Francophiliac to me."

"You got a problem with peanut butter?" Jay says. "Man, sometimes growing up this is all we had. Keeps you full for cheap. I don't know what my mom woulda done without peanut butter back in the day."

"No, I like peanut butter," I say, sensing Jay thinks what I said was snobby. "That's not what I meant—"

Alex hands Jay another sandwich. "Good thing I made extras! You ate that one fast."

"I don't need fancy," Jay says. "I just need my girl."

Alex looks down at her running shoes soaked in mud. Jay takes the rocks and uneven wooden stairs as fast as he can, never stumbling or slipping in the wet dirt. I put my own sandwich in the pocket of my coat in case my stomach can handle it later. Neither of us has anything to say to that.

Jay is a fast hiker, shooting ahead of Alex and me. He never turns around to see if we are still behind him. He knows we're right there, just going more slowly.

As we get farther up the hill, the air gets even colder and windier. The view starts to take shape around us—an impressive, romantic scape of rolling land and small creeks cutting through the clumps of barren trees along the horizon. Mist crowns the hills, dotted every so often with a tall building of some sort. A little village, which must be Montsegur, looks tiny from here. It is hard to imagine that real people, and not dolls, live there.

"Hey, doll, what's the Holy Grail?" Alex wheezes.

"What do you mean?" I ask.

"You know, when people say that—the Holy Grail. What are they talking about?"

"Are you seriously telling me you don't know what the Holy Grail is?"

"Isn't it from a movie?"

I bust up laughing. "Have you ever heard of Jesus?" I tease her. "The Last Supper?"

"Of course I've heard of Jesus," Alex says. She pants as she pushes herself up a particularly steep bit of trail. "My grandparents go to Park Avenue Presbyterian. It's very exclusive."

"How can a church be exclusive?" I wonder, then remember that we're talking about the Upper East Side of Manhattan. From what Alex has told me, even the public restrooms are class-stratified. "Never mind that. They never told you about the Holy Grail?"

Alex bristles. "No, Zack. You don't have to be an asshole about it."

"Just sayin'. You go to one of the best prep schools in the country, will probably get into Harvard and Stanford and Penn based on connections alone, and you can't even tell me what the Holy Grail is?"

"Oh, shove it, Zack." Alex is really pissed. "I don't even care anymore. I just asked because the tourist site says that some people think this was the Holy Grail site. Why are you so rude lately? When I make you pancakes, make you lunch? I mean, I put your stinking ass to bed last night. Do you know what you smelled like?"

"Yeah, I meant to ask you about that, Alex," I say. "Where did you sleep?"

"I slept on the couch," she says. "Why?"

"I thought maybe you slipped into bed with Jay." I whisper it so Jay won't hear. "I wouldn't put it past you."

Alex whirls around, clenching her jaw. "Zack! How could you say such a thing?"

"What? Am I wrong? Is that what this little field trip is all about?"

Alex folds her arms over her black coat, her pink scarf waving in the breeze. "No! I really want to find PJ. I want Jay to be happy. I want to help! Don't you?"

"Of course I do, Alex!" I hiss. "You think I've stopped caring about Jay?"

"Well, kind of. When I saw you in the club the other night, dancing with all those guys, it seemed like you were over him and maybe looking for someone new."

"Well, I am looking for someone new!" How did we get on this topic?

"Good!" Alex says, looking genuinely pleased. "I'm so glad!"

"Yeah," I say. "You know, I liked him, but it didn't pan out. So you know, I'm moving on, just like I said. But I still want to help Jay."

"Oh, sweetie, I know you do," Alex says, throwing her arms around me. "I didn't mean to doubt you. Forgive me?"

I hug her, getting pink angora up my nose. "I forgive you. Balls, Alex.

Of course I do."

"I wouldn't ever mean to hurt you," Alex says.

Wouldn't she? I wonder. With Alex, those are the breaks. But I feel rotten for losing my faith in her. After all we've been through this fall—and just so much in the last week—I can see her growing and changing. Her values are strengthening. The girl might even be growing a conscience. *Maybe.*

Halfway up, we pass a closed tourist office. We keep going, even as it gets darker and more dangerous on the trail. Alex and I each slip and soil our jeans in the mud, but we don't stop to help each other up. We just keep going. I can tell Alex is kicking herself, or at least I hope she is. This Montsegur idea has got to be one of her craziest yet.

Jay waits for us at the top of the mountain, in front of a moldy wooden staircase leading to the arched entryway. He looks a little nervous, but handsome and brave, too. His cheeks are red from the hike. He removes his beanie and wipes his forehead with it. "What now?" he asks.

"Can we even get into this place? It feels like it's been locked up and abandoned for a thousand years!" I say.

"Not to worry," Alex says, breezing past us. "It might be empty, but we can still go in. Come on." She whips out a flashlight from her tote bag. "Good thing I brought this, too."

"You were probably in the Boy Scouts, right Zack?" Jay asks me. "You can handle this?"

I nod, even though I was never in any scout troupe and the closest I have come to hiking and camping has been at religious revival camps where the pastor never leaves the teens alone long enough (wayyyy too risky!) for us to ever have to find our way around the great outdoors without help.

"Awesome," Jay says. "Alex, wait here."

Alex opens her glossy lips indignantly, gaping at Jay. "You'd leave me— the only girl—out here to guard you guys? No way. Zack has to be the lookout."

"Maybe she's right. I'd hate it if anything happened to her," Jay says, a comment I could really have done without at the moment. "You cool staying out here and keeping watch?"

I sigh, knowing I don't really have a choice. "Sure."

Jay nods and gives one last look around. "Alright, man, yell if you see anything sketchy. I don't like the looks of this place too much."

"I will," I promise. "Hurry up, though."

I hear them walk quickly away. From a distance, Alex's shrill giggle pierces the night. I shiver, wondering which part of this is scarier—that Jay is making Alex laugh, or that they are getting farther and farther from their lookout.

"PJ?" I whisper, rubbing my gloved hands together. "You hidin' here, girl? You better show your face if you are. It's damn cold out here."

After a few minutes, I don't hear any more noises coming from inside the ruins. "You ain't in there, PJ. You're not as dumb as Alex thinks you are. Campin' in the ruins of Montségur. As if."

There's a big, glaring moon in the sky, but without city lights shining down on us, it's still dark as hell. I can't stop trembling—from fear or chill, I'm not entirely certain.

"Oh, PJ," I say, feeling peculiar, like I'm being watched with night goggles, the way the killer does in *The Silence of the Lambs*. Speaking out loud, even to myself, makes me a teensy bit less nervous. "I sure hope you're okay out there." Looking out from the back of Montségur Castle, seeing those faint lights from the village and a few other villages beyond it, makes the world feel very, very big. I wonder why we're even on this trip. How could we ever hope to find her when there are so many places she could have run off to?

"I wasn't so nice to you, was I, Penelope Jane?" I ask wistfully. "I could have been a better friend." PJ was an outsider, just like me. Why had I clung to only Alex and Olivia this semester? Why hadn't I ever asked PJ to hang out, just her and me?

In the moonlight I imagine her pale face, floating with eyes closed, in a pool of dark water. I catch my breath. What if she's dead out there? Dead, and no one ever finds her?

I hear a loud noise, like a falling tree, or a gunshot, come from the woods just below the castle. I peer into the dark archway of the castle, seeing nothing but darkness and shadows.

"Alex! Jay!" I yell. "Come on, y'all!"

The only answer is a whistling wind that just brings that mental image of PJ's face, cold and bloated, floating by, over and over.

I can't take it. I pull my jacket around me and tear down that mountain, sliding in the muck and breaking through branches all the way back down to the parking lot. At the bottom, I look up at the castle ruins, breathing hard.

There ain't *nothing* safe about that mountain.

13. OLIVIA

Everyone Has Secret Dreams

I bat Thomas's hand away when he grasps my knee under the breakfast table. Even if Mme Rouille has a committee meeting of some sort this morning, Elise is right down the hall. "Kiss me," he begs in a whisper. "While we can have the chance!"

He reaches out to hold my head in his hands as he presses his moist, full lips onto mine. We kiss for several minutes, and I swear when our mouths separate from one another that I've been to another place in the time that we've kissed. Kissing Thomas just makes me feel so different than it ever felt to kiss Vince. Thomas kisses with confidence and passion, and so much enthusiasm. I feel like I could kiss him forever.

Luckily we break apart just before Elise comes back into the kitchen, her arms full of vegetables she's purchased at the Batignolles farmer's market just down the street from the Rouilles' apartment. Her mesh market bags are full of golden onions, rich squash, and a freshly butchered pink chicken. Thomas immediately rises to his feet and starts poking around in the groceries as Elise unloads them.

"Ah, mes préférées!" Thomas exclaims. *"Les aubergines!"* He holds up two robust purple eggplants excitedly.

"Dehors!" Elise scolds Thomas, waving us out of the kitchen. "Let me do my work."

"Olivia, let us go for a walk," Thomas suggests. "Perhaps we can go to the market before it closes."

"Thomas, we just ate," I remind him. "And Elise just went to the market."

"I'm still hungry," he tells me. "French markets are not just for shopping only. And today it is beautiful, no?"

Thomas is right. Unlike the past few days, when Paris has been hung with a dark, misty fog that won't relent, today is bright and clear. The snow is melting, and I don't even have to button my coat all the way up when we get outside. I still wear my striped mittens and my hat, though. I know I look cute in them, and the hat covers my quickly lengthening dark roots. My mom never did succeed in getting my highlights done while she was here.

Away from the awkwardness of the apartment, Thomas and I can't keep our hands off of one another. I *have* to run my hands through his curly, floppy light brown hair. I have to tap his nose, and then kiss the tip of it, and then kiss his mouth lightly, then kiss him again. I have to play with the underside of his sleeve, tickling his wrist.

Thomas's hands gravitate toward my waist. He lets one of his palms slip under my coat, and then find the edge of my sweater, then under it so that his cool hand is flat against my warm skin. He likes to take my face in his hand, and tell me I'm beautiful. And of course, once we start kissing, we never stop.

Thomas pulls me down the Boulevard de Courcelles. Where the street's name changes to Boulevard des Batignolles, it is crowded with bustling stalls selling fruits, vegetables, fish, meat, bread, soap, and other organic products. I breathe in the rich smells of French cuisine at its freshest, everything crisp in the wintry early afternoon air.

At the end of the long row of merchants is a guy manning a rudimentary grill, pouring a thick, savory-smelling batter onto the black shiny surface. In a few minutes' time, the batter turns into a browned, crispy pancakelike thing. The aroma makes my stomach growl, despite the cereal I had earlier.

"Hmmm, these are very good," Thomas says, stopping to watch the man make his pancakes for a little while. He's an expert at measuring out the batter, at making sure none of them burn, and delivers each one to his customers piping hot, made to order. "Would you like one?"

I smile. "What's in them?"

"Oh, potatoes, onion, some flour . . . and cheese, lots of cantal cheese."

Sounds totally fattening. Thomas motions at the man that he'd like two *Pommes Anna*, and I watch hungrily as ours cook in front of us. When I take a bite, it's pure culinary ecstasy: buttery and salty and cheesy and perfect.

Thomas and I finish our *Pommes Anna* and take a walk around the seventeenth, where it's so quiet I can hear us breathing. Every few steps, I stop to look at him, or he stops to look at me, and we can't help but kiss, our tongues mingling with the strong taste of our French potato pancakes. When the sun starts to dip behind the Sacré-Coeur, we decide to turn back to Ternes. We're reluctant, because then we won't be able to kiss as frequently. We haven't said it aloud yet, but I know neither of us wants to tell Mme Rouille or Elise about what's happened between us.

Despite how good it feels, I don't think anyone—not Mme Rouille, not Mme Cuchon, and certainly not my parents back in San Diego—would approve of our new relationship.

"Thomas, when do your classes start for the semester?" I ask him, suddenly realizing that it is a weekday. Lots of people have gone back to work from the holidays.

"Hmm, soon," Thomas says noncommittally. "I have to check the schedule."

"You don't know when your classes start?" Now that the Revue Bohème is over, getting ready for school again has been totally starting to stress me out. I should be studying French and trig, so that I can keep my average up. Even if I'm not still planning on going to UCLA with Vince right away, I still have goals for the future. And I thought that was something Thomas took seriously, too. That was one of the main reasons I'd initially found him so appealing.

Thomas laughs, stopping in front of a patisserie and admiring the tarts and pastries in the window. "I can think of no things but you, Olivia!"

"Thomas." I stop and look him straight in the eye. "Are you kidding? You can't blow off school like that. Your mother will kill you. She'll kill me if she finds out I have anything to do with it!"

Thomas shrugs. "Look at this one, Olivia." He points to a small puff pastry called a *religieuse*—one fat ball of frosted dough topped by a ring of whipped cream and another smaller ball of dough. "See, it looks like a priest. Would you like to try one of these?" he offers with a smile. *"C'est très délicieux!"*

"Non, merci," I refuse quietly. "I can't keep eating that kind of stuff. I have to stay in shape. Just because the Revue Bohème is over doesn't mean I don't have rehearsals to stay in shape for."

We don't kiss after that. Before we get back to the apartment, Thomas turns to me.

"I will get my bike and go to the dorm," he informs me. "Okay?"

"Okay," I say, a little confused. "But Elise is making your favorite . . ."

"I've let my studies get away," Thomas says. "And I have to start class shortly. You understand?"

"I understand," I acquiesce, not wanting him to see me as needy. And certainly, he's following my advice. But it feels like a punishment for what I said. Later, as he rides away, I feel just a tiny smidgen of the happiness of the day go with him.

I help Elise set the table in the Rouilles' dark-paneled dining room and bring out the food for dinner. She's roasted a lovely chicken, with eggplant, onion, and peppers surrounding it in the pan, soaking up the rich juices. She's also made couscous, fluffed up in a small casserole dish, which I love.

Back in San Diego, I was a strict vegetarian. I ate as lightly as possible—salads, smoothies, and grilled veggies. Mme Rouille expediently ignored this fact when I moved into her apartment, and after a while, I broke down. It didn't even take more than a few days. The food Elise makes is too tasty! I just have to eat smaller portions of it.

Elise excuses herself after we set the table, and I know she's going to meet a friend for dinner. She does that almost every night—makes dinner for us, goes out for a couple hours, and then comes back and does all the dishes and then goes to her little maid's room to watch TV and go to bed. I've always wondered if it's a male friend she's seeing. How totally cute would it be if Elise had a boyfriend?

"Olivia, I cannot tell you the rave reviews you've been getting for your New Year's Eve performance!" Mme Rouille scoops some roasted vegetables onto her blue china plate. "It is my deepest regret that I have missed it. You are the toast of Paris society!"

"Really?" I squeak out, my hands bumping my silverware noisily together as I register this news excitedly. I can't imagine that Mme Rouille's friends are the types to have gone to the Revue Bohème performance, but I guess all Parisians consider themselves among the avant-garde. Seeing experimental dance performances must be within some sort of criteria they keep for maintaining French citizenship.

"*Maman*, she would have took your breath away." Thomas, who spent the bulk of the day at school, has returned for dinner. I had a feeling he wouldn't be able to resist Elise's cooking. "Olivia? Chicken?"

I take a little, but I only manage a few bites. I'm too nervous with both Thomas and Mme Rouille at the big carved dining room table with me. Since the moment Mme Rouille got back from her trip to the Alps with her sisters, I've been on edge. I can't let her find out about Thomas and me and what we've been doing together while she's been out of town. She's *so* into propriety. She'll flip!

"Really, Olivia, I'm so glad you've decided to stay in Paris with us," Mme Rouille continues. "We would have missed you desperately."

Thomas gambles a flirtatious look at me. I stay turned to Mme Rouille.

"Thank you so much for understanding," I say. "It means a lot to me to still be here."

"And the Paris Underground Ballet Theatre!" Mme Rouille crows. "What a marvelous new cultural institution! That is really quite a *coup*, you know."

Mme Rouille has rarely shown me this kind of attention in the few months that I've been living in her son's empty bedroom. She's a formal lady, with a grip of social obligations, and despite the fact that my French is pretty decent, she only talks to me in English. This seems to stunt how much she opens up to me, as if she knows her own English is too limited to make a real connection with me, and she believes that to be the case with my French, too. Not that I spend too much time thinking about it or anything . . .

In fact, I spend a lot of time wondering about the Rouilles, especially now, with all my feelings for Thomas flowering inside me. Since I first came to live here, I haven't quite been able to understand why Mme Rouille signed up to host an American student at the Lycée. Mme Rouille is on the board of the Lycée de Monceau. Thomas was a student there, and she's active in fundraising for the school. And her own son goes to the Sorbonne and lives in the student dorms across the river. So she'd seem like a perfect host family candidate. However, she's one of those adults who takes very little interest in children not her own, and she doesn't try to entertain me as her guest by appealing to any of the things I like or dislike. Mme Rouille rarely solicits questions from me about myself, or how I grew up, or my tastes, or what I think of Paris and France.

Regardless, Mme Rouille, along with her live-in maid, Elise, does everything she can to ensure my comfort, and I feel safe and happy here. The little apartment where we live in Ternes is quiet and calm and a good place for me to focus on my studies after my long afternoons of dancing every day.

But tonight, Mme Rouille is taking an uncommon interest in me. She wants to know how my family enjoyed Paris, and what sights they saw when they were visiting. Then she asks me over and over again about my performance, and how I like André and Henri, and whether or not I've been cast in any of the Underground's spring performances yet.

"Uh, no," I answer that last question. "Not officially."

"But, Olivia—" Thomas cuts in. "They must have their eye on you for something."

I blush. "Well, maybe. I do want to keep in shape, just in case." Henri had been suggesting that I might do a lead in something in the spring. That was one of the major motivations I'd had when I jumped at the chance to do the Revue Bohème. But we haven't had any castings yet. "In fact, I was thinking of going over to the rehearsal space tonight after dinner, if that's okay. I'd like to work on my turns."

"Of course, *chérie*. Thomas, if you don't mind, please take Olivia to the studio in the car when she is ready."

"Bien sûr, Maman." Thomas jumps at the chance to drive me across town alone, just him and me in that big Mercedes. My leg jerks under the table, nearly kicking Mme Rouille in my surprised excitement.

"It must have been just wonderful to be up there, in front of all those people, on such an exciting night of the year," Mme Rouille enthuses, and her cheeks flush a bit. "I did always want to be a dancer myself, you know."

My mouth drops open. Mme Rouille, with her white blond pageboy haircut and rigid posture, seems to me like she'd have made a better head of state than a ballerina.

"I never knew that," Thomas comments. *"C'est vrai?"*

"Oui, oui," Mme Rouille confirms. "Everyone has secret dreams. I just never had the chance. That's why I delight in watching our Olivia dance. You'll have to give me the performance schedule as soon as it is announced. And maybe we could go see the National Ballet one of these days? The new season is just beginning. Perhaps a Sunday matinee, and then dinner. Wouldn't that be nice?"

"Oh, my God!" I exclaim. Tickets to the National Ballet cost a fortune, even with a student discount. "I would *love* that. *Merci,* Mme Rouille!"

"Bon." Mme Rouille looks almost girlish at the prospect. Thomas and I giggle.

"It was totally fun to perform on New Year's Eve," I tell them. "The audience had so much energy, and of course the party after was a riot. But . . ."

"Mais?" Mme Rouille waits for me to finish.

"But knowing that my friends couldn't be there, that was the pits— sad, I mean. Really sad. And knowing that PJ's still missing, and might not be coming back to the Lycée for the next semester, that was a little distracting."

"Your new friends were there," Thomas points out. "They loved it!"

"PJ?" Mme Rouille thinks for a second. "Who is PJ?"

"You've met her. She stayed with us at the beginning of last term, but she was ultimately placed with the Marquets—"

"She was?" Mme Rouille interrupts. "*That* beautiful girl lives with the Marquets?"

"Yes, didn't you know?" Mme Rouille is so involved at the Lycée; I thought that for sure she was aware of the other placements of the Americans around the neighborhood. "Remember? You told me that M. Marquet wants to run for national office one day?"

"I suppose . . . well, I suppose I did tell you that." Mme Rouille's face clouds over. "But I thought your male friend was staying with them."

"Oh, no, it was PJ. But I guess when you met her, she introduced herself as Penelope."

"And you also have a friend PJ who is a boy?" Mme Rouille is confused.

"Not another PJ, but there's a *Jay*," I explain. "I guess those two names sound a lot alike! I never thought about it."

"Oh," Mme Rouille says, and takes a long drink from her glass of red wine. She looks strangely upset, and I'm hoping it's not due to anything offensive I might have said.

"Olivia, there is something I need to tell you. About this PJ. I fear . . . I fear your friend may be in worse danger than you think!"

14. PJ

A Crowd of Three

 slam the bathroom door behind me, my eyes casting about for something I can defend myself with. I turn on the faucet. Maybe I could scald him with hot water.

Who is that guy?

"Penny Lane?" I hear Annabel calling over the running water. "Are you in there?"

I turn off the water. "Annabel?"

"Pen, what are you doing in there? Don't you want to meet Marco?"

"Who's Marco?" I demand, still refusing to open the bathroom door.

"Um, the guy you just ran away from?" Her laugh bounces off the thin bathroom door between us. "Come on! Open up!"

I open the door hesitantly and push it out in front of me.

144

"Good girl," Annabel coos. Her brown hair is in pigtails at each side of her head, like a little girl. She takes my hand. "Silly PJ. This is Marco. I've been dying for you guys to meet!"

Marco is a medium-built, bearded man, as young as Annabel, though he's dressed like a fugitive from the forties—old, strangely tailored slacks and a shrunken vest over a billowy white shirt. His shoes are flat, like something from those Buster Keaton movies my dad likes to watch in the middle of the night when he can't sleep. Marco's dark curly hair spools away from his head in long, wild ringlets, like a clown. He gives me a little wave.

"Who is Marco?" I demand. I stare right at him, daring myself not to be afraid. "Seriously, who are you?"

Marco gives me an impish look and puts a hand on his chest affectedly. *"Je m'appelle Marco Peña. Je suis originaire de Sevilla."* Now that Annabel is nearby, his snarl has turned into a toothy grin.

"He's Spanish," Annabel half-whispers, half-giggles, as if it were a wonderful secret. "Isn't that amazing?"

I'm still dressed only in the mint green, lacy nightgown Annabel gave me to wear to bed. "Amazing."

Annabel's friend's eyes dart around the room as if in a happy trance, taking me in, taking in the strange, old-fashioned furnishings, everything about Annabel's miserable little existence. He seems to like it. He's thrilled with everything that he sees.

All at once I get it. They're high.

"You could have warned me you were going to have a friend over, Annabel," I say. "Don't wake me up in the middle of the night."

"Didn't you want to meet Marco?" She says with a pout. "He wanted to meet *you*. We want to tell you about our plan!"

Marco holds a hand out to me. I shake it, though without feeling. "*Bonjour*, Marco. *Je suis heureuse de faire votre connaissance.*"

"*Ma* Penelope! You are absolutely bewitching. I have been waiting so many months to make your acquaintance," Marco effuses. He takes my hand and kisses it, his lips lingering for way too long on the back of my palm. I wrestle my hand back from him and tuck it safely behind me.

"PJ, my baby," Annabel says. "I have to ask you a favor."

"What is it?" I'm in no mood to give her any favors.

"I can't ask you in here. Can we go into the bathroom?"

"What? Annabel, what are you talking about?"

She nudges me backward into the tiny little bathroom again.

"Don't you love Marco? I met him in Lyon." Annabel perches on the closed toilet. "Lyon is a really far-out city. I was there right after Toussaint. Have you been?"

"What were you doing in Lyon?" I demand, stinging. I didn't go to Lyon on the class trip in November because I'd been kicked off as punishment for having a party. To know that she and I could have crossed paths if I had been able to go makes me feel like banging my head against the wall.

I'm dying to know any details at all of the time between when Annabel left Vermont and arrived in Rouen, but she always seems to avoid my questions. The whole expanse of time is still as much of a mystery as it was when I saw her on the street when I arrived in Rouen.

"It was in Lyon that Marco and I decided that we want to raise sheep. You know, like Mom did. Only we want a whole flock of them." Annabel beams. "Anyway, you've got to sleep in the loft tonight."

"What?" I ask. "No way." The loft above the bathroom is more like a storage space than anything else. It's filled with relics of a pack rat who died without ever cleaning it out. Just because there is a small mattress and an old quilt up there doesn't mean anyone could actually sleep up there. It's disgusting. And lonely.

"Please, Penny Lane," Annabel begs. Her voice drops. "I haven't seen Marco in ages. When I left him in Lyon, he was devastated. I thought I'd lost him forever. Let me have the chance to make it up to him. Please?"

I shudder. "You're kidding, right?"

"He's the most beautiful lover. The Spanish just know things about sensuality that other men don't. You'd be amazed, Pen."

"Annabel." I can't believe her, her wild, red-rimmed eyes, her hair sticking out from each side of her head like an overgrown child, her dirty, baggy clothes doing their best to hide her rapidly thinning frame. She twitches, twirling a strand of her long dark hair around a grubby finger. "Go back to the sheep plan. What are you talking about?"

Annabel giggles. "Won't it be fun? Now that you're here, we can all do it together. Marco will do all the hard stuff, like cleaning the pens. We'll just feed the sheep and love them. Remember how cute Esther was as a lamb?" Esther was one of my mom's two sheep. I bet they've been impounded, or given to one of our neighbors by now. My mom got Esther's mom, Fiona, from a neighbor about five years ago, and a while later Fiona gave birth to Esther. I remember this very clearly because it was after watching Esther come out of her mother that my parents sat me down and gave me the sex talk. Annabel, of course, had beat them to it. I already knew everything. Annabel's version, of course, had been a lot racier.

I don't answer. I don't even know where to begin.

Sheep? Lyon? The loft?

I apply Chapstick to my dry lips and rummage around the toiletry shelf idly, not wanting to leave the bathroom. If we leave, he'll be out there. I'll have to come to some sort of terms with the fact that my sister is sleeping with someone I wouldn't even sit next to on the Paris métro if I could help it.

Annabel stands back up, a little shaky on her feet, and huddles against me. I've always been tall, but she still has at least two inches on me. "I'm so glad you caught up with me, Penny Lane. You're my sweet. And you'll love Marco when you get to know him. I promise. We're going to have the best time together. He knows about Mom and Dad. He knows about Dave. I've told him everything."

"What do you mean?" I ask her. "What is everything?"

"I was so alone when I met Marco," she tells me carefully. "I hadn't spoken to anyone—*anyone*—in months. You know me, PJ—I can't live like that, without friends, or family . . . I was running out of money, and he let me into his life, no questions asked. He was so . . . welcoming."

"Okay," I say, about to gag. I pat her clammy hand. "But I'm here now. You don't have to keep him around anymore. You won't be lonely now that we're together again."

"It's not about loneliness!" Annabel cries, her voice rising a bit. "I want Marco to stay because I told him everything! I had to tell *someone* . . . I had been holding it all in for *so* long. I couldn't help it! It all came out one night."

"*What* all came out?"

"That I . . . that Mom and Dad . . ." Annabel begins. I hold my breath. I know we have to talk about it eventually, but I don't want to just yet.

Can't we wait a little longer for things to settle down, for me to figure out a way to get Marco to leave? So that we can handle this alone, together?

"I didn't know then that they were selling drugs," I rush to say. "I thought we were just looking for you. I didn't know the whole story. I know it's my fault. But I really didn't know!"

"Penny Lane, what are you saying? What do you mean, it's your fault?" Annabel stares at me, perplexed. "You didn't know what was going on. That was the whole point! I didn't want them to get you involved."

"I know—I wanted to find you. So did Dave, and Mom and Dad. We all drove up there one night, I don't know why they agreed to it—they must have known it wouldn't be safe—and then I had to stop to pee—"

"I don't know what you're talking about."

I take a deep breath. "It's my fault they got arrested, Annabel. I'm so sorry I didn't tell you till now. I wanted to wait until we were settled." I search her eyes for empathy. "You might have run I know you probably can't forgive yourself for taking off right before everything got out of hand . . . but it was *me* who made the stupid mistake of making them stop to pee so close to the Canadian border . . . I knew something felt wrong as we were driving back. I should have just held it till we got to our house. But I didn't. It kills me. But how was I supposed to *know*?"

"You *still* don't know the whole story, PJ," Annabel interrupts. "I *always* knew more than you. Dave did, too. We knew everything, from when I was like, fourteen. I told them to stop dealing before you found out. I wanted to keep you out of it," Annabel tells me. "They promised me they would. And they did stop. But then I found out that they were doing it again, PJ, and I was *so* mad. So flipping pissed, you have no idea."

"I was mad when I finally figured it out, too. How couldn't we be?

But I wasn't mad at you. If you felt like you had to go, I understand."
I look around the bathroom with a rueful smile, remembering my old
bedroom at the Marquets', remembering the thick carpet on the floor of
their living room, as cushiony as a mattress when you walked across it. "I
definitely get that. I left them, too, you know."

I'm starting to relax a little bit. I realize then that Annabel and I both
have incredibly complicated feelings about what happened last summer.
It's so comforting to think that we can now sort through them together,
one day at a time.

"No, you're not listening, PJ! Mom and Dad didn't get caught just
because you stopped to pee. How can you be so obtuse? Cops don't just
pull folks over for being near the border—have you never heard of the
Fourth Amendment?"

"The Fourth Amendment?"

"Search and seizure, PJ! Jesus. The cops, the DEA, they all have to have
a reason to get a warrant to question people, to raid their house. They
have to have *evidence*. I was so mad that before I left Vermont, I went to
the cops, I told them. I told them they were endangering you, and that
I'd testify against them and throw them in jail. I was so pissed! I couldn't
even see straight."

"What?" I get that strange feeling I sometimes get when I stand up too
fast, or when I take a shower before I've had any coffee in the morning.
Annabel is still talking, but I can only see her lips moving, hear the most basic
noises coming from her mouth. It was like this when I first got to France—a
strange vertigo from not yet having any experience listening to Parisian
French. It came to me slower, and took me several minutes to ascertain the
meaning of simple phrases. "Slow down, Annabel. I don't understand."

"Because then I couldn't get caught, too," Annabel goes on. "Because then I wouldn't go down with them. I was helping them all along, PJ, and I wanted out. But they wouldn't stop. All their convictions and politics, and . . . and . . ." She's hiccupping and choking so much she's having trouble getting the words out now. "And I was so afraid . . . that we'd all get caught, that we'd go down together. Dave, too. Dave didn't think it was a big deal—he thought it was noble of them; I was afraid if I married him, my life was going to be just like Mom and Dad's. And I couldn't, I just couldn't . . . So I told the cops." Tears stream down her pale face, and her dark hair is matted and crazy. She looks awful. "I told them everything they wanted to know—"

"Annabel! You turned in *our parents* to the cops? To federal agents? You purposefully tried to put Mom and Dad in *jail?*"

Annabel nods. "I did, Pen."

I remember my mom carefully sewing Annabel's sleeveless satin wedding dress, embroidering tiny flowers around the neckline and stitching *To my angel—don't fly too far away* into the inner hem. I remember my mom and dad swooping in from out of nowhere when we were kids and Annabel fell out of a tree in the backyard and broke her leg. My dad hoisted her into his arms and told her jokes to make her laugh all the way to the hospital. We'd all painted her cast with my mom's expensive oil paints, the ones she'd gotten as a gift and was saving.

"How could you?" I clap a hand over my mouth. In seventeen years I've had many crises of faith when it comes to figuring out my sister. It never occurred to me, however, that she might really be malicious. Vengeful. "Please tell me this isn't true."

Annabel starts to cry.

"Stop it!" I scream at her. "Stop crying! You don't deserve to cry for them!"

I turn away from Annabel, unable to look at her without slapping her. I am afraid if I stay in the bathroom I'll lunge for her, rip out her long pigtails in thick clumps.

To think I took a Greyhound bus from Vermont to New York, believing the whole way that my parents were soon going to lose everything all because of *me*. Every time the bus passed a cop car, I held my breath and imagined my parents in handcuffs inside it. When Dave filled me in once I got to Paris, I wanted to die.

Instead, I chose to start a new life. But never once did I realize that what happened to them had been expressly *Annabel's* fault.

Annabel leans forward, grasps my arm. "Please, PJ, try to understand this was for *you*! They were about to ruin your life, all of our lives. What if you'd spent the rest of this year there, turned eighteen, gotten embroiled in it?"

I shake her off and wipe my face on my sleeve. "Please stop talking, Annabel. Just stop."

I feel it then, a crack deep in my heart where Mom and Dad and Annabel all used to live.

Numb, I ask her to finish. I know it can only get worse, but I need to know the rest.

"So, you left Vermont after telling on them."

Annabel doesn't lift her head up but she answers, "Yes. They thanked me for my information and told me they'd be in touch. They told me I was doing the right thing. When I got back to my car in the police station parking lot, I sat there wondering if I should just drive off a bridge. It was so wrong. I know it was wrong."

"Why didn't you? Drive off a bridge, I mean?" I know I'm being cruel, but I hate her right now. I really, really despise her.

"I sold the car and went to Ireland," Annabel says. "I thought I still had something to live for, if I could get out of there."

"Can't the cops just find you over here?"

"Probably, eventually. In Dublin I bought a passport. I used it to get here because I knew they wouldn't look that closely coming from another EU country."

"But Marco knows that passport isn't yours?"

"Yes—that one says *Megan* on it. I destroyed the one that says *Annabel*. See?"

Annabel pulls a red passport out of her pocket. MEGAN O'LEARY, it says. It has Annabel's photo in it, pasted in clumsily inside the front cover.

For some reason, I'm no longer getting upset, even though the story gets worse and worse. Annabel is in trouble, and is making it worse for herself every day. When the cops do find her—and I know they will—she'll be doomed for her international flight.

The crack is widening, that spot deep inside me getting bigger and bigger. Where I used to feel solid and safe, now that I'd finally found my only sister, it now feels like a dark river of pain and fear. When I close my eyes, I see myself in jail next to my parents, next to Annabel.

"You haven't told anyone you're in Rouen, right?" Annabel asks me.

"No," I say, still as stiff as a board. I feel disembodied, in a way, like I no longer care what happens to me if I can only get this dark feeling to go away. "No one knows I'm here."

"Okay, good," Annabel says. "PJ, please try to understand. I feel horrible about it, but we can start over. We can!"

I look at her for a long time. Her face still looks just like mine. Maybe she's right. We both made mistakes. We both have to move on.

"I'll sleep in the loft," is all I say.

"Thank you," she whispers. "I love you."

When we come out of the bathroom, Marco is no longer on the couch. The bedroom door is open. Marco's asleep face-down on the bed, stripped down to his black underpants. Annabel looks at me in delight and gratitude.

I sigh and climb up the ladder to the dusty loft.

When I wake up in the morning, the door to the bedroom is closed. I can't take it anymore. I have to go outside. I leave a note for Annabel and greet the fresh, cold morning. It feels good to be out of that stuffy little apartment. Just a ways down the street is the river walk along the Seine, a parklike path for biking and running. There are benches there, and little docks for houseboats and barges, much like in Paris. In Rouen, however, from the banks of the Seine, you could be anywhere. In Paris, you always know you're in Paris.

Annabel is three years older than me, a wild child since her first moments on this earth. My parents adored her, spoiled her rotten. She came out screaming, my mom likes to tell us, while I came out with a wondrous look on my face, completely taciturn. When I was born, Annabel took me under her wing as if she would be the mommy. She tried to snatch me from the crib and take me into bed with her, like a doll. When I was a very little girl, she would snip off my blond hair and hide locks of it in her pillowcase. And with the other kids at school, she was always fiercely protective, making sure I never played with anyone she deemed unworthy.

As a teenager, Annabel's intensity never faded, but her focus did. She didn't like school as much as she adored reading, and she plowed through every book my parents owned. She liked music but only wanted to strum a guitar, never take lessons. She wanted to teach herself. And when she met Dave, a few years older than her, seventeen when she was fourteen, she fell madly in love with him above all other things. Like Dave, who hadn't been able to hack school, either, she dropped out halfway through her junior year—exactly the same level in school that I am now.

And I guess now I'm kind of a dropout, too, I surmise as I lower myself onto an empty bench, curling my knees up to my chin. It's true. Now that I've run away from the Lycée, I'm no longer a high school student. And that makes me, at least in the eyes of the colleges, not to mention society, a high school *dropout.*

I take a long, slow breath. I fix my eyes on the rapidly flowing Seine, trying to imagine the water as all these bad feelings rushing away from me, toward Paris. All the way down to the Mediterranean Sea.

I shiver, stuffing my bare hands into my coat pockets for warmth. There I feel a small piece of paper—a business card. I pull it out and read, *Binet Nagou.* That curly-haired social worker from the train station. She was so kind.

I gaze sadly at the card. No one can help us now. We have no one to turn to.

I lean over the railing and let go of the tiny rectangular card, watching it catch in the wind and fly through the air above the water, before disappearing.

I climb back up the steps to Annabel's attic apartment a few hours later, weighed down by heavy shopping bags. The stale air in the building makes me wrinkle up my nose. My sudden goodwill, my desire to make this whole thing right, inspires me to clean up the apartment after I finish cooking breakfast. Annabel and I could make this place a home, at least for a little while, till we figure out what to do next.

I creak the door open. Annabel and Marco are awake.

More than awake . . . Annabel's draped in Marco's big, poufy white shirt that he was wearing when I met him in the wee hours of the morning, and Marco's clad only in his boxers. Seated on the kitchen counter, her legs wrapped around Marco's waist, the two of them are locked in a hot, steamy embrace, Marco's hairy hands firmly gripping Annabel's behind. They part lips when I walk in, and flushing red, Annabel grabs to close Marco's unbuttoned shirt over her chest. Marco, for his part, looks very pleased to see me.

"¡Joder! Penelope!" he cries. "Bonjour! Comment vas-alles tu?"

"Très bien, merci," I choke out. I avert my eyes to avoid his near-nudity.

"PJ! I'm so glad you're back. Where did you go?" Annabel hops off the counter and finishes buttoning his shirt.

"I thought I'd make some food for us . . . all of us." I gesture at Marco. "Him, too."

"You are too precious," Annabel replies. "Marco, isn't she precious?"

Marco reaches out and, too disgustingly for me to comprehend what he's doing before it happens, actually wraps his snaky arms around me and holds me in a close, nauseating hug. "Muchas gracias, Penelope," he whispers in my ear.

"Ew!" I shriek. "What is wrong with you? Don't touch me!"

Marco jumps back. "*Ay Dios mio.* What did I do?"

Annabel looks back and forth between us. "Marco, baby, why don't you get dressed? PJ and I can start cooking. Maybe you can run out and buy a bottle of wine? A nice dry Chardonnay would be really yummy right now."

Marco slinks off to the bedroom to put his pants on. "PJ!" Annabel hisses. "Marco's just trying to get to know you."

"Annabel, I'm going to say something to you and I really don't want to say it again after I say it."

Annabel's face is horrified confusion. "What?"

"Don't let him touch me again. Don't ever let anyone touch me without my permission again."

"Oh, Pen," Annabel whispers. "Okay. He's really just trying to be nice."

"I don't care. I really don't care."

Marco comes back. "May I please have my shirt back, Mademoiselle?" He's trying to be light but it comes out forced and a little intimidated. I start putting away the groceries.

Annabel ducks into the bedroom and comes back wearing a high-necked dress that looks about a hundred years old. She hands Marco his shirt and a ten-euro bill. "Don't spend it all, okay?" she asks him.

Marco leaves and Annabel goes into the bathroom to wash her face. Once back in the kitchen, I see that she's combed out her bedroom hair and pulled it away from her smooth, pale face in a way that highlights the beautiful arch of her cheekbones. Her skin is flushed a little pink, and despite the awkwardness still lingering in the apartment, I can tell she's in a great mood.

"I'm totally in love with Marco," she confides as she reaches for the carton of eggs and a bowl. She cracks each egg perfectly into a splash of cream, without getting any shell at all into the mixture. With a whisk and some salt, she beats them to a fluffy consistency, just the way our mom does it.

"That's ridiculous," I say coldly. "You don't even know him."

"I know everything I need to know about him to know that I love him," Annabel insists. "And last night was out of this world." Annabel watches me chopping the leeks and takes the knife out of my hand. "No, do it like this," she instructs. "See? It's easier."

But she doesn't give the knife back to me. She just cuts up the rest. She's always going to think she knows better than me. "I knew he was planning to come see me, and he'd told me to meet him at the cathedral at six P.M., just after the evening Mass lets out. I didn't have any idea that he'd even show up! The last time we were together he'd said he'd be there on New Year's Eve. And there he was. Isn't that romantic?"

"He's a pervert," I say. "What drugs were you guys on last night?"

Annabel glares at me.

Marco returns with the Chardonnay. I notice he doesn't give any change to my sister, just opens the bottle and pours himself a huge glass. Annabel pours some for herself, and a tiny splash for me.

She demands that we toast to new beginnings

"To organic wool!" she cries.

The idea is so preposterous that I laugh. I can better imagine Alex and Zack herding sheep and shearing them every spring than Annabel and this Marco. I can see it now: Annabel, suddenly full of free love and happy living, deciding to free the sheep in the middle of the night. As soon as she realized how hard raising them would be, she'd come up with some excuse for why they were better off in the wild.

And Marco? I watch him pick his teeth with the steak knife Annabel just used to chop asparagus.

Annabel assumes the position behind the stove, contending she's the better omelet maker. She puts me on juice duty. You know, the hard job.

By the time we're ready to eat, Marco is drunk and Annabel looks like she'd like to go back to bed with him this very moment. I shove bites of omelet into my mouth and stay quiet. Finally, after the dishes are done and Annabel has relocated to the couch, where she's settled into a nap, I ask Marco to please leave.

"Why?"

"Don't you have anywhere else to go?"

"Not really," Marco says.

"You're staying here? Like, permanently?"

"*Oui*. Until we find a plot of land to start our farm," Marco replies. "Annabel told me it was okay."

It is not okay. "I'm going into the bedroom now," I say as evenly as possible. "When I come out, please don't be here."

"What do you—"

"Just go!" I snarl. "Just go away." I can't bear the thought of being in this apartment with them for the rest of the day. I need to think about how to extract my sister from the hold Marco has on her.

I make the bed and try to tidy up the minuscule space.

When Annabel got to Rouen, she met a man who needed someone to look after the apartment where his recently deceased mother used to live. If she'd keep an eye on the apartment until he was able to sell it, most likely in the spring, she could have the apartment rent-free. But he wouldn't pay her. He assumed that she'd get another job, and in truth, giving her a free place to live was generous. She has been able to earn a little money cleaning houses a few days a week. Not much, but enough to eat.

And, apparently, drink. Empty wine bottles are piled high around the sink.

The idea of Annabel cleaning houses makes me laugh. She's notorious for her messiness. Look at this place. Her side of our room at home used to be like a disaster zone. Someone—my mom, Dave, me—was always cleaning up after her.

The dead woman's things have all been pulled out of the closet— apparently by Annabel, looking for some hand-me-downs to wear—so I hang those back up and try to separate clean from dirty. There's an old washing machine in the bathroom that I'll use for laundry. In the summer, there's a clothesline outside the apartment window to use to dry your clothes; in the winter, I suppose you have to just hang them all in the bathroom.

This is so Annabel. I'm mad at her, and yet here I am doing her laundry. A while later, I hear Marco and Annabel leave again. I come out of the bedroom and eat some more cheese and bread. I slice up an orange for dessert. I don't want to write in my notebook. I don't want to read whatever book Annabel's got around, I and certainly don't feel like cleaning Annabel's apartment anymore. I stare into space as the apartment darkens in the dusk, wondering how this could have happened.

I can't believe my sister has given some sketchy Spaniard free access to our safe place.

Like last night, I fall into a fitful sleep in the loft, wondering about what trouble Annabel could get into with Marco. The possibilities, it seems, are endless.

I wake in the middle of the night. The apartment is dark, but Annabel and Marco have come home. I can tell because it smells like smoke and onions, a scent I'm quickly associating with Marco.

I creep down the ladder and switch the bathroom light on.

In the bathroom, I find a sight so disturbing and odd that I don't believe it's real.

Floating in the toilet, steeped in fresh, bubbly urine, is my periwinkle hand-knit hat.

15. ALEX

Father Figure

I crack the backseat window a bit for some air and pull my warm fur hat more snugly onto my head. The hat is the best souvenir from my dad I ever got. I become truly ill sitting in the back of the car, which Zack *knows*. But after he was so *obviously* suicidal on our last trifecta excursion—I mean, we found him at the bottom of Montségur, fuming—I suggested that he drive today and Jay take shotgun.

The French countryside rolls by the car window as we turn south toward the shore, toward Cannes. The flora changes as we get closer to the Riviera—less forest and more palm trees. A little bit of giddiness bubbles up in me. I know I should care, but I don't anymore if we're on a wild goose chase after a hapless blonde who doesn't even want our help. It's fun to have a mission, and look at us—traipsing about France like bohemians. It's amazing, really!

Montauban was a bust, yes. Toulouse didn't get us anywhere but tipsy-ville. And the ruins of Montségur really left us in a big cold heap of nada. So much for the Holy Grail. But I knew I had to suggest something to keep Jay's hope alive. As long as he believes he can find PJ—that she's what he wants—I can keep on being what he *needs*.

Which is why I had the brilliant idea for us all to go to Cannes. If PJ could be anywhere, why not there? Zack was much easier to convince than Jay, but given that he didn't have any better idea, he finally agreed. So this morning we repacked our bags and headed out.

Of course, I had special reasons for suggesting Cannes. When my mom moved to Paris and met my dad at a club on the *rive gauche*, they fell in love instantly and she moved into his apartment on the Rue de Miromesnil in the eighth arrondissement a week later. Within a month she was pregnant with me. My dad was so thrilled to be procreating (I mean, it was Baby ME we're talking about!) that he took a suite for her at the Grand Palace Hotel in Cannes.

And we all know that didn't work out too great. But I also know that Cannes is a magical place, one that my mom loves to return to. When we're there, her bitterness, that hard edge she has about her that makes her so good at her job and such a prickly mother, softens. As comfortable as my mom is still going to Cannes, to cover the film festival for *Luxe*, or to visit old friends, or just to take me on a little vacation, she still can't bear to go into the Grand Palace Hotel. Somehow, that's just a little too much for her. So I haven't been back *there* since I was just a mere fetus in the womb.

Thinking about my mother gives me a pang. I have fourteen missed calls from her by now. But I'm not going to think about that. Not today.

Using the GPS system on my BlackBerry, I figure out exactly how to get to Cannes. I lean forward to dictate directions to Zack every once in a while, but mostly I feel quietly peaceful and excited inside.

I can't wait to get to Cannes. For some reason, it just feels so right.

My hunch was brilliant. Of course Tuan Nguyen still has an account at the Grand Palace Hotel! And it is just as fabulous inside as I always dreamed it would be. The front desk checks me in just as easily as M. Garty let us into the penthouse apartment in Montauban.

"The usual room, Mademoiselle Nguyen?" the pretty, pert desk clerk asks me cheerfully.

"*Oui, bien sûr,*" I answer. I snap my fingers at Jay and Zack. A bellhop follows us, my suitcase and the two boys' backpacks lying on his rolling cart.

"This is the same suite my mom lived in the summer she was pregnant with me," I tell Jay and Zack when the bellhop lets us inside. I'm not exactly sure if that's true. But I like the way it sounds.

"This is fantastic, Alex!" Zack says.

"Yeah," Jay agrees, but he sounds less interested in the luxury surrounding us. He wanders through the two-bedroom suite, with a full wet bar and two enormous bathrooms, one with a spacious Jacuzzi. We have a balcony patio overlooking La Croisette, the boulevard that runs along the waterfront. The sun is just setting as we are arriving, and the lights of Cannes are starting to glow along the sea's edge. It's truly breathtaking. I can see why my mother was so happy here.

I cross my arms over my chest.

"Zack, can I talk to you alone for a minute?" I ask him. "Will you join me on the balcony?"

Jay gives us a puzzled stare, but I just smile. Pulling open the broad French doors that lead us to our private patio, I breathe in that delicious smell of the sea. I let the freshness fill my lungs and exhale slowly, loving every molecule of the Mediterranean air. Then I light a Gauloise.

Facing the beach, Zack and I stand there for a while.

"Zack," I say. "Are you okay?"

"What do you mean?" he asks.

"Well, I'm worried about you. You seem so down lately. Are you mad at me?"

Zack sighs. "Oh, Alex. I don't even know."

"You are!" I say. Deep down, I know the reason. He can tell. Since the moment I met Zack it was like he could read my mind.

"Alex, don't let's get into this right now," Zack says. "We both know you're going to do whatever you want."

It's pretty windy out here and my hair is whipping my face wildly. "What do you think I want to do?" I ask carefully.

"Jay," Zack smiles ruefully. "If you haven't already." His tone is joking, but there is real pain under his eyes. "Isn't that why you guys were taking so long at the ruins? How far did you get with him? Kissing? Making out? As far as you got with George?"

"No!" I gasp. "Zack, Jay is a *friend.*" Jay and I wove in and out of the ruins, getting lost among the piles of crumbling stone. Yes, of course I thought about making a move, but I know that wouldn't work with Jay.

But how obnoxious is it that Zack knows me that well? He stares out at the roiling sea and I can't see his expression.

"Zack, you are absolutely paranoid," I say. "I don't like Jay!" I laugh. "I mean, I do like him, I want to help him, but just because he's a great guy. Not because I want to take him to bed. It's not like George at all!"

Zack looks at me without saying anything for a minute. It's a long minute.

"Oh, jeez, Zack, what? Why are you looking at me like that?"

"It's not like George?" he asks. His voice is shaky. "You promise?"

"I promise."

"Then why are we in Cannes? Why the big show? You really think PJ is in Cannes?"

"She *could* be here," I reason. "If I were going to run away from Paris, this would be the first place *I'd* go."

"It really is incredible," Zack accedes. "Look at all the people down there." There are hundreds of brightly dressed tourists strolling along as the last rays of the sun disappear for the day. It's freezing out here, but for some reason, it feels good to be outside.

Zack looks through the sliding glass doors at Jay, who's sprawled on the couch, watching French TV.

"Because you know with Jay, it won't work," Zack says. "He'll see through it. He's smarter than that."

I know what he means is, *he's too good for you.*

"And, you know, it didn't really work that well with George either. If it had, we wouldn't be having this conversation." Zack stalks across the patio and goes back inside. "Think before you leap, Alex. It's a long drop."

I finish my cigarette and look back over the edge of the railing. A long drop is right.

I suggest we begin the night at the hotel bar. That way, we can charge everything to the room.

Zack is dressed to the nines, in the same suit he wore to my birthday dinner in Paris. His hair is gelled so it stands up in chunks, very chic. Jay has on beautiful gray wool pants and a black crewneck merino sweater that hugs his broad shoulders. He cleans up so nice.

I chose silky black stockings and a crimson and black sleeveless chiffon dress that gathers at the neck, leaving my back bare. I bought it last year, and this year it fits even better than before, my chest filling it out better than I'd hoped. I wear my little black booties, with their spiky heels that set me at least four inches above my normal height. In them, I'm almost as tall as Zack and easily see over the top of Jay's buzz cut.

"Ready, boys?" I ask them as we wait for the elevator doors to part and take us downstairs.

"Let's go," Zack says. I smile at him, and despite the conversation we had earlier, he smiles back. "I'm on celeb-watch. I cannot wait!"

Jay folds us each under one of his powerfully built arms and squeezes us with affection, a gesture that's uncharacteristic as of late. I knew this trip was a fantastic idea; I just knew it!

At the bar, I order us each a Bellini and a shot of vodka.

"You'd really have come here if you wanted to run away from Paris?" Zack asks me.

"Look around you. Of course I would have. This is *the* place to be."

"I just don't know if the Riviera's the place *PJ* would go." Jay sighs, leaning over the bar. "But I guess I don't know her as well as I thought I did. . ."

"And anything's possible," I say, putting my arm around him chummily.

"There's only one way to find out," Zack says. "Let's drink! If we're loud enough, having enough fun, she'll find us."

"My thoughts exactly!" I chime in. *"Un, deux, trois!"* We down our shots and clink our Bellinis. The bartender brings us another round. These go down even more easily. I'm about to order a third, when the bartender comes over with a bottle of champagne—Veuve Clicquot.

"Pour vous, Mademoiselle," the bartender says.

"Hmmm, yummy! I love champagne!" Zack squeals.

"Isn't that what we've been drinking already?" Jay asks.

"No, this is the *good* stuff," Zack tells him.

"Who sent this?" I ask the bartender sharply. I look wildly around the room. "Who sent this bottle?"

Discreetly, the bartender cocks his head toward a handsome, fit Asian man in a striped suit and a dark gray, partially unbuttoned shirt at the end of the bar. He winks.

I'd know that man anywhere. My throat falls into my stomach. It's my dad, the one and only Tuan Nguyen.

It's funny, that feeling I get sometimes when I'm not being careful. My first instinct is to run into his arms. The second is to sock him, right in the teeth.

Jay catches the sound I make, but Zack doesn't. "Alex? Who's that guy?" But I've already started walking away from them.

"Dad?" I say quietly when I make my way over to him. "I didn't know you were here tonight."

"I noticed," my dad replies. "Imagine my surprise when we arrived to find that my suite was occupied for the night."

"We?" I ask.

"You look stunning, Alexandra, darling." My dad leans forward to kiss me on the cheek. "So much like your mother."

"Yeah, well, Dad, it's been, like, ten years since I saw you."

"Has it been that long?" my dad asks mildly. "Ah, Camille. Come meet someone."

Dad reaches out to a person walking up behind me. She's a petite blond woman in a long black dress, her shiny mass of waves trailing down her back.

"*Bonsoir,*" she greets me, her lips only making a tiny crack at a real smile. "Hello."

"*C'est* Alexandra," my dad says quietly. If you looked away for a moment, you'd have missed the slightest hint of Camille raising her eyebrows. "She's the one who took our room."

"We can leave the room, if you want it," I say hastily. "I didn't think you were going to be here. I thought you'd be in Vietnam, or Thailand."

"Oh, Thailand. I never go there anymore. Too popular now." My dad has his arm slipped around Camille's midsection and his eyes are half closed and no longer directed at me but sort of grazing Camille's décolletage. Is he drunk?

"Oh. Well, I wouldn't know. I've never been there." Or Vietnam, for that matter. I feel woozy. Camille never takes her eyes from me. It makes me all too aware of how much bigger I am than her, how close to me she probably is in age. There isn't a wrinkle on her face, and her dress would be a crime of indecency on anyone over twenty-eight.

"I've got to go, Dad." I rush out. "Nice seeing you." I can barely form the words. My voice dips in and out, like a cell phone with bad reception. "Happy New Year."

"*Bonne année*," Camille replies, but my dad just smiles. By the time I stumble blindly back over to Zack and Jay and turn around, Camille and my dad are gone. I keep the smile frozen on my face. My heart feels pinpricked, over and over again.

"Who was that?" Zack shrieks. "Because I want to thank him myself! This champagne is heavenly!"

"Yeah, Alex," Jay says, putting his hands on my shoulders to steady me. "Who was that? Are you okay?"

Just the fact that after watching my first encounter with my dad in over a decade, my friends *still* can't tell that we are blood relations is enough to send my emotions into a tailspin. "Just some guy I used to know," I choke out. I grab my glass of champagne and drink the whole thing.

Jay and Zack stare at me when I grab for the bottle and pour another large glass. "Watch it, Alex!" Jay warns, but I take the whole glass and swallow it in one gulp, too.

"Alex, what the hell are you doing?" Zack looks really concerned. "You keep that up and you'll throw up. Come on. I thought we were having fun tonight."

"What the hell am I doing?" I repeat. "That's a good question." I look at my champagne glass for a while, studying it, wondering what would happen if I threw it on the ground. If it shattered, would I get kicked out of the bar? Kicked out of the hotel?

Would they get my dad back down here to pay for it?

I don't get to find out. Jay sees me pitch forward, the world suddenly starting to go dark, and he hoists me up and hauls me straight out toward the elevator.

I almost never puke, but those shots of vodka put me on the wrong course tonight. I throw up all over the elevator, crying the whole time. Jay takes me to the suite, wipes a hot wet washcloth all over my face, and puts me into bed, still wearing my dress and my tights.

Zack bursts in.

"Alex!" he yells at me. "I can't take this anymore! What the hell is going on here? All day you've been acting bat shit crazy!"

My face crumples. "Don't worry about it, Zack. Just leave me alone."

"Why can't you just be straight with us? Why can't you ever just tell us the straight, honest truth?" Zack runs his hands through his coiffed hair. "Come on!"

"Zack, just leave her alone, like she said!" Jay yells at Zack.

"What do you know about being straight, anyway?" I mumble.

I'm not even sure that I actually said that out loud until I open my eyes to find two very shocked faces riveted on mine.

"Oh, Alex." Jay shakes his head. "*Ay Dios mio.*"

"That's it!" Zack screams. "I'm finished with you, Alex Nguyen. Fuck you and your time-shares, your fancy hotels. Fuck you and your twisted mind games. You are, and always have been, a spoiled *bitch*! We're done. For real this time!"

Zack storms into the other bedroom and grabs his backpack. "I'm leaving."

"Where are you going?" Jay asks, panicked. "I thought you were going to help me!"

"I can't help either of you," Zack announces. "You two are pathetic. Help yourselves. This isn't about PJ, is it, Alex? This is about you on a poor-little-rich-girl tour of the South of France. I'm over it. I'm going to

Amsterdam. See you back at the Lycée. If you two don't get kicked out of there for your stupid schemes in the meantime. Good-bye!"

The door slams with so much force I can hear someone in the hallway gasp.

"Forget him," I mumble at Jay, and paw at the light switch next to my bed until it goes dark.

Room service knocks at our door around seven A.M. The guy leaves a tray on the desk with a café au lait and a croissant on it. At first I think maybe Jay ordered it, but he's fast asleep when I put my robe on and go check on him in the other room.

Under the napkin is an envelope, presumably for the receipt. I open it, wondering if this was supposed to be for the suite next door.

I almost drop the contents of the envelope when I get it open. In thin, crisp, 500-euro denominations, is more money than I have ever had in cash in my life.

"From your friend at the bar," reads the hastily scrawled note. "Have fun in Cannes."

I call down to the front desk. "I need to speak to Monsieur Nguyen," I tell them. "Put me through to his room."

"Monsieur Nguyen checked out earlier this morning," the clerk tells me. "We do have a Mademoiselle Nguyen staying with us. Can I connect you?"

"No, no thank you." I slide the money back and tuck it away in a pocket of my bag along with the envelope holding my letter from the Lycée.

I rush to the bathroom, feeling like I need to puke or drink water, or both, and then do it all over again.

My head hung over the toilet, I see Zack's toothbrush hanging over the edge of the sink. He forgot it when he stormed out last night.

I crawl across the bathroom and climb into the glass bathtub. I let the water rise up around me, covering my tights, then my dress, likely ruining the silk.

The roar of the running water drowning my sobs, I slip my head under the water and wonder if I'll ever get my best friend back.

16. OLIVIA

Family Histories

"Thomas, I think I would rather take Olivia to rehearse," Mme Rouille says. "Olivia, are you ready to go?"

"Give me five minutes." I run into my room and change into a black leotard, tights, and Lycra shorts. I slip a hooded sweatshirt on over my dance clothes and jump into my UGGs. I'm still full from dinner, but I don't want to miss the chance to get a ride over to the Place d'Italie. It's at least forty-five minutes by métro. And I really should get in some extra practice. Since performing the other night, I've been slacking off. I feel like a lazy bum!

Something also tells me that Mme Rouille really needs to get me alone right now. When Thomas pressed her to explain herself a few minutes ago, she went white and ran into the kitchen. What does she mean when she says that PJ is in more danger than I think?

The doorman of the Rouilles' building brings their cream-colored Mercedes around to the front door.

Mme Rouille takes the busy Avenue de la Grande Armée to the Porte Maillot and gets on the *Périphérique* heading south. There's gnarly grid-lock on the ring road around Paris. Mme Rouille honks urgently on the horn.

"Mme Rouille? Are you okay?"

"Olivia, I've made a terrible mistake," she says haltingly. "I didn't realize . . ."

"Mme Rouille! What do you mean?"

"Your friend. Your friend who was here with us—Penelope. She is so beautiful."

PJ's beauty is a truism people never seem to be able to quite wrap their minds around. How can someone that beautiful be real? And sitting at their dining room table? Sleeping in their bed? Sitting next to them in class? It's hard to get used to.

"I know. She's a knockout. I really—I really hope she is okay." I feel a sharp pain in my gut, that feeling I get when I realize I haven't thought about her in a little while, and she's *still* missing.

My life goes on: I go to the Batignolles market with Thomas; I have dinner with him and his mom; I worry that I'll be found out for going out with someone who's not entirely kosher with my host mother. I ride through Paris traffic; I go to the Underground studio space in the thirteenth and worry about when I might get the chance to perform for Henri again. And PJ is *still* gone. How can that be?

"I cannot believe I did not adequately prohibit that girl from leaving us to go live with M. and Mme Marquet. I had no idea when you told me that you knew someone who had been assigned to them for a homestay that you were speaking of a young woman."

"Why? Why does it matter?" Mme Rouille has the seat warmers on in the Mercedes, but suddenly I'm freezing cold.

"I will tell you something, and I need you to never repeat it to Thomas, or to anyone. Can you promise me that?"

I just stare at her, this woman who is the picture of good breeding, good manners, even temper. Her voice betrays extreme fear, and her hands are shaking.

"Of course," I murmur.

"I have known M. Marquet for a long time—since before Thomas was born. We went to the Lycée de Monceau, and he took me out on some dates when we were young. He flirted with too many other girls, and so in college when I met M. Rouille, I was so glad to be with someone who was loyal, and so kind, and I no longer accepted to go on dates with M. Marquet. But we stayed in contact; we were in the same social circles."

This is the first I have ever heard Mme Rouille—or even Thomas—mention M. Rouille, Thomas's father. I stare at the long line of cars in front of us, creeping along. I wait for her to tell me more.

"M. Marquet was at one point interested in becoming a doctor and had his family arrange a place at the Sorbonne for him. M. Rouille was a medical student there at the time, and the two men became friends. M. Marquet was very flashy, and M. Rouille very conservative. I guess one was a good foil for the other, for a time." Mme Rouille flicks up the heater. I notice again that her hand is shaking.

"M. Marquet dropped out of school. His grades were terrible. M. Rouille and I got married, and M. Rouille went to work at Saint-Rémy hospital. Then, M. Marquet came back into our lives. He began dating a much younger woman, and, as was his want, he began to throw a lot of parties at that country residence in the Dordogne. He begged me and my husband to come down to one of the parties, a Christmas party. His younger girlfriend was so drunk that she went to bed. That left *me* to make sure the staff ran the party properly. I was in the kitchen, sorting out the catering company, when M. Marquet came in and asked me to get some wine from their cellar with him."

"Oh, my God," I say breathlessly. I don't want to hear what's next. I know it's going to be awful without even seeing the look on Mme Rouille's face.

"He tried to kiss me, and I pushed him away, and he heaved himself on top of me, and . . ." Mme Rouille's voice drifts off. She's looking straight out the windshield, but I can tell all she is seeing is that awful Christmas night. "When he was through, I found M. Rouille and made him drive me all the way back to Paris in the middle of the night. I went to the doctor and got some pills and stayed in for a few months. I was so humiliated." I can hear Mme Rouille swallow a sob.

"M. Marquet did that to you?" I repeat. "How could he?"

I've never met PJ's elusive host dad, but I've seen his photos and had heard that for all his absent ways, he was an okay guy. By all of PJ's reports, he had far more personality than his wife, a petite, hard-faced woman who seemed to put PJ on edge.

"It was a different time."

My heart starts hammering. Does she think M. Marquet assaulted PJ, too? Could that be possible?

We finally get to what is holding up all of the traffic—a bad accident involving an overturned delivery truck. *Les Fleurs de Paris*, the driver's-side door reads. Roses are spilled all over the blocked-off pavement.

I try to imagine what that must have been like for Mme Rouille and find that I can't. I can't even imagine it. I should reach out to my host mother, try to comfort her. I've never shown her any affection. I ache to hold her hand, remind her that it's all over now. But I stop myself. Somehow, I fear that Mme Rouille wouldn't necessarily welcome my condolences.

"M. Marquet was very angry that I'd been unwilling to accept his advances, even though I was married, *putain de merde*! He confronted my husband at the hospital. He told them we were *done* in Paris society."

"What do you mean?"

"At first, we thought he was just angry. But then, when we had Thomas, we found that it was hard to get our son into a good kindergarten, and harder still to get him into a respectable school after that. M. Rouille was passed over for several promotions, so that he soon reported to a much younger man as his boss. No one ever confirmed it, but we knew it was because of M. Marquet."

I try to imagine Thomas, just a young boy, in long navy shorts and knee socks, completely unaware of the drama of the adults. Did he know as a kid that he wasn't going to a good school? Did he care? From looking around the apartment at pictures of the cherubic Thomas, I have a feeling Paris society was the very furthest thing from his mind.

"I felt so guilty," Mme Rouille goes on. The traffic has thinned out, and she's driving faster now. Almost too fast. "I'd ruined our lives! Stéphane's father died, and he'd been left very little—most of it had gone into trust for Thomas's education. There was no way we could keep the house we'd bought when we'd married. But Stéphane did not seem to care—he found the circumstances inspiring."

"Inspiring?" I ask. I see that our exit is coming up. I wonder if Mme Rouille even remembers where we are going.

"*Chérie*, my husband was an idealistic man. Not unlike Thomas in many ways. In very many ways. He loved France, but he was drawn to other places. He applied for a job doing medical work in a remote part of Tunisia, and we moved there. I taught Thomas at home, and every once in a while was able to take him into Tunis or another city for a concert or some other cultural event. Stéphane flourished in Tunisia: He learned Arabic; his patients loved him. Thomas loved it, too—he painted, and wrote poetry, and read every book we could get for him in French. Only I detested living there. I missed my friends, and my sisters, and, of course, Paris itself."

I'm so absorbed in her story I realize I'm holding my breath. "When Thomas was fourteen, Stéphane got a call in the middle of the night. A Bedouin man—a nomad—had gone into convulsions in a small village quite far from where we lived in Gabès. Stéphane jumped into his jeep and went looking for the man. Three days later he had not come back. Thomas and I just waited and waited for him, until finally, a man from the French Embassy came to the house and told us that Stéphane had hit a slick part of the road, going much too fast, and flipped the jeep over." Mme Rouille wipes a discreet tear from her face. "His neck snapped," she went on, her voice quieter, "and it being so late, no one found him till the next morning. He didn't even have his passport with him. But when some locals hunted through the wreckage, they found his doctor's bag and in it, a prescription in his name. They took it back to the village where the

Bedouin man had been having his seizures—he had died by then—and called the Embassy." Her voice has dropped to a whisper. "They were too afraid to come tell me themselves."

"Oh, Mme Rouille." I'd had no idea that Thomas's dad had been killed in a car accident. What a devastating sight the man from the Embassy must have been at the front door. "Watch out!" Mme Rouille almost misses our exit. Just in time, she scoots in front of a station wagon.

"*Désolée*. I decided immediately to return to Paris, and out of desperation I contested my father-in-law's will. How could Thomas have a trust for his education but not for a roof over his head? The civil court took pity on me, and, of course, Stéphane had life insurance. My only worry, after finding this apartment, was that no schools would accept my Thomas, because of M. Marquet. But shortly after we moved back, I got a note from a Mme Marquet. I was shocked. I'd been so far away—in Tunisia there had been no news of the society weddings. Apparently M. Marquet had disappeared for a while. When he returned to Paris, he had a fiancée from Marseille. And this woman reached out to me, offered her condolences for my husband, and offered to help me secure a spot at the Lycée de Monceau for my son. She was on the board of admissions. I don't know how."

"Is she still?"

"Yes, very much so. That's why she signed up to be a host parent this year. It must make her look good to our committee."

"And now that M. Marquet is running for office . . ."

"I always thought it was odd that they hadn't had children yet. Maybe she can't have them; maybe she wanted a stand-in daughter for the campaign trail. The French love families; they love beautiful women."

"Not PJ," I say, tears running down my cheeks. I should have been there for her. I could have stopped this. But I was too wrapped up in Thomas; too wrapped up in my dancing. "That can't be what's happening to PJ. Please, no."

Mme Rouille is crying too. We pull up in front of the rehearsal space, its interior lights glowing. I can tell that it is empty; they leave the lights on even though few people ever practice here at night. I can't go in there; I can't spend another moment doing a turn, or a leap, or a lift.

"Mme Rouille, what can we do? Should I alert the police? What can we do for PJ?"

"The police? And tell them what? The Marquets will squelch any scandal and ruin all our lives in the process. I cannot face them again. You must not face them, either." She shakes her head, still very shaken by the confession she's told me. She sighs. "There is nothing I can do for your friend, Olivia. It is too late."

"No! There must be something!" My thoughts are so jumbled I barely register what I do next. I don't think. There's too much to think about. So I just act.

"We have to go home," I tell Mme Rouille, thoughts of dancing completely forgotten. "I have to warn my other friends. Drive as fast as you can!"

The ride home takes less than half the time that it did on the way over; they've cleaned the accident off the road. There are still roses, wet and dirty from melting snow on the highway, everywhere.

"Thomas!" I scream as I run up the stairs two at a time to the apartment, Mme Rouille following close behind. "Call Xavier! Tell him we need the moped—and we have to leave town *tonight*!"

LE JOUR DES ROIS

Twelfth Night

17. ZACK

Queers on Wheels

alfway to Paris, I look down at my hands clutching the steering wheel, and I'm cracking up like an old crank that just broke out of the loony bin.

I pass the Lyon exits, the signs pointing out where to get off the highway to visit all the sights Madame Cuchon took us to see on our field trip in November. Buried in those medieval streets is a McDonald's—the place where I first detected that Alex was capable of deep disloyalty. I shiver, remembering how much it stung when she told me that Jay doesn't go for my kind.

I'm driving very carefully, not flying the way I would down a Tennessee back road at four in the morning. If this were Pierson and me, we'd be kicking up dust and turning up Johnny Cash. But I'm not about to risk getting pulled over—and the only getaway soundtrack I can access from the rental-car radio is a sad-sack mix of Christmas songs and classic opera arias.

Alex is going to be a damn hot mess when she realizes that I am not coming back. And I have their car, too. They'll have to take—*gasp*—public transportation to get back to Paris now. Alex will freak.

And guess what? Jay's gonna see what his new "best friend" looks like in the midst of a mental breakdown. Just watch.

I return this hunk of teal-painted junk to Eurauto in the basement of the Gare Montparnasse as the sun is coming up. Then I head straight to the Gare du Nord. I'm delirious with fatigue. On the métro, the stops of central Paris pass by me in a blur. I can't believe I've been gone for more than a week!

And for what? To make myself into even more of a fool in Jay's eyes. To cater ever further to Alex's insane demands. And, of course, we didn't find PJ.

That's the worst part. PJ's still out there somewhere. And I know Jay won't rest until he's found her.

Is it atrocious of me to say that I always had a feeling something like this would happen? I know, I know.

She never fit in, that Penelope Jane Fletcher. She done came to Paris with just about *everything* going for her: PJ's drop-dead gorgeous, the kind of girl who gets plucked out of a crowd to work runway shows for a million dollars a day. She's *wicked* smart—easily the best French speaker in the entire Programme Américain, including all the American kids with French parents. And her talent flabbergasted everyone—her paintings could easily hang in the lauded galleries of the Louvre.

But she's an odd cookie, that PJ. She flaps her mouth too much, but then stays quiet for long enough for you to wonder what on earth the little minx could be thinkin' about without telling you. And she's fidgety—she *never* stops moving around, poking at her clothes, flicking her hair, cracking her knuckles, and just looking dang *uncomfortable*. If I didn't know better, I'd have thought she came straight from a crack house in a seedy Memphis slum, jonesin' for a fix.

PJ was all right. I don't hold anything against her, let me just say, but she *did* take it for granted that everyone wanted to be her friend. Especially Jay.

And no matter what kind of bug about Paris had gotten up her ass, if you walk away from Jay—you are just a straight-up *fool* in my book. A no-good, uneducable *fool*.

Not to admit my bias or anything.

I grin as wide as the back of a truck when I look at the timetables from Paris Nord to Amsterdam. First train to Amsterdam has spots left for sale, and wouldn't you know it, it's just about to board.

Sweet Jesus, would you look at me! I bet no one clapping their hands and praising the Lord this Sunday at Christ's Message Baptist Church in little ole Germantown, Tennessee, would recognize me speeding like a bandit straight up to Sin City, Euro style. What kinds of trouble could I get up to in Amsterdam?

Holler back, y'all! I say to myself. *Mamas better hide your sons!*

I can't help it: I'm peering out the window like a puppy in a pickup as the train enters the Amsterdam station. I see Pierson before he sees me:

grinning like an idiot, wearing his hair slicked back under a hat like the hot Euro guys he's brought along with him to meet me. They look like an ad for Calvin Klein: clean, crisp shirts and starched jeans and each of them decked out in dark glasses and trendy railroad-worker style hats.

"Is this theme dressing?" I exclaim broadly as I disembark the train. I pull Pierson's cap right off his head and square it jauntily on my own head. *"Bonjour, bonjour, mon ami!"* I kiss him, flamboyantly, on both cheeks. Then I barrel into him for a real hug. Oh, *Lord*, is it good to see him. It's been four months!

"Well, ain't you a sight for sore eyes, brother!" Pierson says, just as happy to see me as I am to see him. Pierson loves to call people brother—just like the elders at our church. "Dang, you look *good*."

"You're just bein' nice," I say, making a face. I look like I've just spent all night in the car and half the day on a train next to three old ladies who had nothing good to say about the world—they just went on chattering and complaining for *four hours*. But hey—at least I'm here.

Pierson, meanwhile, looks so hot he might actually be *crispy* to the touch. "Hot damn, boy!" I say. "Amsterdam does you right!" He's lost a few pounds of that baby fat he's been carrying around with him his whole life, and between that and his new, streamlined look, I'd say he's doin' darn well for himself.

"Thank you kindly. I do enjoy myself in this here town." Pierson gestures to the tallest, blondest man I have ever seen in all my seventeen years. "This, my dear, is Hannes. Make your acquaintances, boys."

I lean in to shake Hannes's massive hand. "Um, hi," I say up at him. He's got to be near seven feet tall. "Great to finally meet you. I've seen your picture."

"*Hallo*," Hannes responds in what I guess is Dutch. "*Welkom in Amsterdam.*"

"Oh, Hannes, speak English!" Pierson wheedles. "Zack ain't gonna know what you're saying if you go on with that nonsense." He reaches up and pats Hannes on the cheek. "You plucky bastard."

I'm *very* taken aback by how comfortable Pierson—the smart aleck chubby kid I grew up defending and protecting from all the redneck bullies we went to school with—is with his new(ish) boyfriend. Already they strike me as being as close as Pierson and I are, except even closer, since they are, you know, *intimate*. Picturing the two of them together, sleeping snuggled up in a bed somewhere, with no one else around, fills me with a warm, fairly unpleasant sensation—I feel bashful for even thinking of it, but it's more than that.

But I'm also elated for Pierson. *I wanted this for him,* I remind myself. *He's an amazing person and my best friend in the entire world. He deserves this.*

Even if *this*—Hannes—looks like he belongs on a superhero movie poster, saving the world so that all the short people will be safe.

Pierson leads the way to the Amsterdam métro. Apparently, he shares a dorm room with the other kid he brought along to the train station, an American guy named Bobby. Bobby, like us, is a Southerner and is actually the conduit who introduced Pierson to Hannes. I quickly glean that he, too, is gay. I wonder if *everyone* here leans that way.

Pierson's program works a little differently from the one that I am doing at the Lycée. All of the kids in the Programme Américain are juniors in high school and live with Parisian host parents. Pierson's program is open to kids between the ages of fifteen and nineteen, and everybody lives in a giant dormitory that is connected to the school.

Bobby, whose parents are Dutch, is doing this program in order to take the Dutch baccalaureate test so that he can go to college here in the Netherlands. He's already graduated from high school in the U.S., he tells us as we take the train back to their campus.

Bobby grew up in Atlanta, the son of the Dutch consul general there.

"I was one of the lucky ones," he tells us, grinning. Either he just had his braces off or God gave him the straightest teeth in the world. His smile is a true feat of amazing orthodontia. "Most kids of foreign service officers have to move around a lot. But my dad stayed in his same job for fifteen years. So don't let anyone tell you I'm not a true Southerner just because I have an EU passport. I lived in the South nearly all my life. I bleed peach-tree flowers, you hear?"

"True Southerner. Dyed-in-the-wool," Pierson confirms. "Ain't no question."

"All right, all right!" I say. "I get it. You don't have to prove it to me. I know one when I see one."

If anything, Pierson and Bobby bring out the Southerner in each other. Pierson's accent is more pronounced than I remember, while I feel I've worked hard to bury my own Memphis roots while I've been in Paris, correcting myself whenever my speech slips into those stereotypes of slow-talking idiot bumblejacks. I'm amazed, and a little impressed, that Pierson has held onto that part of himself here.

"You got all Yankees on your Paris program, huh, brother?" Pierson asks me. "You ain't never told me about no other folks from down South. You got Vermont, New York . . ."

"Uh, well, we got Texans."

"Texans don't count. They don't see themselves as nothin' but Texans," Bobby jokes. We hop off the train and head over to a low-slung brick building that looks more like college-campus housing than a high school. Tapestries and political bumper stickers are everywhere. Out one window flies an enormous rainbow flag that reads PACE on it—Italian for peace. It feels like my own personal welcome mat.

In Pierson's dorm, we take a few minutes to get organized before going out to get some lunch. I stash my backpack under Pierson's twin bed. Pierson's decorated his side of the room with large, goofy posters, like the one that says, BEER: HELPING UGLY PEOPLE GET LAID FOR YEARS. He's also got his autographed fan photo of Dolly Parton hanging right above his bed. Dolly is Pierson's idol.

I can't believe this place, not the posters or the tapestries or the flags, nor the fact that Pierson rolls out a little package of a brown, cakey substance and packs it into a glass pipe.

"What's this?" I can't help asking.

"It's hash, brother," Bobby tells me. "Little slice of happiness. Enjoy."

I wrinkle my nose. I notice that Hannes passes on smoking any, too, so I feel better. I can't believe Pierson is doing drugs! Even if they *are* legal here. I never! Pierson's done gone and become a badass.

"Let's go eat, man," Bobby says and giggles when they're done, and we set out to see Amsterdam. If my first hour here is any indication, this is going to be a *wild* city.

"You ready for some ass-kickin' eats?" Pierson asks as we sit down to a late lunch. He's lead us into a dark restaurant with low tables and with pairs of traditional Dutch clogs hitched to the walls as decoration. "You're gonna love this place, I promise. It's so . . . *old world.*"

The four of us order boiled-beef stew and potatoes. Our waitress speaks perfect, almost accentless English, and brings us icy cold mugs of Amstel beer. It's not like me to drink during the day, but the other guys seem to expect that a meal such as this will be accompanied by a large, frothy brew, and I can't complain when one is set in front of me.

The food is simple and easy to eat after such a long trip. Pierson and Bobby pepper me with questions about Paris and ask what the hell took me so long to get to Amsterdam.

"Why couldn't you come sooner? What changed your mind?" asks Pierson between bites of stew. "Medusa finally run you out of town?"

Pierson knows that PJ is missing, but in our texting, I've kept from going into too much detail. I know this would be a good time to bring him up-to-date, but the idea of launching into an explanation of what exactly it is about Alex that made me take the car back to Paris and charge my "emergency" Visa card with a round-trip train ticket to Amsterdam, seems like a decided bore at the moment. I just want to relax with this cold beer and these new friends, and bask in the ease of being surrounded by guys—gay guys at that.

"You don't want to know," I finally answer. "All I can say right now is by the grace of God in heaven my host parents don't give two hollers about how I spend my winter break. And now that I'm here, I plan to enjoy it."

Bobby raises his half-empty mug to me, and we all tap his glass with ours. "Amen, brother," Pierson says, and Bobby looks at me as he takes a long swallow. *"Welkom in Amsterdam."*

After lunch, as the sun sets, we take a long walk around the canals and small alleyways of Amsterdam. The city is quiet, and surprisingly, it's not as cold as Paris was when I returned the car early this morning. The buildings, row houses, and elegant, plump little offices, are low to the ground and just too adorable for words.

Hannes, Bobby, and Pierson know their way around like pros. I find out that Hannes is actually from Rotterdam and goes to University here. The connection between him and Bobby is that they met in a club and hit it off. Bobby brought Hannes home, and Pierson was in their dorm room studying for a test late into that Saturday night. Hannes and Pierson started talking, and Bobby soon realized that he wanted to take himself out of the equation. Goofy Pierson and sweet, quiet Hannes were perfect for each other. Hannes left that night with a quick hug to both guys and Pierson's cell phone number in his pocket.

"This is the Red Light District," Pierson tells me, and when I look up, I see rows upon rows of windows, each lit up with a woman, or a man, or some mixture of the two, on display for all the street to ogle.

"You're joking," I say, more to myself than to the other guys. I can't stop staring at the prostitutes, none of which are particularly beautiful, or even look very interested in enticing their prospective customers. One woman, on the second floor of the house right in front of us, meets my eye but doesn't smile.

"Crazy, right?" Pierson giggles. Hannes rolls his eyes affectionately at him.

"Pierson can never get enough of the Red Light District," Hannes intones.

"No," I gasp. "You come here? Like, for services?"

Bobby and Pierson bust up. "No, stupid!" Pierson wheezes. "You really think that little of me?" He slings an arm around Hannes's broad shoulders. "Besides, why do you think I would need to?" Hannes kisses Pierson's cheek.

"Then, why?" I ask, looking back up at the woman who won't stop looking at me. "*I don't pitch for your team, darlin'*" I want to tell her. "*You're wasting your time trying to entice me up there.*"

"Because it's *different*." Pierson shrugs. "Because it's not Tennessee, and I love to be reminded of that. As often as possible."

Bobby smirks. "For some people, there's no place like home. For Pierson, there's no place like the Red Light District. It brings the man comfort."

"That's creepy." As we walk away, headed back toward the dorms, the woman in the window lifts up her skirt, and I realize her legs are very hairy . . . and that *she* is a *he*.

Pierson and Bobby want to do something surprisingly cheesy the next morning—they want to go on a bike tour of Amsterdam. I balk at the suggestion. I don't even remember how to ride a bike.

"Will they provide helmets?" I ask.

"Shut up, prissy pants," Pierson answers. "Bobby and I have been waiting for someone to visit us so that we could do this. It's *so* Amsterdam!"

So Amsterdam indeed. The little canal city is chock-full of bikers—each rider blond and rugged and ripped—atop expensive-looking cruisers. Skeptical, I trail Bobby and Pierson to the tour shop inside Centraal Station. There's a tour leaving in about ten minutes.

"Let me just text Hannes to make sure he has enough time to get here," Pierson says, excusing himself. Bobby and I wait by the helmet rack, trying to find some that aren't still damp from this morning's sunrise tour. When Pierson gets back, he's all smiles. "Hannes is on his way!"

"Hallelujah," I say. After walking all over central Amsterdam last night, Pierson and Hannes made out for at least a half hour before Hannes went back to his own apartment. "I wish I could come with you," I heard Pierson whine to Hannes, but to his credit, Hannes just smiled and left. At least *he* has some manners when it comes to friendship over sex! But the way Pierson is acting now, you'd think he hadn't seen Hannes in months.

Oh, wait a second, that would be *me* who Pierson hasn't seen in months.

Hannes dashes up just as we're hopping on our bikes and gives Pierson a quick kiss on the mouth as a greeting. Once again, I'm blown away by how open they are.

"Look out, Amsterdam, we're queers on wheels!" Pierson shouts as we set off down the Spuistraat, away from the station. "Comin' at you!"

"Well, ain't you in a good mood?" I call to him.

"Ain't no question," Pierson responds. "I've got my three most favorite people in the world right here with me, and after this we're going to have the best *frites* you've ever tasted. *Velkom in Amsterdam*; welcome to paradise, am I right?"

It's a cool morning, perfect for a little bit of exercise, a great time of day for taking photos with my digital camera. From Cannes to Amsterdam overnight. It's incredible. In the less than twenty-four hours since I got here, the anxious pulsing of my blood in my ears—that suspenseful, nervous feeling I get when I'm around Jay, and worrying about upsetting Alex, and always, always wondering in the back of my mind *where on God's green earth is PJ Fletcher, and what if something really bad happened*—has subsided.

"Ain't no question," I shout back, feeling a grin spread across my face. I pedal faster, surpassing Pierson, just as I always had in childhood. As I pass him, I stick out my tongue.

"That's right, brother Pierson—Zack's back!"

I join Pierson's laughter as I leave him trailing in the dust.

18. PJ

A Chance Worth Taking

"So, Penny Lane, tell us what it's like in Paris," Annabel coos at me from the couch, where she's curled up next to Marco. "You've been so quiet ever since you got here. It's been what—a week and a *half* and I still don't know what you've been up to since we last saw each other."

There was a time—any of the dozens of times I sat by myself, wondering where my sister was and whether or not I would ever see her again—when the idea of getting to pour out the confusions and glories of the last semester in Paris to my sister would have brought me great comfort. Living in the Marquets' town house on the Place des Ternes, so often spending all evening by myself since my host parents were out of town at their house in the Dordogne, I sometimes spoke out loud to myself as if Annabel was there.

"I'm not sure *what* I think about Jay," I would say aloud giggling as I heated up packaged soup for dinner. "He's really good looking and smart but he's so different from me. What would we talk about if we went on a date?"

I'd imagine Annabel hopping on the kitchen counter and watching me stir clumpy lentil mix into the hot water. *"You should go for it, Penny Lane. He's hot! Besides, what do you have to lose?"* When we lived at home, Annabel was always bugging me to find a boyfriend.

"All you need is love," she'd tell me back when she was head over heels for Dave, dancing around our bedroom in her flannel pajamas.

It's true. But it's also so wrong.

"What do you want to know?" I'm up in the loft so I can't see them, but I can tell what expressions they have on their faces. Annabel is doing that thing where she's interested, but also teasing me. Marco just wishes I would go away. The last time he saw Annabel, there was no Annabel's little sister. There was just a promise, an invitation. As impetuous as Marco's bohemian spirit might be, I'm pretty sure I was a surprise not to his liking.

"Is it beautiful?"

"Extremely."

"Are the people nice?"

"Most of them."

"What did you do for fun there? Did you have friends? A boyfriend?"

I snort. "The usual stuff. Some friends. No boyfriend."

"Did you like it there?"

"Very much." I close the magazine I was flipping through, an old copy of *Marianne* from several years ago, its pages lined with dust.

"Then why did you leave?" The singsong quality Annabel's voice has held so far in her line of questioning turns serious. She really does want to know. Without being able to look at her, I can still tell this is something she's been dying to find out.

"Nothing's perfect," I say flippantly. "I wanted to find you. You know that."

"No, really, PJ, why did you leave? Why then? Why now?"

"I had school. This is the only time I could get away without being noticed."

"I don't believe you."

I scowl. What is she up to? I crawl over to the opening of the loft, swinging my legs over the ladder, and look down at her until she feels my gaze and stares back at me.

"What are you getting at, Annabel? You didn't want me to come to Rouen? You didn't want me to come find you, living in a dump, cleaning houses for beer money, and listen to you cry in the night?" My words come out more harshly than I meant them to.

"Jesus Christ, Penelope," Marco swears at me. "I cannot believe the things that you say. You should have more respect for your sister."

I roll my eyes and go back to my magazine.

He comes over to the bottom of the ladder. "Do you hear me?"

"Yes, Marco, I heard you. I think everyone in our building heard you. Ever heard of volume control?"

Marco glares at me, stroking his black, wiry beard. "Penelope, what is the matter with you? Are you crazy? ¿Loca? ¿Estúpida? Why you treat your sister so cruel?"

"Me, crazy?" I laugh. "No, Marco, I'm not the crazy one here. I'm not the one who wants to go raise sheep in the south of France. I'm not the one who pees on other people's hats!"

"Penelope, you know that wasn't my fault you dropped your hat in the—"

"I didn't drop my hat! I didn't do anything! All I am trying to do is help my sister! And she doesn't want to be helped! She just wants to get high or drunk with you all day!"

"Pen-EL-O-pee, why can't you listen?" Marco slams his hairy fist straight into the plaster wall of the apartment, right next to the ladder leading up to the loft. "¡Joder! Look at what you made me do!"

Annabel jumps off the couch. "Oh, sweetie, are you okay?" She grabs some ice from the freezer. "Put this on it." She looks at me. Don't you dare take this any further, her eyes warn me. "Let's just go in the bedroom for a bit, okay? You're so tired. Let's just go rest and calm down."

"I don't want her to come with us, Annabel," I can hear Marco say to my sister behind the closed bedroom door. "I won't go if she goes!"

"Don't worry, baby, there's no way I'm going without you. This is our dream. I want it as much as you do," I hear Annabel soothe him. "I'm not going anywhere without you."

I have to get out of here. I bolt out of the attic apartment door, leaving my bag there, just grabbing my coat and mittens. I refuse to wear my hat now, even though Annabel insisted that it had to be an accident and took it and boiled it and stretched it back into shape so that it would be clean. The wool felted a bit, and now it's like a whole different hat. I still can't forget what it looked like in the toilet.

I find myself back at the cathedral square, the same place where I found Annabel. It feels like years have passed since then, though it's only been around ten days. I must have been so sick and demented when I was wandering around this new city. I still don't feel entirely comfortable here, but I've learned my way around a bit. When I feel down, I sneak over here without telling Annabel where I'm going. Sometimes, seeing Jay on Gchat or reading his emails to me, I am so tempted to just tell him what happened, what's going on, and have him meet me somewhere, anywhere.

Jay's offline. If he were on, would I be able to stop myself from just writing "ROUEN" in the chat box?

Jay's emails tell me he's gone with Zack and Alex to some place called Montauban, then Toulouse, and even the ruins at Montségur. I look at what I last wrote to him.

Jay,

Please don't waste time trying to find me. Just enjoy where you are. Wish I could say the same. Things are pretty bad here but I can't explain because I am still figuring out what to do. There is no way you can help me right now, except by sending me these emails. Thanks for being there.

PJ

Jay wrote back only a few minutes after I sent that one.

PJ,

I'm glad you are still writing to me. Please don't stop. Please just tell me where you are. I'll come find you. I KNOW I can help if you let me.

Jay

PS Alex's dad has a suite at the Grand Palace Hotel in Cannes. We'll be there if you need us. But somehow I have a feeling I am never going to see you again. I'm so worried about you alone like this.

PPS The sunsets here are like a painting—a painting only you could paint.

I shake my head. If only I'd been able to make a clean break! But no, I had to go and leave Jay a note, keep writing to him because I can't let go of the Paris I left behind.

I reply.

Jay,

Cannes sounds beautiful. And who knows? Maybe someday I'll get to paint sunsets after all. Don't say that you'll never see me again. One day, you will.

I head toward the Église Saint-Maclou, another of Rouen's gorgeous churches. I keep thinking about why Annabel is so into Marco when clearly he's so skuzzy, and suddenly it hits me: Annabel simply *needs* a man in her life. Whether it was our dad, or Dave, or this Marco. As independent as she always seemed to me, it finally dawns on me that she can't function without someone else breathing life into her wild schemes, fanning her flames.

I step into the church for a little respite from the cold as I try to figure out what to do with this new insight about my sister. All this time I'd thought that if only I found Annabel, she'd help me get through the chaos my life has become. It never occurred to me that *she* might be the one who needs *me*.

In a back-row pew, I let my face warm up, rubbing my mittens against my cheeks. The church is full of tourists, and I feel anonymous enough here. It's a good feeling. Most of the time I'm paralyzed with fear, unwilling to leave the apartment. Annabel and I are just two of lots of Americans here. Even if the Marquets did come looking for me, asking around for me, how would any of the locals know which American to point to? I could be anywhere. I could be any one of these people. Somehow, that's not so easy to remember in the middle of the night, when I wake from nightmares about the Marquets finding me.

Sometimes, I forget that my exile is self-imposed. That I brought myself here, that I fled Paris and the Marquets and the Lycée. Now, hindsight being 20/20 and all, I wonder if it had to be that way. Could I have gone to Mme Cuchon when I decided I couldn't take living with the Marquets anymore?

But when I think of Mme Marquet, with her steely blue eyes, her taut, thin face and long nose always pointed up toward the ceiling in disgust at what she saw, I know for certain that she'd *never* have let me stay in Paris if I offended her. My value to Mme Marquet was that I was there to play the part of the American student completing her perfect little family. If I rejected her family, or if I told anyone about all the wacked-out stuff that had happened last semester, she'd see to it that I was sent home and placed in a miserable foster home until I turned eighteen. She'd make sure that I left France, and then I would never have been able to find my sister while I still could.

I know I did the right thing. Everything I did was to find Annabel, for us to be together. It's all worth it.

Outside the church, I'm a little lost in thought. I can't help but wonder what is to become of Annabel and me, living like this, with so little money and shrouded in so much secrecy.

At the corner of Rue d'Amiens and Rue Armand Carrel, I momentarily lose my sense of direction. Is Annabel's apartment to the left or to the right? Rouen is not a large city, but like those of Paris, its streets turn and curve in unpredictable ways. I take a few steps to the right, then backtrack, looking around for a landmark that might guide me home.

All of the sudden, I remember how best to get back to the apartment, and I whirl around to go back in the direction I had originally thought. I stop short and find a car stopped in the street behind me, a vaguely familiar face behind the wheel,

It's the guy in the baseball cap, the one from the train on Christmas Day. He lifts a gloved hand off the steering wheel and waves to me, smiling a little.

I'm nearly knocked off my feet by the shock of seeing him again. It feels so long ago since I boarded that slow train to Rouen, but this guy, still wearing that American-style hat, seems to recognize me. He doesn't even seem surprised to see me at all.

"Bonjour," I choke out instinctually, my skin prickling into bumps beneath the wool sleeves of my sweater.

His window is rolled up but he registers my greeting.

I suddenly feel very threatened and exposed. The guy's face is nowhere near as friendly as it was that afternoon on the train. That day, his pale, sunny features were open wide with a casual, inviting rapport, but today, cast in the shadows of the streetlamps and church candles flickering through the tall stained glass windows of the Église Saint-Maclou, he looks capable of something hateful.

The guy reaches forward, his car still idling in the street. Maybe he is just rolling his window down, maybe reaching for a knife or a gun. I don't wait to find out. Whirling back toward the church, I dash away from the Rue d'Amiens and weave a zigzagged pattern through Rouen all the way back to Annabel's apartment.

19. ALEX

Addicted to a Smile

sit on a lounge chair on the balcony in the cold, watching the sun go down and smoking Gauloises while wrapped up in my coat and an old black pashmina. Jay comes outside. I stub out my cigarette. I get the feeling he disapproves of smoking.

"You okay?" he asks me, his voice casual but still caring. He doesn't look at me, I think in an effort not to appear confrontational. "Last night was pretty crazy."

"I'm fine," I say brightly. "How are *you*? Can I get you anything?"

"I'm okay," Jay says, crossing his thick arms in front of his chest. It's pretty cold out, even this far south. The sea rolls ferociously under the powerful winds. "As good as can be expected, I guess. This hotel is off the hook. But I feel like I can't even enjoy it, no offense.

Until we find PJ—until she sends me an email that makes any frigging sense—I'm never going to really be able to have fun here. Pretty pathetic, huh?"

"Oh, Jay, that's not pathetic," I say, getting off my lounge chair and walking over to him near the balcony railing. "You really care about her. It's really beautiful."

"No, I know it's pathetic. She won't even talk to me, you know? At this point, you know me better than she does."

My face colors. So Jay's been feeling our bond grow, too.

"I don't really know that much about you. I don't even know where you're from."

"I'm from all over," Jay says. "My parents are from Guatemala, and most people think I was born there too. I was actually born in Chicago. Then we moved to Minneapolis so that they could find work in one of the meatpacking plants there. We've also lived in Texas and Fresno, California. My parents—they go where they can find money. I've got five little brothers and sisters. Man, when I go to college, my parents are going to be so relieved just not to have to feed me anymore!"

As much as I love my steak tartare, a meatpacking plant sounds like a fresh vision of hell to me. I feel a little uncomfortable about the turn this conversation has taken, embarrassed to be having it on the balcony of our all-expenses-paid suite at the Grand Palace Hotel. From this deck you can see the shining white line of Cannes's resort hotels around the bay, plus marinas and yacht harbors stretching out from the coast like so many long, glittery fingers. Even in the depths of winter, Cannes sparkles with money, fame, and charm.

"Where do you want to go to college?" I ask.

"Wherever gives me the best scholarship." Jay shrugs. "Probably University of Minnesota. You?"

I think of the Final Comp and how that letter from Mme Cuchon likely wiped out my chances of ever getting into any college, nonetheless one that I would actually want to go to.

"I'm not really into college. I'll probably just come back to Paris and start working right away. Like, for a fashion house or a magazine or something." Somehow, this line of conversation feels like a minefield, too. Jay must think I'm the most spoiled person in the world!

Jay laughs, though not unkindly. "Wouldn't that be nice? Coming to Paris was the best thing I ever did in a lot of ways. I mean, there's been some drama, but man . . ."

I look at him and smile. "I know. Traveling is the best."

"I miss my family and all, but seeing the world . . . that is something else."

"Do you ever miss Guatemala?"

"How could I miss somewhere I've never been?"

"You've never been to Guatemala?" I went to Lake Atitlán with my mom a few summers ago. It was beautiful. I decide I won't tell him that I've been there when he hasn't.

"It was a civil war when my parents left. They felt lucky to get out of there alive. That's why I have to get into a good school and get a good job when I graduate. I've got to make sure they never have to go back there again."

I don't say anything. For some reason, I'm bumbling through this conversation with Jay, and all I want is for him to see how interested in him I am, for *him*. Not for his looks or money or popularity, like I was with

George. I like Jay for every reason he just mentioned: because he's responsible, practical, friendly. Because he has a history. Because he works hard for what he wants.

His smooth, dark head of close-cropped hair and his bright, shiny smile, of course, don't hurt either! When he smiles, his eyes crinkle like you've just shared the most hilarious moment that ever happened. I'm addicted to making that smile happen. I swear. Sometimes I just stare at him, willing his face to brighten again.

"What are you doing out here, anyway? It's freezing," Jay says finally, tousling my hair. "*Que bonita!* Come inside and let's go eat somewhere."

I watch Jay walk inside and check his email on his phone for the thousandth time today. He still thinks about PJ all the time. I wish *I* was the one who took that place in his heart.

Jay's wrong. You *can* miss somewhere you've never been.

"So what do you want to eat?" Jay asks me as we take the elevator down to the lobby.

"Definitely a steak," I say without hesitation. "Cooked *bleu*."

"Hmm, that sounds good." Jay casually slips his arm around me. "I'm starved, man."

"I want it with plenty of sautéed mushrooms, too. And creamy mashed potatoes. Can we make that happen?" I ask.

"*Pourquoi pas?*" Jay says and steers me down a street that looks a little less touristy than the one we were just on.

"And can we have wine? A nice Burgundy?" I ask.

"Alex, I will get you absolutely anything you want," Jay says. "You should know that by now."

I shriek with surprised giggles. Oh, Jay honey, if you only *knew* what you're getting into with that statement!

"But you said, back in Montauban . . ." I tease him, remembering how he accused me of never being able to understand what it is like to go without.

"You convinced me that you don't get everything you want," Jay tells me, leading me into a cozy steakhouse overlooking the pier. "You didn't convince me that I couldn't try."

I tuck into our feast with gusto. This might be the last piece of good French *boeuf* that I enjoy for quite some time. When I get back to Brooklyn, I just know my mom is not going to be feeling very generous with me. She'd never resort to something so pedestrian—so TV movie— as actually grounding me, but I could see her disallowing me from any European travel for a while. And how will I live without Europe? How will I live without the delectable cuisine, rich and fatty but perfectly won- derful in moderation? How will I live without the shoes? How will I live without . . . all of this?

In between bites, I keep looking at Jay's handsome face and resolute yet relaxed upper body. He's so strong. But he couldn't save PJ, could he?

Could he save me? Could anyone save me from the mess I've gotten into with school?

"Well, this has been some trip," Jay comments as he steals the last bite of steak from my plate. *"Quelles vacances super!"*

"It hasn't been all bad."

"No, you know, it hasn't." Jay winks at me. "We've had some fun, haven't we?"

"I'd say any extra time spent with me cannot possibly be a loss," I say.

Jay considers this, pretending to not be able to make up his mind if I am right. Then he laughs. "No, man, you are really something. I never would have expected to be such good friends with you when we met in the fall. I remember you walking into the first day of school like you owned the place. I've been the new kid enough times to tell who the Queen Bee is right off the bat. I was like, *Ay Dios mio!* That girl is gonna be *muy peligrosa.*"

"I don't know what that means," though I get the idea. I laugh.

"But then I find out you're just like the rest of us—lovesick and lonely and looking for action in Paris. I should have known—why else would anyone come here?"

"You weren't lovesick till you met PJ," I remind him. "That's not why you came here, it was something that happened on contact."

"Oh, man, I guess you're right. But I've had my share of *problemas.* With the ladies."

"The ladies? Plural? I should have known! The truth comes out!"

Jay nods with mock overconfidence. "Yup. Plural."

"I doubt it!" I screech, but in truth I imagine every girl in Fresno, Minneapolis, and all the other sad places he's lived are still nursing their abandoned broken hearts and will be for a long, long time.

"Naw, man, I'm joking. But there was one girl—Tanya. Drama city. She liked me all sophomore year. I was the class president and she was the VP. People told me she ran just to do student government with me. The sophomores put on the winter formal for our school, so as soon as we were elected, we had to start working on fundraising, themes, etcetera."

I listen, fascinated. Brooklyn Prep has some of those school activities, I think, but since my cousin Emily has been inviting me to hang out with her friends in Manhattan since I was in the eighth grade, I've never paid any attention to them.

Jay clicks through a photo album on his phone screen and shows me a snapshot of a big group of kids lined up in front of what looks like a really, really long Hummer. Good God, it is a *limousine*. How tacky! And one of the girls, a chubby blonde standing next to Jay, is wearing a *tiara*.

I mean, I expect to go to the prom one day, except at Brooklyn Prep it's called Promenade, and everyone wears either vintage or couture. There are *no* tiaras involved. And definitely no combination SUV-limos!

"Don't tell me that's Tanya." I laugh. "In the tiara!"

"That's her, man," Jay says. "That night, she told me she wanted to be my princess. I felt so bad for her I said yes."

I take a sip of wine when he says that; it nearly comes straight out my nose.

"Be quiet, you did not."

"I thought I could make it work," Jay says. "She was cute—"

"Not really," I interrupt.

"—smart, and sweet. And good at school. I didn't have a lot of friends, man—"

"I thought you'd just been elected sophomore class president!" I interrupt again.

"I had been, but I only ran because I knew it would help my college apps to be on student council," Jay explains. "And hardly anyone else was running!"

"And Tanya's dreams came true!"

"For a while," Jay says. "But it doesn't work when one person sweats the other too much, or not enough. And she had this funny way of talking."

"Oooh noo," I say, making fun of how I've heard Minnesotans talk. "Like this?" I can't believe I'm making such a goof of myself, but the wine and the giggles have made me act a little less poised than normal.

"Exactly. At first it didn't bug me, but then when we had to make announcements over the school intercom, I started to listen out for it. If she did it, if I noticed the accent, it would make me crazy!"

"Jay!" I say, hysterical. "She couldn't help it."

"I know. It's terrible, man. I finally broke up with her, and she's all, 'What went wrong? What did I do?' And I couldn't say it was her accent. So I told her I didn't want to commit when I knew I was coming to Paris. I told her then it would be too hard for me to leave."

I snort, wiping tears out of my eyes. "That is too hilarious. You came to Paris to escape Tanya!"

"It was just a great excuse to tell her adios."

"Jay Solares, dirtbag ex-boyfriend. Never would have guessed it."

"We all have our stories, man."

"So I see." I take another sip of wine. "So how do you feel about the trip now? Do you feel resolved, or restless, or what?" I really do want to know.

"I feel—I don't know what to feel! I just can't believe these emails PJ keeps writing to me. I never took her to be the type that played mind games. Did you?" The laughter disappears from Jay's face. He looks genuinely at a loss.

Um, definitely. "No. But you never really know anyone," I say morosely. "People are like that. Quick to disappoint when the going gets tough."

"Are you thinking about your dad?"

I set down my glass of wine. "What?"

"That guy at the bar a few nights ago. The one who sent us the champagne. Zack and I knew he was your dad. Who else would it be? But you wouldn't admit it. You wouldn't even acknowledge that he was anything to you."

I stay quiet, furrowing my brow.

"Alex? Come on," Jay beseeches. "You can tell me about it."

I sigh.

"A lot of people have deadbeat dads, crazy parents, family troubles. Why do you feel like you can't tell your friends? After all we've been through in the past few weeks?"

"Oh, really?" I finally ask him, my voice shrill despite my trying to keep it under control. "A lot of people's dads skip the country with their daughter's nanny? They move to London and never invite their kids to visit? They call them twice a year? Reporters at the *Financial Times* know more about my dad than I do. The staff of the Grand Palace Hotel knows more about Tuan Nguyen than I do."

I realize I'm gripping the table with both hands, leaning forward toward Jay, and getting right up in his face. Jay never loses my gaze.

"It wasn't me who wasn't acknowledging him," I choke out. "He would barely acknowledge *me*."

"That's not your fault," he says in a low voice. "You know that."

I close my eyes. I'm in that red and black dress. I'm sipping my Bellini, and I see my dad winking at me at the end of the bar. All of the sudden, I'm awkward, with braces and a double chin like I had when I was twelve. I'm unsteady on my feet as I walk over to him. As I get closer, he registers me as I really am—ungainly, overfed, wearing too much makeup, reeking of cigarette smoke and perfume. "You just don't understand," I whisper.

When I open my eyes, Jay's are still fixed on me.

He wipes the tears from my cheeks with his fingertips. "Oh, man, Alex, if you could just see yourself."

I let go of the table and put my wet face into my clammy, cold hands.

"That came out wrong!" Jay exclaims and jumps up from his chair. He crouches next to me, encircling me in his arms. He smells like red wine, cologne, and the cozy wool of his black sweater. "I just meant, if you could see yourself the way I see you, the way the rest of the Lycée sees you . . . You're a star. You're so beautiful, funny, and glamorous. . ."

"Really?" I ask him, having wanted to hear these words but not believing him once they've been uttered aloud. "I mean, *you* think so?"

Jay sets some money on the table and lifts me out of my chair. "Let's get out of here."

Jay keeps me wrapped closely to him as we walk back to the hotel. It's raining now, and all I can think is that nothing at all could save me from this mess that I've gotten myself into. It's not just this crazy Jay/PJ mix. It's that letter from the Lycée sealing my fate. The envelope of cash it makes me ill to even think of opening. The fact that my mother has been trying to reach me for nearly two weeks and I don't know *how* I'll ever face her again. Where will I even *go* when this break is over?

I cry silently into his chest as we wait for the walk signal at a crosswalk near our hotel. The rain comes down harder, echoing along the rooftops as it falls. Small puddles begin swirling around our feet and into the gutters, totally soaking my cream-colored suede platform pumps. Across the street, the Mediterranean Sea crashes against the docks of the marina, soaking the sandy beach. Watching the storm brewing, I can't help but feel like this time, I'll never dig myself out. For the first time in my life, I have no survival plan.

By the time Jay unlocks the door to our suite, we're both wet and shivering. He grabs some fresh towels that housekeeping dropped off while we were out. He yanks off his drenched sweater and T-shirt, then pats my hair dry and lets me wipe my nose on the towels.

"Alex, Alex, shhhh, it's okay," he tells me softly, holding me against his chest, now bare. "It's okay." He pushes me back and looks into my eyes. "What is it? Why are you still crying? Everything will be okay."

I look wildly around the suite, which is as messy as my life has become.

"No, it won't," I say, shaking my head. For some reason, his sympathy makes me feel even worse. I wish Zack were here. He'd cry with me for a second, then start laughing and telling me to pull it together. He'd hand me a glass of gin from the minibar and put on a bad movie.

"Zack . . ." I weep. "Zack's gone. My dad's gone. When you find her, you'll be gone, too . . ."

I'm crying so hard I'm not sure if he can understand me.

"You and Zack will make up, Alex . . ." Jay soothes me. "Let's just sit down, maybe order some tea from room service . . ."

I collapse onto the soft king-sized bed, burying my face into the sleek brushed Egyptian-cotton pillowcase. Jay lays down next to me, patting my hair until I can't remember anything and sleep consumes me.

The next morning, I wake up lying flat on my back, my hair matted against the sides of my face. The sun glimmers in the sky, pouring in bright yellow light through the glass patio doors. Jay is passed out with his head on my chest, his arms wrapped around my waist.

Like a baby's, Jay's lips are relaxed and slightly parted, every once in a while emitting a deep, restful sigh. I burrow deeper into the covers, sliding my body farther under the warmth that his creates.

Jay, still asleep, responds by shifting his weight and hugging me closer to him. I can feel his bare chest against the skin of my arm. "Shhh," he says, still trying to comfort me after having that breakdown last night.

I look at his closed eyelids, willing them to open. I could almost brush his eyelashes with my lips if I just moved ever so much closer to him. . .

Jay's head lifts, his eyes still closed. I hold my breath, feeling his mouth coming toward me as he drifts slowly back into consciousness. "Alex . . ." He breathes softly.

I feel shivery, like every nerve in my body is fully awake. I close my eyes and swallow hard, anticipating the moment when Jay will finally kiss me. I can already feel his stubbly chin on mine, his hands grasping my back and pushing my body closer to his. His body is so warm, seems to fit mine so perfectly. I feel my breath coming in shallow.

When I open my eyes, Jay's dark brown eyes are fluttering above me. He grins just a little bit—maybe he's nervous.

"I can't do this," I suddenly whisper, my lips still tingling from the kiss they long for. My body is crying out for this, but I can't, not when I think of everyone I could hurt—everyone I've *already* hurt.

"Alex? What's going on?!" A harsh voice interjects.

Jay and I turn our heads and squint to see someone, haloed by sunlight, standing in the bedroom doorway.

20. OLIVIA

Behind Closed Doors

"*A*lex?" I say again, stepping farther into the master suite, Thomas right behind me.

Two pairs of familiar eyes, arranged in a very unfamiliar composition, bounce in my direction. Jay and Alex, entangled on the king-sized bed, gape at me in horror.

"Olivia!" they cry at the same time. "What are you doing here?"

Vince would have hemmed and hawed and told me to wait till the morning, but no. Thomas totally supported my rash decision to head out on the road immediately.

In his huge, unheated studio in Clichy, Xavier handed Thomas and me his two motorbike helmets and the keys to the Vespa. I hugged him gratefully. His solid, strong hug was very soothing despite everything, and I appreciated fully for the first time how lucky I was to have met all of Thomas's wonderful friends. "*Merci*, Xavi," I whispered to him. "I'll pay you back somehow." Xavier shook his balding head with a smile.

"I can tell when you have to follow your heart," he told me, and it sounded so totally simple, so totally *right* when he put it like that.

"*Allez-y*," Thomas said as he gunned the Vespa. "*À Cannes!*"

Hopping on the back of the Vespa was thrilling. "*Allez-y!*" I repeated after him.

Thomas screeched away from Paris. The wind was bitter and cold, making my hair whip out behind my helmet and my clothes billow full of air. I gripped tightly to Thomas's waist, the adrenaline pulsating between us.

Don't worry, PJ, I said to myself. I reached into my jacket pocket and touched the rosary that Alex gave me at the cathedral in Lyon a couple months ago. *We'll save you.*

Alex had told me that they were going to the Grand Palace Hotel for a few nights. It turned out the Grand Palace Hotel is the largest, most ostentatious façade of all of the hotels that overlook the Cannes seafront. Made from crystalline pink and green mosaic tiles, the swooping art nouveau architecture announces the Grand Palace as *the* place to stay in Cannes.

"Which room are they in?" Thomas asked me as we tucked our helmets under our arms and stepped through the revolving doors of the hotel in the early hours of the morning, after driving through the night.

"I'm guessing a penthouse suite," I told him. "This is Alex. I can't imagine anything less."

Security at the front desk was a little intimidating, so we followed my hunch and went straight for the elevators, pressing the top button to take us to the most lavish suites. In the hallway where the elevator let us out, I saw four doors before us. Three of them looked perfectly normal, but in front of the door to one, the suite directly in front of the elevator, there was a room-service tray, heaping with the remnants of a pastry basket, along with several empty cans of Diet Coke waiting to be picked up.

"Got it," I said. "That's Alex in a nutshell." We found them.

Just then Thomas's cell phone starts ringing, startling the four of us out of our shocked silence.

"It's *Maman*," he whispers to me. "Let me go talk with her outside." He crosses the room, avoids looking at Alex and Jay, and steps onto the patio. *"Bonjour, Maman!"* I hear him greet her.

"You guys?" I don't want to get any closer. I literally cannot believe my eyes. "I, um, didn't mean to interrupt . . . but I found out something . . . really bad . . . about PJ . . ." I stare at the floor. Alex's clothes and shoes are *everywhere*.

Jay jumps off of Alex and pulls a sweatshirt on. "What? What did you find out?"

"I don't want to betray Mme Rouille's confidence, but—but Mme Rouille told me the scariest story about the Marquets last night," I tell them. "She was crying and told me there was nothing we could do. I just felt so bad for her, and I had to get here as fast as I could. PJ might be in more danger than we think! Mme Rouille thinks this could be really serious!"

"Danger? Really?" Alex asks, motioning for me to hand her a sweatshirt. The sweatshirt can't be hers—it has a big purple V on it.

Vince would be proud that I know that means it is a Minnesota Vikings sweatshirt.

"Yes, Alex, that is what I am trying to tell you. The Marquets are *bad* people—really, really bad. If something happened, if she had to run away from them, they could take her future and crush it. They are capable of *terrible* things. PJ is in *way* over her head. I was praying the whole way down that we'd find her here, with you."

Jay looks at me, his face an etching of terrible guilt. "No, she's not."

"Have you guys . . . given up looking for her?" I say awkwardly. It certainly looks that way, I think, trying not to be angry. How could Alex and Jay be . . . together? What about PJ? What about Zack?

Then again, I remember feeling that same guilt when I first realized that I liked Thomas. It wasn't enough to stop me from kissing him, from falling in love with him.

Alex looks at Jay, then back at me, then pulls the sweatshirt over her head. I can see from the way she looks at Jay that this might be the same for her. And who am I to judge *that*?

Thomas comes back in from the balcony. *"Bonjour,"* he says timidly. "Hello."

I smile at him, so grateful that he brought me here. He looks so beautifully disheveled right now. "Thank you," I mouth at him.

"We haven't given up," Alex says, reaching for Jay's phone. "PJ's been in touch. She might even come here. Right, Jay? Show her the email you last got from her."

Jay takes the phone and logs onto his Gmail. "See—here it is. Oh, wait. I got another one from her!" He waits for the screen to load. "Alex, how did I miss this last night?"

Alex gulps. "I don't know, Jay."

"What does it say?" I ask. "Read it to me."

"Dear Jay," Jay reads. *"Things have just gotten too complicated. It's really better if we just forget each other. Just forget me."*

"What does that mean?" Alex asks.

"Oh, no," I say. "I should have gotten here sooner!"

"She wants me to forget her," Jay says, not looking at us. "What am I supposed to do anymore? I can't keep going like this. I love her, but man . . ." He goes into the bathroom, slamming the door behind him. I hear him turn the shower. on

Alex winces.

"Alex, where's Zack?"

Alex laughs ruefully. "Zack's in Amsterdam. He couldn't deal with me anymore, and you know what, I'm glad he went."

"Alex, don't say that!" I scold her. "How did he get there?"

"Get this, Livvy, he took the rental car! He stranded us here!"

"So why don't you guys get another one?"

"We were out of cash. Sort of," Alex explains. "Can we get some coffee? You guys want anything? I'll order some room service."

Alex orders coffee, fruit, and toast, which is delivered within only a few minutes. When the waiter asks Alex if she needs anything else, I notice that she just smiles obliviously. The waiter asks her again what he can get for her. Does she even know what he's saying?

"Rien, monsieur," I cut in quickly. *"Merci beaucoup."*

Alex perches on the sofa and stirs some sugar into her *café crème.* "Wow. I really needed this. I was dying. Literally dying. Okay, now we can talk. So what were you asking me before?"

"Alex." I can't believe this. There is no way that Alex could have not understood that man. She's been taking French lessons her whole life. She goes to the best program for Americans in France! How on earth did she ever pass her Final Comp?

Realization hits me like a bucket of ice water over my head. "You didn't."

"What?" Alex licks a bit of jam off of her finger.

"Pass the test. Final Comp. You didn't pass. Did you?"

Alex rolls her eyes and stands up. "Livvy! The test is *finally* over. Why are you still talking about it?"

"Alex." I take her hands in mine. "Tell me the truth." Thomas watches us, enthralled. He knows how hard I studied for that test.

"Whoo, Livvy, your hands are cold!" Alex says. "Let me get you some coffee. How about a banana, too?" She leans forward and starts scooping some sliced banana into a bowl for me.

"What are you going to do? Alex, please talk to me about this. I'm so scared for you!" I take her shoulders and square them so she's facing me and is forced to look me in the eye. "This is serious, Alex. This could affect college—this could even make you not be able to graduate high school on time. Isn't there anything I can do to help you fix this? I'll help you, Alex—I'm sure there is some way you could study, and retake the test." I'm ashamed of my own selfishness. I should have helped Alex before, when we were all getting ready. If only I'd known that she was really having a problem here!

"As long as we're on the subject," Alex says with a sigh, rolling her dark eyes disdainfully at the whole situation. She looks like she has even more bad news. She wriggles out of my grip. "Jay's not going back either. They might have covered his tuition but he spent all the rest of his scholarship money on the rental car. That cash he had at your house on Christmas? That was his entire disbursement for books and food and everything. We're *done* at the Lycée de Monceau."

I gasp. "No!"

Alex grimaces. "Honey, would I *lie* about something like this?"

I fold onto the couch next to Alex, tucking my knees under my chin. I reach stupidly for my nylon wallet, counting the bills my parents gave me for Christmas. I'd been saving them to perhaps get PJ something— anything she would need when we finally find her.

"Maybe if we all pool our money, Jay wouldn't have to go . . ." I mumble. "Maybe Zack and I could tutor you…and find work—and you guys could stay…"

Alex puts her head on my shoulder. Her black hair smells like stale cigarette smoke. I cough harshly and start to cry.

Alex looks at me, shocked. "Oh, not you, too, Livvy. I need you to stay strong. Everything is a mess around here. Please don't you lose it, too! You're our rock, Livvy! You're the only sane one in this bunch!"

"Okay, okay," I say. I suppose I do need to be strong for her, and Jay, and Thomas, and definitely for PJ. And Zack, too, when I finally hear his side of things.

"You're mad, huh?" Alex says, standing back up.

I get up, too, and head for the balcony. "Alex, it's not about being mad at you. It's about loving someone—a bunch of someones—you can't fig- ure out."

"What do you mean?" Alex says indignantly. "I'm an open book!"

"I gotta go," I say, motioning for Thomas to come back in so we can leave. "I'll talk to you later."

"What were they *thinking?*" I screech at Thomas as we take the elevator back down to the lobby. "What were any of us thinking?"

I'm not angry at my friends, I'm angry at *myself*. If only I had been there for them more! In looking for PJ, they all seemed to have just lost *themselves*.

I wish I had just gone with them, kept things from getting so out of control. But no, I had to dance in the Revue.

"Olivia," Thomas says gently. "Let them go. Not everyone has the drive to do special things like you. You are more special than your American friends."

Tears well up in my eyes and I don't force them back down. "No! They *are* special. They've made a mistake but they could still fix it! I know they could fix this! They've given up on looking for PJ and they've given up on the Lycée. How could they?"

"Do you believe the email that you saw from PJ?" Thomas asks me.

"Like, believe that she wrote it?"

"Well, yes, but also, do you believe what she says in it? Or was she under some kind of duress, do you think?"

"Oh, my God, Thomas." I ask, "Do you think she's been kidnapped?" For a moment my mind goes white, like a blank, bright screen at a movie theatre.

"Let's think about this, Olivia. Let's not give up on your instincts."

I am so grateful for his steadfast loyalty that my tears dry.

"*Je t'aime*, Thomas," I tell him. "I really do love you."

★ ★ ★

Thomas uses his credit card to get us a room at the much cheaper hotel a few blocks away from the Grand Palace Hotel. In a musty room lined with shaggy pink carpeting and grandmotherly florals, Thomas and I close the drapes to keep the sun out so we can try to rest. The place reminds me of the cheap motels my mom and I used to stay in whenever I had to travel for dance competitions or regional ballet theater auditions. The towels in the bathroom are threadbare and dotted with faded stains, and the shower curtain is moldy at the edges.

We nap for several hours. My sleep is haunted by PJ—images of her being bound and gagged. I imagine someone forcing her to write those words—*Forget me.* Throughout the haze of my sleep, I hear the words of the email she sent to Jay as he read them at the Grand Palace Hotel this morning.

When I wake up, it's starting to get dark. I shake Thomas awake, too. "I just can't not try. Not after what your mom told me."

"What did *Maman* tell you?" Thomas is alert, suddenly inspecting me with intense interest. "You still haven't told me anything."

I promised Mme Rouille I wouldn't reveal the tragedies of her past to her son. I intend to keep that promise as long as I live. That's a story, a terrible story, that a son should only hear from his mother, not his new girlfriend.

"Your mom told me that the Marquets aren't fit host parents," I offer simply. "I'm afraid they may have done something to alienate PJ, and that she felt too ashamed to tell anyone. I'm afraid that she's just wandering around somewhere with nowhere to go." I don't tell him that I'm worried there might be repercussions for PJ if she did really have an altercation with the Marquets. Repercussions that could destroy her future, or her life in France, the way that M. Marquet had held a grudge against Mme Rouille for all those years.

If it wasn't for the ambitions of Mme Marquet, Thomas himself may have never been able to crawl out from under M. Marquet's vendetta against his family. And that was only because socially, Mme Rouille still had clout in Paris, at least in some circles Mme Marquet found important. But PJ . . . she has no clout, no power of any kind.

She's helpless.

Thomas reaches for me and holds me—it's only then that I realize I've been shaking. "Okay, Olivia." He knows I'm not telling him all I know, and he's so supportive anyway. I could weep with gratitude.

"I can't sleep," I tell Thomas. "I'm going to go check my email."

The lobby of our hotel is a cramped, linoleum-floored space that reminds me of the waiting room at the child services office in San Diego, where my mom sometimes has to go to arrange for the school district to cover some of Brian's special tutoring. Whirring in the corner is an ancient computer monitor. A paper sign posted above the computer offers fifteen minutes of Internet service for two euros. I dig out a heavy two-euro coin and ask the bearded man behind the desk to access the Internet for me. The connection is slow, but thankfully it works.

I scan my email for anything from *Fletcher, Penelope*. During fall semester we would sometimes email one another, asking for help with math homework, or to share a funny joke, or to point out a cool Web site. But today, as in the past two weeks, there's nothing.

Filled with hopelessness, I download a photo of PJ from my Web album and tool around on the computer until I have a flyer ready for the front desk to print.

"*Monsieur*," I tell him. "I need to make five hundred copies of this poster. Don't worry, I will pay you for it. Just make sure the photo is as clear as possible."

The picture is from when PJ was staying with Mme Rouille and me, and PJ and I went out for a Saturday of sightseeing together. We had an Italian woman on the Ile de la Cité take our photo with the twin towers and the gargoyles of Notre Dame in the background. For the poster, I cropped myself and the background out of it, so it's just PJ's beautiful, smiling face: big, soulful eyes; her thin nose and high cheekbones, the pale, clear skin; and the wide, almost bluish lips that always made her look like she was cold.

I spend the rest of the evening papering Cannes with MISSING posters of PJ.

Somehow, I know it's hopeless, but I just don't know what else to do.

21.ZACK

Baptism

"Brother men!" Pierson calls to Bobby and me across the wide avenue lined with trees and benches packed with locals in front of the Rijksmuseum, Amsterdam's enormous palace of art masterpieces. The museum looks like a castle or a church, with impressive spires, cathedral windows, and a huge arched atrium as you enter the building. The museum was swelteringly hot, but now that we're back out in the cold, we have to quickly bundle back into our coats. I admire Bobby's rust brown parka with envy. Not everyone could pull off such an idiosyncratic color. But that's just the kind of thing that looks terrific on Bobby. On me, it would look like a litter box.

Bobby and I have just finished an exhaustive tour of the Rijksmuseum,

Bobby playing tour guide with me as the enraptured student. Bobby clearly just adores the old Dutch masters. There are plenty of those beautiful-maidens-in-a-charming-meadow pictures, the kind that make you think of shepherd boys courting and singing to milkmaids. In art class, I often saw PJ painting dreamlike, angelic women like those, surrounded by flowers or silk pillows. But the paintings Bobby pointed out to me were more disturbing, realistic portraits, each one a little creepier than the last.

We stopped and looked at one of an old, craggy woman in a dirty white head scarf. She was smiling, but her missing teeth and her yellowing gums made her look scary, not jolly.

"Just imagine the stench coming off of her, dude," Bobby whispered in my ear just as I was thinking how blessed I am to live in the age of modern dentistry. The museum was as quiet as a funeral for someone nobody liked, but I burst out laughing and couldn't stop. Whoever that artist was, I'm sure he didn't expect no hayseed American would one day laugh at his masterwork and then ask when lunch was. But that is just what I did. Luckily, Bobby gave up on the tour and took me to the café—and the super-fantastic gift shop, where I bought a groovy red salad bowl for my host family. On the card, I think I'll write—*Thanks for having so little interest in me that I can get away with doing whatever I want for all of Christmas break!* or something to that effect.

Meanwhile, Hannes and Pierson spent the morning at Hannes's apartment, and now Pierson looks delightedly rumpled as he jogs over to us, his hair mussed and his cheeks rosy and bright.

"Well, brothers, how was it? Did you want to put a stick in your eye the whole time?" Pierson asks me after giving us each a burly hug. "Y'all can tell me the truth."

"Not at all." I sniff, straightening my glasses back into place. "I enjoyed every minute of Bobby's tour. He's a very learned docent."

"Not to mention an incredibly sexy one!" Pierson adds, chucking his roommate on the shoulder.

"Why, Zachariah, I had no idea you were enjoying yourself so much," Bobby responds, flashing his bright white teeth in a huge, goofy smile. Once again, I marvel at how good we have it what with our fluoride and orthodontics these days. "Shall we go in again? Our tickets can be reused for admittance all day." He playfully starts to steer me back toward the Rijksmuseum entrance, his exuberance for the place causing him to nearly break into a jog. "I'm always up for more!"

"Um, no!" I declare. "Once was enough!"

"I thought so," Pierson notes smugly. "My brother Zack doesn't care for your highfalutin ideas about the arts and whatnot. I told you!" He smirks at Bobby, who shrugs.

"I did all that I could," Bobby says, adjusting his newsboy hat so it's cocked just so, like he's highly offended by my ignorance. "I tried to enlighten you, but you know what they say about taking a boy out of the country . . ."

"Hey," I finally stick up for myself. "I *did* like the Rijksmuseum. It was great. I'm just ready to do something else. No more museums, for a couple hours, at least. Okay?"

One of the best things about having Bobby as my personal tour guide is that he's so confident, I don't feel like I have to pretend to like it just to be nice. He did make it way more interesting than it would have been by myself, but that's not necessarily because he's a brainiac. It's also because he doesn't seem to let anything get to him. He loves everything about

Amsterdam, and after a while, it starts to rub off on you.

I'm getting this feeling like I've known Bobby a long time. We can joke around like we're old friends. But at the same time, I also feel like there are a lot of things I would still love to find out about Bobby, things I definitely don't know about yet . . . like whether or not he's a good kisser. It's just one of the things that I found myself thinking about in the Rijksmuseum! I also thought about it this morning, when we all went down to the dorm dining hall to eat cereal. And I thought about it last night, when we were all sitting around talking about things we love about being away from the South. When he told me that he'd be fine without ever seeing another Monster Truck Rally commercial again, I told him that I could kiss him right then. It's just a saying, just something you might say when you want them to know how glad you are they aren't a bleeding idiot, but I kind of meant it in another way, too.

"*Pas de problème,*" Bobby promises, jumping up and down a bit to get warm. He smooths some Blistex onto his lips, which are red from the wind and dry air. "It's a beautiful day; we should be out and about, not stuck inside some museum."

"You got that right," I agree. "Gosh darn it!" It's cold, but the sun is cheerfully pouring over the city and making the frigid air much more bearable.

Hannes and Pierson walk ahead, toward the Leidesplein, an open-air square filled with outdoor restaurants, souvenir stands, and coffee shops off any of the side streets. Bobby and I trudge along a few paces behind them. It's a nice walk, not too far, and I'm excited that I feel like I have a little bit of a sense of direction here in Amsterdam after our bike tour yesterday.

"I do like art, you know," I tell Bobby. "I just don't love museums. I wish all the good art wasn't locked up like that."

"Really," Bobby answers, giving me an amused grin. "Where do you think it should be kept, then—on the street, so people can vandalize it?"

I know he's just teasing. "I'm not sure what the alternative would be, but I just find the museum scene to be so . . . stifling. I mean, when I see a painting like some of the ones we saw in the Rijksmuseum, it makes me want to do anything but sit and be quiet. I want there to be, like, music playing. I want to know what it was like back then. I don't know."

"You could just watch a period movie."

"I guess," I say. I remember the party we'd had at PJ's house, all of us drunk and dancing among the Marquets' fabulous pieces of art. "I guess I just wish the paintings could be in a more familiar part of our lives. Like, if they gave one really nice one to every family in the world, and then you could have a party, and everyone would come over and look at it, then get distracted, and think about something else. And then you'd look at it again, and you'd have had a chance to think about it, process it. You know?"

"So you're saying we should redistribute the world's wealth of art, socialist style? I didn't take you for such a Marxist, Zack!" Bobby pinches my ear. "Sounds like a great plan. Now, who's going to implement it? The government? A rebel faction led by Zack Chandler?"

I laugh. "If only I could be in charge of making sure everyone got something decent to decorate their apartments and houses with. Houseguests like myself wouldn't then get subjected to posters of kittens playing with balls of yarn as the wall hangings, like I have in the bathroom of my homestay in Paris. And people like my parents in Tennessee wouldn't be allowed to decorate their McMansions with bad art they buy at the Christian frame shop in the mall."

"Saving the world, one badly decorated home at a time," Bobby muses. "Sounds like a project I could get behind!" And just like that, I feel it: a slight brush of his hand on my lower back, almost like he was about to put his arm around me.

We stop in front of a neon-lit hash bar, dark and sinister in the light of day. Unlike some of the hash bars we've passed so far, this one doesn't have crowds of college-age tourists taking pictures of themselves smoking pot. It's littered with some sketchy-looking punk kids and an old hippie guy with no teeth. My eyes go wide with fear.

"You guys, *no*," I say. "If the Lycée found out, I'd be kicked out. I *can't* get sent back to Tennessee. I'm serious. I'm already not even supposed to be in Amsterdam! I'm supposed to be in Montauban with Alex and her dad!"

"How in Jesus's name is your fancy school in Paree going to find out about a teensy bit of hash? It's totally legal here. Right, Hannes?" Pierson and Bobby look at me hopefully.

Hannes nods. The kid never talks, he just stands there like a silent Greek god. Which is fine by me.

"If it's such a good idea, how come Hannes never does it?" I ask them.

"Hannes is an athlete," Pierson says. "He can't smoke anything or he'll ruin his time."

"His time at what?"

"Running." Pierson groans. "Track or whatever."

"Hannes, do you run track?" I ask Hannes. This is the first I've heard of

Hannes having any other extracurricular activity besides Pierson.

Hannes, again, just nods.

"Well, why don't you guys go in," I suggest, "and Hannes and I can go shopping or something?"

"Shut yer trap, brother," Pierson says. "You can't run away with my Hannes. Have a little hashish and relax. Then later you and *Bobby* can go shopping."

I sigh. "Fine, I'll go in. But I don't want any."

If it were Alex offering me the hashish, I would have been all over it. But for some reason, because it's Pierson and because it feels so weird to see him having so wholeheartedly embraced a totally new life, one that includes dating guys, and drugs, and drinking beer during the day, I want to resist it.

Bobby gives me a wry smile. "You'll like it. And it's part of the quintessential Amsterdam experience, you know?"

I follow Bobby and Pierson to a table. Hannes slides in next to Pierson and orders a glass of orange juice while Bobby and Pierson pore over the *other* menu, the one with the drug offerings. They settle on something called Great Beyond, which is supposed to produce an intense high that takes you to a whole new world. Yeah, right.

When the hashish comes, Bobby rolls it into a joint with some tobacco and takes some deep puffs. Pierson does the same when Bobby passes it to him, though much less expertly. When they pass it to me, Bobby swivels to face me and expertly shows me how to hold it and when to inhale. I notice how confident his dark hands are, like he's rolled thousands of these. I wonder what it would be like to hold those hands, kind of like Hannes and Pierson are doing now.

"Seriously, I'm not into it," I reiterate.

"Just live a little," Pierson says. Just to get him to be quiet, I roll back the sleeves of my gray cardigan and decide to do it.

When the smoke hits the back of my throat, I feel like I can't breathe. It stings and makes me very dizzy all of the sudden. I sputter and cough, sending Pierson into gales of laughter.

"Come on, brother, try it again," Pierson cajoles me obnoxiously. I glare at him, but I do try to hit the joint again. This time, I inhale the smoke more easily and let it drift down to my lungs and back up to my brain without coughing so much. In a few minutes, I find myself relaxing, my eyelids drooping stickily, and my smile coming at almost nothing.

"See what I mean?" Bobby laughs. "I knew you'd like it. I wouldn't lie to you."

Hannes and Pierson are whispering to each other, and after the joint is done, they ask if they might be excused.

"Again?" I exclaim. "Balls, you guys!"

Pierson laughs and pulls Hannes out the door. "Have a lover-ly afternoon, friends! See you back at the dorm!"

I roll my eyes. There he goes, ditching me for Hannes again.

"He's just in love." Bobby smirks, showing a hint of his bright white teeth. "He'll snap out of it, I'm sure."

"Pierson is definitely in love. I just wish he could chill out with all the midday sessions with Hannes. I mean, I'm leaving soon! I have to get back to school by the fourteenth! And he's making *you* show me around Amsterdam," I say, though I'm enjoying Bobby's company immensely. "That's not fair."

"I don't mind," Bobby says mildly. He leans toward me, nudging my shoulder with his. "You want to get out of here?"

"Yeah, let's," I say. "We'll have more fun without them!"

Back in the late afternoon sunshine, Bobby makes a left. "I want to show you something really cool. It's my favorite place in Amsterdam. You up for another tour?"

"Sure," I say. "I'd love to see it." Bobby strolls ahead with a big smile, leading me toward this special place of his. I wonder, for a moment, if Bobby might be my first kiss. I'm starting to think that he might be into me, too.

We walk in a comfortable silence along the canals, north, to an area I don't think we covered on our bike tour. After several blocks, we stop in front of a little town house.

"This is the Anne Frank House?" I ask Bobby, reading the big square placard out front. I'm starting to feel tired. I kind of wish we had just walked back to the dorm. I think my pleasant buzz has worn off. "This here is your favorite place in Amsterdam?"

All I know about Anne Frank is the story of her hiding with her family for two years during World War II. She kept a diary, and our English class could read it for extra credit. I was too busy with swim team to do the project, but listening to other kids do their presentations about her gave me a bad feeling. I can't explain exactly why, but whenever I started to think about it for too long, I would immediately have to push the thought away. The Frank family hid for all that time, then they were discovered, and the whole family except for the dad was killed in concentration camps.

"Yeah, it's really interesting. Let's take a walk through it," Bobby says, leading me inside to the ticket booth. Inside, we watch a short movie about tolerance. The screen flashes pictures of skinheads, burning crosses, people marching in the street crying for blood. I feel nauseous and tell Bobby I want to go look around.

We walk through the main town house to what they call the Secret Annex—hidden rooms where the Franks had to live with another family. The house is simple, and cleared of most furniture. The wall exhibits explain how the families were completely dependent on resistance workers for food, clothes, and news of the outside world. They didn't see sunlight again until they were taken to concentration camps.

In one room there is a collage of photos of Anne Frank, and I feel like I can't take my eyes away from hers. I've been staring at one photo, a large one where she can't have been more than twelve, for a long time when Bobby turns back and pokes me.

"Dude," he says. "Are you okay? What's going on?"

I start hyperventilating all of the sudden. The encolsed space, the beautiful face of this little girl who died when she should have been allowed to grow up and have kids and have a life. The museum, being as it is in the actual place where the Frank family hid, is tiny, relatively speaking—and the people have to flow through speedily if they want to avoid getting stuck. I'm holding up the flow. I don't know how those people managed to live here for all that time. Visitors from all over the world surround me, trying to get around me. But I'm riveted to one spot, right in front of Anne's photo. I can't stop staring at her.

"Dude!" Bobby says more vigorously.

"I've gotta get out of here," I burst out. Spotting the emergency-exit door, I barrel through to a back staircase. "Sorry!" I yell to a security guard. "I'm not . . . I'm not feeling too good . . ."

"Zack, wait!" Bobby chases me onto the back staircase and down into the alley behind the museum. Once a safe distance from all the tourists, I finally stop and give him the chance to catch up to me.

"I felt like I couldn't breathe. You know? You ever feel that way?"

"Of course, dude. Don't sweat it. I guess it wasn't such a good idea to smoke hash and then go to such an intense museum," Bobby says as he guides me to a bench along the canal a few blocks from the Anne Frank House. "I didn't think you were stoned anymore."

I don't answer. I just watch the little tugboats tied up along the edges of the canal, bobbing in the murky, dirty water.

"I just really wanted to show it to you before you left," Bobby continues. "I feel like such a jackass. I'm so sorry, I didn't think it would upset you."

I flush red and get to my feet. "It didn't upset me!"

I start walking toward the bridge, suddenly wanting to be as far away from the Anne Frank House as possible. How can all these people just visit the house, the place that witnessed so much terror, and then go about their day? Why don't any of these tourists get how messed up that is?

Bobby jumps up and follows me, catching up to me at the arch of the bridge. "Hey, slow down. Let's just hang out for a minute. Okay?"

"Okay," I agree. "You want to sit?" We both take a seat on the ledge barrier of the bridge wall and look out over the dusky system of thin, perfectly planned canals. Amsterdam is so different from Paris. It feels so much smaller, so much more contained and planned out. There's none of the grandiosity of Paris here. Paris sprawls out with adventure and fantasy, and Amsterdam is quaint, with a seedy undercurrent. Paris wants to enchant you, love you, and leave you wanting more. Amsterdam wants to expose you, scare you, show you what's real and terrible and try to nor-malize it into daily life.

Give me Paris any day of the week.

"You wish you were back in Paris, huh?" Bobby asks me, as if he can read my mind. He's a really smart guy.

"Totally."

"You absolutely love it there, I can tell. I can't wait to go there myself one day."

"Yeah, you should. It's spectacular."

"Hey, maybe I could even come to Paris while you'll still be there! For spring break or something! Because I'm thinking of maybe . . . maybe going to university there. Of living there. You know, next year."

"You're thinking of moving to Paris?" I turn and stare at him. "Why?"

"Well, you make it sound really great." Bobby laughs. "Actually, I've been wanting to go there for a while. In fact, *you* should think about tak-ing the baccalaureate exam next year, so you can come back and go to university in Paris, too! I mean, who really wants to stay in America after this?" He gestures out over the water and the quirky city of Amsterdam I'm still getting used to. "Aw, man, Zackie. We could go to university together. Maybe get an apartment or something that year. Keep up the good times!"

I'm speechless. Bobby wants to move to Paris . . . with *me*? Over a year from now? I feel my panic attack coming back, a slow contracting of my stomach that creeps up my esophagus and clenches my throat.

"Brilliant plan, yeah?" Bobby continues, his smile turning a little shy. "Hey . . ." he reaches out to pinch my ear again but doesn't let go as quickly this time. It feels terrible, his touch hot, unpleasant, invasive. I try to shake him off me, but I feel like he's still there. I feel like I can't get away from him, like there are still too many people surrounding me.

Bobby laughs. "Zack, dude, relax, everything's okay now. Right?" He leans in, hovering so close to my face I can still smell the hash on his breath.

"No!" I scream, finally unable to take it for a second longer.

With all my might, I push him off of me, *hard*.

He can't kiss me right now—shouldn't he know that? What kind of freak from freaktown is this guy?

Not after that hashish and the Anne Frank House. It feels like the walls, even though we're now sitting outside, are still coming in on me.

"Hey!" Bobby shouts, and all of the sudden, he loses his balance. Bobby's arms flail wildly as they reach out for something to hold on to. I see his face contort in fear as he realizes that—oh my sweet Jesus—he's about to fall over the edge of the railing. "Zack!" he shrieks, his voice not the confident Georgian drawl I've come to know from him, but a girly, truly frightened screech that recalls my grandmother when she realizes a dog's killed one of her chickens. Bobby's legs kick forward, slipping and sliding on the smooth stone of the bridge, damp from the melting snow. Amsterdamers must have been shorter back in the day because there Bobby goes, clearing the railing easily and falling several feet down into the canal. It happens so swiftly that I'm still fumbling to steady myself when I hear the splash and look down to see him upside down and crashing into the disgusting water as brown as Bobby's parka.

"Lord have mercy! Bobby!" I cry. What did I just do? Bobby just faceplanted into three centuries of sewage, oil, and garbage.

I run off the bridge to the canal bank and leap in after him. The water feels slick and oily when it makes contact with my skin under my heavy coat and my jeans. I clench my lips together so none will get in my mouth, and swim frantically. I realize as my foot hits the soft floor of the canal, that I can actually stand up in this water. It only goes about waist high.

I'm pulling him toward the shore, splashing and crashing and causing a huge crowd of people to gather above us on the bridge, asking if we are all right, when Bobby pushes me off of him.

"I'm sorry, Bobby!" I cry. "I am so, so sorry."

Our faces streaked with dirt, we flounder back onto Amsterdam's quaint, brick-laid streets.

"Well, jeez, dude, I get your drift," Bobby says, wiping grime off of his face. "I can take a hint. No need to *push* me into the canal."

"Bobby, I didn't—" The winter wind against my wet neck makes me shiver.

Bobby shakes his head and stamps away, dripping a trail of canal water behind him as he goes. "Find your own way home, dude. I'll catch you later."

22.ALEX

Truth and Tabloids

"Don't you get it, Livvy?" I ask Olivia as she, Thomas, and I walk along the wintry Cannes waterfront this morning. The sea couldn't be bluer, shining vividly in the winter sun.

I pull my fur hat down over my ears and tuck my pink angora scarf wherever the cold air can still reach my skin. Olivia and Thomas wear their wool coats open, as if it's not cold at all. Just because the sun's out, they feel like it's an early spring. They aren't alone. After the storm two nights ago, the sun has come out in full force, and tourists from all over the world are doing the same thing we are this morning: strolling the paths along the bay, admiring the fancy yachts docked for the winter, and reaching down to touch the soft sand, still wet from all the rain last night. But me, I can't seem to get warm. Not since yesterday, when I woke up under Jay, chilly and sleepy and afraid of what we might do together.

"PJ's fine," I continue. "And even if she isn't, she doesn't want our help. She wants to handle it on her own. *'Forget me.'* How much more direct can she get?"

"How can you be so sure?" Olivia asks. Her eyebrows are furrowed tightly together. She can't let go that she might be able to fix everything. "How can you guys just give up like this? Not just on PJ, on everything, like the Lycée. What happened to you two?"

"Livvy, doll, I wanted to find PJ, too."

Olivia gives me a look like she doesn't believe me.

"I did! And yes, I'd love to be returning to the Lycée—I didn't *want* to fail the test and get kicked out of our program. And Jay didn't *want* to spend all of his scholarship money. But that's how it happened. And for whatever reason, PJ *wanted* to get the hell out of Paris, and now, she doesn't *want* us around."

Olivia looks out at the Mediterranean sadly. Thomas puts his arm around her shoulders.

"Olivia, you have worried too much," he says. "*Maman* can be very dramatic when she wants to be. She does not like to make you so upset, I think." I feel a pang, seeing them together, a happy couple despite all the chaos and drama of the last two weeks.

The posters Livvy made are all over Cannes. PJ's everywhere, her picture making her look like very much the waif in distress. I, for one, think she'd be horrified if she knew Olivia had done that. I mean, really! How tacky!

Olivia shakes her head. "You don't understand, either of you!" She looks out at the Mediterranean for a minute, not saying anything.

Finally, she asks Thomas if he will give us a minute.

"Is anything the matter?" Thomas asks, immediately concerned and doting over her, stroking her face.

"No, Thomas, nothing is the matter. I just really need to talk to Alex alone for a minute, okay?"

Thomas's face falls with disappointment. "Okay. I go to look at magazines. Let me know when I can return." He sulks and heads over to a nearby newsstand that sells toy boats and overpriced bottles of Evian.

"The Marquets are *shady*," Olivia says in a loud whisper once Thomas had stepped inside the little shop. "Even if PJ is telling us to leave it alone now, I know they've done *something* wrong. I'm convinced of it. Alex . . . M. Marquet . . . he tried to rape Thomas's mom. He forced himself on her at a party! She's so terrified of him, she won't say anything, even after all these years!"

I stop dead in my tracks and gawk at my petite friend, who's wringing her mittened hands. Olivia is in obvious turmoil.

"Olivia, what are you talking about?"

"I swear, it's true. *Please* don't tell Thomas—he doesn't know. No one should know! Not even you! But no one believes me when I say I need to help her! Don't you see now why I have to find her? Why we have to save her?"

"You think PJ ran away from the Marquets because he attacked her? His *host* daughter?"

"I don't know—maybe! The Marquets are very powerful. What I'm fearful of is that if something happened, if she made them angry—what if they try to exact some kind of revenge?"

"Olivia, this is complete madness. Are you positive? Are you sure you're

not overreacting?" We stand very still on the boardwalk, people maneu-
vering around us in their big jackets pushing strollers, walking dogs, trying
to keep up with their friends.

"The only thing I am sure of is what happened to Mme Rouille.
The Marquets ruined most of her life. They banished her husband. They
ruined so many opportunities for Thomas that he doesn't even know
about. I've never felt so bad for anyone, *ever*. You know Mme Rouille!
She was crying. In front of me!"

"That's tragic," I say breathlessly.

Olivia scrunches up her sweet little heart-shaped face and heads over
to the newsstand. "Come on, I don't want to make Thomas worry."

"Well, speak of the devil. Look at *Gala*," I say, pointing to the glossy
weekly tabloid as we walk up to the overflowing magazine racks in the
window. "There they are."

On the cover of *Gala*, in a collage of photos, are the Marquets—M.
Marquet in a tux and Mme Marquet in a forest green satin ball gown. If
I had to guess the designer I'd go with Escada. It's stunning, though not
to my taste. *"La Saint-Sylvestre très prestigieuse!"* the headline screams. It's a
society piece about all the most important New Year's Eve parties.

"Oh, my God!" Olivia yells and runs into the store to buy the magazine. I follow her. Olivia tears through the magazine to find the article.
"They went *out* on New Year's Eve! When PJ is missing! They don't even
look worried."

I laugh ironically. "There's all the proof you need, Livvy. Where was
that photo taken?"

"At the Château de Reime-Claude, in the Dordogne. It says it was a
ball for over three thousand people."

"Livvy, get serious now. The Marquets were at a ball on New Year's Eve, in the Dordogne. If they were at a ball, how could they have kidnapped our princess?" I take a closer look at M. Marquet's ruddy, handsome face. "Funny. He doesn't look like a lecherous skeeze. But I guess you never know with politicians. My mom says they always hit on her when she interviews them, especially the conservative ones!

"When you go back to the Lycée, I bet she'll be there, all sheepish because she tried to run away and they found her before we did. That's probably what that email was about—she wanted to stop making such fools of us, and herself! She just wants us to forget about it and let the whole thing blow over before school's back in session."

Olivia can't stop staring at the photo of the Marquets. "Maybe," she says.

"Mme Rouille wouldn't make something like that up, though," I say, flipping to an article. "It just doesn't make any sense."

The words printed on the page swim in front of my eyes. I'm starting to feel very tired.

"Guys, I think I'm going to head back up to the suite for a nap. Do you mind if I excuse myself?" I hug Thomas and prepare to hug Olivia. "Can we meet for dinner or something later?"

"Alex, I was hoping we could spend some time figuring out how to get you back into the Lycée. I know if we just put our heads together, we could figure out how to convince Mme Cuchon—"

"Olivia!" I snap, my face growing warm under my scarf. "Please quit! You are *so* naïve if you think there's anything you can do about it!"

Thomas looks up from the magazine he's perusing and takes a few steps closer to us. "Alex, she is helping," he says. His broken English suddenly seems much less charming than usual.

"You are both so naïve!" I burst out. "This whole thing. Thomas's mother is right—you should stay out of it and mind your own business!" I close the magazine and toss it back onto a rack.

"Comment?" Thomas says. "What does she say?" he asks Olivia. "What do you know of *Maman*?" he asks me.

Olivia's face goes pale. I didn't mean to mention Mme Rouille.

"Maman says what about minding business? *Qu'est-ce que tu dis?"* Thomas is frozen. He won't move.

"Thomas, you should really ask your mom about this . . ." Olivia says, trying to get Thomas to look at her. But he won't stop staring at *me.* "I don't want to break her trust!"

"What does Alex know of *Maman* that I—*son fils*—do not know?"

I grimace. "Oh, God. I'm sorry . . ."

Olivia pulls Thomas back onto the boardwalk. I can't hear everything she says to him over the roar of the crashing waves, but Thomas is visibly perturbed. Once Olivia finishes talking to him, he grabs her hand and starts to drag her back toward their hotel.

"Come on, Olivia!"

"Wait, Livvy, where are you going?" I shout after them.

"You really think the Marquets are going to be in the Dordogne?" she yells back.

"That's what the article says. Don't you think they're probably staying through Epiphany?" The French like to drag out the twelve days of Christmas for as long as possible. That's why we still haven't had to go back to school yet. Well, not *we*—but the Programme Américain. Those who haven't been kicked out or dropped out. "I'm sure they're still in the Dordogne. Don't you think?"

"Then I guess that's where we're going!" Olivia races after Thomas. I can tell from her face that she's still mad, but glad the truth is out in the end. "I'll email you!" And she's gone.

"Hey," I greet Jay when I spot him in the plush atrium at the hotel. He's staring out at the water, seated in a white wicker chair. I notice that he's shaved since the other morning, when his skin was scratchy against mine. "How are you?"

Jay gives me a weak smile. "Not great. I haven't heard anything yet today."

I sit in the chair next to him. I study my nails, wondering if I should say something about the other night. About that morning.

"Jay—" I begin, just as he says something, too. "What?" I laugh nervously. "What were you about to say?"

"We got carried away, huh?"

"You could say that." It's amazing how blue the water lapping up on the shore is right now, under the midday sun. "These are crazy times, no?"

"Man, you're telling me."

"I don't think I should help you anymore," I tell him, both of us still looking forward at the sea, instead of looking at each other. "All I did was distract you. Make a bad situation worse."

I open my bag and dig out the envelope my dad had room service send to me before he left. Jay opens the envelope and whistles.

"You'll need this." I say. "For next semester."

23. ZACK

You Only Hear What You Want to Hear

*T*he line to get into the Van Gogh Museum stretches around the block. Pierson groans when he sees it. "You really want to wait that long?"

"Yes," I say decisively. "I don't know when I'm going to be back in Amsterdam. I might not get another chance to see it."

The line moves ahead in spurts, the guards letting in a small group of people at a time. We finally make it to the stairs of the museum, and Pierson dramatically lowers himself onto one of the steps, making a lot of noise about how tired he is.

"Busy night?" I ask.

Pierson giggles. "Ain't no question."

"Lord-a-mercy," I complain. "Haven't you two had enough by now?"

"No," Pierson says. "Shows how much you know about the birds 'n' bees. The more you *do*, the more you *want* to do."

I seethe at his imperiousness, and also at his loud voice, which carries around to the other people waiting in line.

"Got it," I mutter. "Thanks for that tidbit."

Finally we're allowed in, but we find that the crowd control outside has not lessened the impact of the claustrophobia inside. Van Gogh's paintings are amazing, but some of them are so small, and have so many people clustered around them, that I can't enjoy them at all. The crowd is as bad as the Anne Frank House was yesterday. Except today, I'm not on hash. And I had a feeling the Van Gogh Museum would be like this—he is, like, the most famous painter in the world—but I'd stubbornly clung to the idea that I visit it before I left Amsterdam and went back to school.

Besides, I'd really been anxious to leave the dorm room this morning. Bobby had woken early and played computer games loudly all morning. When we invited him to join us, he barely even answered.

"Hey, brother, I can't even walk in here," Pierson whines. "Do we really have to stay?"

"Just ten more minutes," I promise him, feeling irritated by the whole scene.

Pierson nearly trips over a stroller he doesn't see. "Honestly! Zack, this is total BS, brother! I'm leaving."

Pierson navigates his way around the swarm of people, out the double glass doors and down the cement steps back onto the street.

"Pierson! Where are you going? I said just ten more minutes!" I call after him, following his route out the door.

Pierson inhales a few lungfuls of fresh air. "I can't hang."

"I only wanted you to stay for ten more minutes!" I know I look like a queen, my hands on my hips and my voice an octave higher than normal. "Why can't you just spend ten minutes doing what *I* want to do?"

Pierson shakes his head. "Sorry, brother, I was just not feelin' it. Can we come back later or something? When the space is less cramped?"

"It's cramped because it's popular!" I say, nearly shouting. "Because everyone wants to see Van Gogh's paintings! Including me! You can't just walk out on me!"

"Shhhh," Pierson interrupts me. "Stop screaming at me. I was just not into it."

"Not into the museum, or not into me?" I demand, not lowering my voice at all. I don't care who's watching. "Ten minutes! That's all I asked— ten minutes!"

"Zack, what is this about? The Van Gogh Museum, or somethin' else? Because I'll be tied up on a fire pole if I'm gonna stand here while you wail like a banshee at me in the middle of Amsterdam for all the world to see. You are *embarrassing* me."

"Oh, please forgive me," I spit out at him. "So sorry to pull you away from the magnificent Hannes and then embarrass you in public. How could I? How thoughtless of me."

"This is about Hannes?" Pierson says in disbelief.

"No!"

"Are you sure this isn't about . . . Bobby?" Pierson's skeptical look makes me want to smash his teeth into his skull.

"What about Bobby?"

"Why do you hate him so much?" Pierson asks. "Why did you push him in the canal yesterday?"

"What? Is that what he told you? I didn't push him into the canal. He *fell.*"

"He tried to kiss you, so you pushed him. Real mature, Zack."

"That is not how it happened. And Bobby's hardly being very mature himself. He spends a few days with me, and then suddenly he wanted to move in with me! In Paris! He was planning a whole future with me, and I barely know the guy!" I peer past Pierson to the long line behind him. A lot of people are watching us, wondering how this argument will end. I don't even care about them. I just want Pierson to admit how crazy his friend is.

I mean, he told me he wanted to *move* to *Paris!* Can't Pierson see that he was moving way too fast?

"Bobby is thinking about going to University in Paris, Zack, that's it. Last I checked, you were thinking about doing the same thing a year later. Why wouldn't he speculate on the idea of you two being roommates some day?" Pierson is almost laughing, he finds me so ludicrous.

"No! You don't get it! He wasn't talking about roommates, he was talking about . . ."

"No, Zack, he was talking about roommates. But you didn't hear it like that, because you only hear what you want to hear," Pierson says flatly. "You won't let your guard down for even a moment to find out that there's a whole world of people out there who are fun, and nice, and easy to love. People who will accept you for who you are. But you won't let them in."

"I do have friends who accept me for who I am!" I shout, furious. "My friends in Paris know who I am! They like me for me."

"If they like you so much, why'd you end up in Amsterdam? Why'd you run away from them in the middle of the night?" Pierson's tone becomes milder. He puts his hand on my arm.

"Don't touch me!" I shriek, tears scalding my cheeks in the brisk air. I take off down the street toward Pierson's campus.

Bobby is still sitting at his desk when I barge into their dorm room, but now he's reading emails and the *New York Times* online instead of blowing up onscreen warships or whatever.

"Nice to know you, Bobby," I say. "Thanks for everything." I grab my backpack and throw their spare key onto Pierson's bed. "Wish I could stay, but I've got a train to catch."

I skulk down the street to the Amsterdam Metro station, remembering how excited I was when Pierson, Bobby, and Hannes came to pick me up a few days ago. When we were riding the train over to the dorm, I felt almost drunk with the possibilities of what could happen here. Maybe I'd meet a guy, someone I'd like enough to kiss . . .

What is wrong with me? Why did I freak out at the last minute?

Alex would be so pissed at me if she knew about this. She was always my number one cheerleader, especially when it comes to me getting busy with guys.

Ha. I wonder what she's up to right now. Somehow, I have a feeling she's doing okay without me.

When I get to Centraal Station, I try to buy a ticket back to Paris, but the agent tells me there aren't any seats available on the direct trains back to Paris this late in the day.

"You can take the train to Brussels, then switch from there . . . to Rouen. That is the cheapest route if you have to leave tonight," the station agent tells me through the little speaker above her window. "From there you can take the regional service to Paris. *C'est agréable?*"

"Sure, whatever," I mumble, taking my tickets from the sliding tray she puts them in.

"Have a good trip!" she calls to me. I push my hair out of my eyes and wave at her, wishing that it had been.

24. PJ

On the Edge

"Wait a second." Annabel looks around frantically. The owner of her apartment is coming over today to cart some of the old stuff in the closets to the Rouen flea market. Annabel is trying to clean up at the last minute. "Where's the clock?"

"What clock?" I ask her, on my hands and knees scrubbing the grimy bathroom floor tiles. I know how important it is to keep this place nice. The owner can't think anything sketchy is going on.

Marco, of course, is drinking beer at the kitchen counter. He alternates between leering at me and leering at Annabel. "Marco, you're going to take off before he gets here, right?" I ask as politely as I can. "I mean, we don't want him to know three people are living here for free. He wouldn't like it, right, Annabel?"

Annabel doesn't answer me. "Seriously, where is that clock? It was right here on the table a couple days ago." She starts taking the plaid cushions off the couch and digging her arm into all the cracks. "A clock doesn't just grow two feet and walk away."

I stand up and help her look. "That brown clock with the gold numbers?"

"Yeah. Ivan said it was an antique from Kiev or something. It's worth a lot of money. He was gonna take it to the flea market with him today."

I go in the bedroom and look everywhere—in the dresser drawers, the closet, under the bed, between all the pillows and blankets. I still can't find it.

"Marco, have you seen the clock Annabel is talking about?" I ask him when I come back out into the living room. I try my very hardest not to sound patronizing.

"No," Marco grunts. He's got a three-day-old Spanish newspaper in front of him. To watch him read it, you'd think it was the most fascinating thing he'd ever laid eyes on.

"Are you sure?" Annabel asks. She chews on her lip nervously. "I'm sorry to keep asking you, baby, but it is really important that we find it. Ivan will totally kick me out if he thinks I'm stealing his stuff—especially when he just told me the other day how he specifically wanted that clock for today's market." She dashes into the bedroom to look again.

Marco laughs. "Ivan! What a buffoon!" He does a quick impression of Annabel's portly Russian landlord waddling up the attic steps. "Who cares about his foolish clock?"

"Annabel cares, Marco," I tell him. "I do, too. You should if you had any—"

"Shut up, Penelope!" Annabel interrupts me. "Leave Marco alone!"

She gives me a warning look. "It's no big deal."

"Annabel, you happened to just *lose* a *valuable antique*? I don't think so. Are you sure Marco didn't take it and sell it? Especially if he realized it was worth something?"

"Why do you think that I stole it?" Marco shoots back. "How do we know that you didn't sell it? You're the one who is always disappearing in the middle of the day."

"How dare you!" I scream at Marco. "How dare you accuse me of something that we both know—that we all know—you did!"

"*Yo sé* you did it, Penelope!" Marco throws his empty bottle into the ceramic sink, splintering it into shards. "*Yo sé* you did!"

"Get out, Marco!" I yell at him, not even caring what the neighbors will tell Ivan. "Get out right now! We've had enough of this! You're a liar! Just go!"

I start pushing Marco toward the door. Stronger than I realize, he turns around and pushes me back. "Let me go!" I scream. "Marco, let me go!"

"Marco, no!" Annabel shouts. "Marco, let her go!"

Marco grasps my wrists and doesn't let go. My wrists sting with pain and I can see my hands turning purple under his grip. My heart is racing. "You think I want to go selling things, Penelope?" He shakes me roughly. "You think I want to make some money, eh? How about I go sell your secrets? Annabel told me everything, Penelope. How about I go sell those at a market? I think they'd fetch a good price, no?" His olive face is red, his fat lips in an angry sneer.

"Marco, please let her go," Annabel cries, dissolving into sobs. "Don't hurt my sister."

Marco finally lets me go and I'm dizzy. Marco takes his coat. I hold both my aching wrists to my chest. Annabel rushes to my side, inspecting me for damage.

"Annabel, I won't forget this. I'm through with being kind to you and your *puta* sister. You've made a mistake, accusing me. I'll destroy you both!"

"No, Marco, no!" Annabel says, dropping me out of her arms and trying to keep Marco from leaving. He flings her off of him and bounds down the stairs.

I grab Annabel and hold her back. "Stop, Annabel! Just let him go!"

Annabel drops to the floor, repeating "Marco, Marco" over and over again. I slide down next to her. She's lost weight. Her shoulder jabs me under the arm, as bony and pointed as it has ever been. What has become of us?

I don't know how much time goes by. Annabel and I stay on the floor, me rocking her back and forth and holding her tight.

Suddenly, there's a knock on the door. Annabel shoots up off the floor.

"Ivan!" she whispers. "What am I going to tell him about the clock?"

"Let me answer it," I say. I go to the door. I'll tell Ivan that I broke the clock and didn't realize it was an antique. Just like I told the Marquets after my party.

Behind the door, I don't find Ivan. Instead, it's the guy from the train again, still wearing his baseball cap.

"*Bonjour*, PJ," he greets me without a smile.

Oh, God. This can't be good. "What are you doing here?" I ask him.

"And this is your sister, I presume?" A chill runs down my spine as the guy reaches out to take Annabel's hand. How does he know who she is?! "You are just as beautiful as PJ. It's a pleasure to meet you."

"Don't touch him, Annabel."

Annabel looks confused. "Who is this guy, PJ?"

"*Je m'appelle* Denis," the guy tells her. "Denis Marquet."

I gasp. "Marquet?"

"*Oui*, Penelope—Marquet."

Annabel gapes at me in terror. "Do you know him from Paris, PJ? How does he know about me?"

"Please sit," I tell the guy. "Annabel can get you some water if you want."

Annabel fills a mug with tap water. The guy removes his baseball cap, and I see that he is more handsome than I realized. Like a younger, less formal-looking version of M. Marquet. He couldn't be much older than twenty or twenty-one. His hair is dark and elegantly floppy, and there's something aristocratic in the way he holds himself. His teeth are all perfectly straight. He sits down at the kitchen table. I stand next to the stove, not wanting to be any closer to him.

"What do you want?" I ask him again. "Have you been following me?"

"I've come to tell you something important," he says. "A message from your host parents."

My throat constricts. "What, then?" I urge him. "Just tell me."

"The Marquets feel that they, well," he looks a bit uncomfortable with what he's about to say. "They gave you security, two homes to stay in, despite your tantrums and your . . . your past in America. And yet you are determined to humiliate them."

Annabel takes a seat at the table. "PJ—what is he getting at?"

"What took you so long?" I ask Denis.

"You are not so easy to pin down, *ma belle*."

"You want me to go back to the Marquets. They told you to find me and tell me to come back. So that they won't have a scandal," I say, my voice quavering. I clear my throat, trying to sound more confident. "Is that right?"

"Right." He grins—a weird grin that reminds me of M. Marquet. "M. Marquet is a public figure. He is going to be campaigning for a national office soon. It would be better for everyone if you would return to Paris and to the Lycée. Furthermore, they will need you to participate in some campaign activities. In the true spirit of *fraternité*, the Marquets will adopt you as their daughter, as your drug-lord parents are no longer able to legally care for you."

"That's not true!" I interject. "I don't need anyone. I'm almost eighteen. And my parents are not drug lords!"

"Save it for the authorities, PJ," the guy says dryly. "If I understand you correctly, you do not wish to return to Paris under my supervision. When that would provide you and your sister with all the protection you need."

Annabel squints at me anxiously. "The Marquets will protect *me*, too?" she asks hopefully. "I won't have to testify against my parents if we just go back to Paris with you now?"

"I'm sure once M. Marquet takes one look at you, Annabel, he would be happy to host you in his home and take care of whatever extradition issues you are facing." The guy gives a little knowing chuckle in my direction. "My uncle loves beautiful women."

Denis leans in to touch Annabel's cheek.

"No!" I scream. I rush at him frantically, grabbing the tea kettle in my hand, knocking him out of his chair and away from my sister. "Don't touch her!"

Denis's head hits the floor with a sickening crash. His eyes roll back into his head.

"Oh, my God!" Annabel shrieks. "What did you do?"

I look down at the kettle in my right hand—there's a spot of blood on it. I stare at my wrist, both covered in bruises from when Marco grabbed me. "I don't know," I say, not recognizing my own voice. "I don't know."

"PJ, his nose is bleeding! I think he's unconscious!" Annabel leans down and slaps at Denis's cheek. "Denis! Wake up!"

Denis doesn't respond.

"I don't get it, PJ. What is going on?"

"I just . . . I just can't live like this anymore," I say, swaying. I suddenly feel so tired I am not sure if I can stand up. The room seems to spin. I look down at Denis's limp body, wondering coldly if he might be dead.

Suddenly the future looms before me like a black tunnel. For a second an image of a girl—one who looks just like me but with cropped hair—flashes in my mind. It's the girl who gave me the ride on Christmas Day, the art student. In that moment, it's as though this alternate life, a totally other reality, swims by me. I could have been her. I could have had a different life than this.

But I only have this one. It's hopeless. It's all so hopeless.

"What are we going to do?" Annabel asks in a shrill, panicked voice. Her skin is deathly pale against her shiny dark hair.

"I don't care." I look down at Denis again, dark red blood pooling around his face. I feel like I may puke, or pass out. "I just can't keep living like this. Come on. We have to get out of here. And we're not coming back." I grip the table for support, a chilling certainty numbing me. "Ever."

L'EPIPHANIE
Epiphany

25. OLIVIA

Great Men

___

*T*homas is scarily calm the whole drive to Périgueux. The only way I can tell he's upset is that when he lets go of the Vespa handles, the leather on them is slick with his palm sweat.

For much of the drive, I look longingly toward the Mediterranean Sea. I'd always dreamed of going to the French Riviera, but not in January. Not under circumstances like these.

At a supermarket in Nîmes, Thomas stops to make a call. I step away to give him a little privacy. Grazing the magazine rack, I see it again—the issue of *Gala* that has the Marquets on the cover.

"Non! Il ne s'agit pas seulement de toi, Maman. Il s'agit aussi de moi—et Papa," Thomas abruptly shouts into his phone. I run to his side.

"Thomas! What's going on?" I lay my head on his shoulder, trying to impart comfort through my touch. Obviously, Mme Rouille is not excited about Thomas and me going to Périgueux. I can hear her tinny voice through Thomas's phone, demanding that he turn around and come back to Paris.

"Papa *died* because of M. Marquet," Thomas says in English, apparently so that I can understand how strong his feelings are, too. "Please do not worry—I won't do anything stupid."

Mme Rouille is still talking, but Thomas hangs up.

"Thomas, what are you going to do when you see M. Marquet? If you threaten him, he might hurt you," I say shakily, getting that familiar chill. I want to find PJ, but this might not be the best way. I know I should support Thomas, but this seems reckless.

"I want to speak to him," Thomas mutters. "Face *à* face."

I nod. "*Je te comprends.*"

A few words around the town of Périgueux point us in the direction of the Marquets' château. Everyone knows where the local magistrate lives.

We drive up to the enormous darkened house. Far afield, in a smaller house, some lights are on. After pounding on the heavy front door of the main house for a long time, Thomas starts walking briskly toward the small one.

"*Bonsoir,*" a woman greets us at the door. "*Est-ce que je peux vous aider?*"

The anger in Thomas's face is clear, and I can't blame this woman for clutching the side of the doorframe in thinly veiled fear. I try to soften the tension with a small smile.

"*J'essaie de trouver a mon amie,*" I explain. "I'm trying to find my friend, PJ. Penelope. Do you know her?"

"Ah, Penelope," the woman says. "*Oui*. She is the adopted daughter of *les Marquets*. They are all on vacation together in Normandy."

"*Normandie?*" Thomas echoes. "What are they doing in Normandy? Who are you?"

"Penelope has family visiting," the woman says. "*Je suis* Marie. My husband and I take care of the estate for *les Marquets*."

"Nice to meet you." I force a smile. "*Mais je ne comprends pas. Mon amie* Penelope—she is on vacation with them? But weren't the Marquets in the Dordogne just recently, for New Year's?"

"*Ah, oui*," Marie replies. "Mademoiselle Penelope went to visit her sister, *apparement*. And then the Marquets joined them. The whole group is *actuellement* traveling with the Marquets' nephew, Denis. He is a friend of my son. They grew up together, always playing here at the château. Do you know him, too?" Her noticeable fearfulness seems to abate as the conversation carries on. The mention of her son brings a smile to her tenderly wrinkled face. "They are a bit older than you two, I believe. Denis lives in Paris now, *je pense*."

I shake my head. "*Non*, I don't know him. I don't know your son, either." I'm confounded by what Marie is telling us. For the last couple days, since Thomas and I took off toward Cannes, through everything that Mme Rouille had told us about the Marquets, I'd been more and more certain that PJ had run away because the Marquets had presented some sort of danger to her. And now, Marie is saying that PJ—and her sister, who I've never once heard about before now—is on a family vacation with them?

Thomas interjects roughly. "So *les Marquets*—they are not here?"

Marie shakes her head. "*Non, chéri.*"

This woman makes me feel so much better. I trust her for some reason.

Mme Rouille's story, though. She wouldn't have gotten so upset if she didn't truly believe my friend was totally in danger!

We return to the dirt road where we left the Vespa parked at the edge of the drive. I want to look on the bright side. Whatever is going on with PJ, it sounds like she's with her sister, so she must be safe. Right?

"Fuck!" Thomas suddenly screams into the cold night, kicking the Vespa tire, then kicking it again, even harder. "Fuck!!!"

"Thomas!" I rush to him, trying to contain his thin, wriggling body in my arms. "Thomas, it's okay!"

"It is never okay," Thomas says, his face hard like a stone. "These people, this man. He hurt *Maman*. He killed *mon père*. My whole life—my whole life is a *lie* because of this man!"

"Thomas, what do you mean?"

"We moved to Tunisia because of M. Marquet. I know that now because you told me," Thomas spits out. "But what I have never told you is why I'm studying to be a doctor. I only do it for my mom, so that she can be proud of me. I hate science. I hate the bodies we have to touch, the horrible lights in the lab. I hate the textbooks and *je déteste* the other medical students. I do it because my dad was a doctor, and I know the only thing that could make *Maman* happy again is if I became one, too!"

I try to reason with him. "But Thomas, you don't have to do that. This thing between your parents and M. Marquet—it isn't about you. And besides, it's over. It was a long time ago."

Even as I hear myself say the words, I know how impossible it will be for Thomas to put these recent revelations behind him. His childhood in Tunisia, the death of M. Rouille—these are the things that define him.

But unlike yesterday or the day before, when I felt like I could comfort him, protect him from this pain, today I am at a loss.

Thomas sinks down, crouching on the Marquets' white gravel driveway for a long time. I crouch next to him, rubbing my hand up and down his back. He's wearing Xavier's leather jacket. It makes him look not tougher, like a leather jacket ought to, but even more baby-faced. Despite having been together for so many days in a row, I feel a strange distance growing between us, like I am thinking about things that I don't necessarily want to share.

Finally, Thomas gets to his feet. He gives me a light kiss on my lips. "Olivia."

"*Oui?*"

"We don't know what we are doing anymore," he says. "Let's go back to Paris."

I nod. "Okay."

Mme Rouille and Thomas have a long talk, late into the night, as soon as we get home. I know I don't need to be a part of it, and besides, I'm aching with exhaustion. I go to bed with a cup of chamomile tea.

As I fall asleep, I try to find solace in the fact that despite not finding PJ, at least I spoke to someone who's absolutely sure of where she is. Besides, school starts in another day, and according to what Marie said, it sounds like she'll be there.

But it still doesn't make sense. Why did PJ not tell me that her sister was coming to France? And why would she leave Jay that weird postcard if she was just going on a trip? And why did she email Jay to forget her?

Sunday morning, Thomas is asleep on the couch in the living room. I sit in the easy chair and wait for him to wake up.

"*Bonjour*," he finally groans sleepily. "Come here."

I go and kiss him. "Good morning."

"Get dressed. I want to take you somewhere."

Once I get dressed, Thomas and I take the métro to the Left Bank. We aren't as affectionate as the last time we were in Paris together; I notice that right away. It's like our souls are too tired, too worried, too upset, to find pleasure in one another.

Thomas pulls me up the stairs and out of the Cluny–La Sorbonne stop. When we reach street level, the Boulevard Saint-Germain is packed with people. Along the fences surrounding the church are little booths selling souvenirs and jewelry. There's a cozy feeling to the shops and the restaurants in the area. This is, after all, one of the most visited neighborhoods in the entire world. You can hear as much English as French spoken, but also Japanese, Italian, Russian, and many other languages.

Thomas turns down the busy Boulevard Saint-Michel, where the area begins to feel like a college campus, with inexpensive chain eateries filling up with students on break from school but without much else to do, and used book and record stores selling paperbacks in bins on the street for only a euro each. "Are you going to show me around your school?" I ask Thomas.

"I can, if you want." Thomas turns another corner. "But let's go inside the Panthéon first."

"Okay," I agree, despite not really being in the mood for tourist attractions.

The Panthéon is, of course, one of the main sites of Paris, but whenever I read the description of what it was in my guidebook, it never seemed that interesting to me.

The Panthéon is a neoclassical hall wherein many of France's "great men" are entombed. (One exception is Napoleon, whose final resting place is across town at the Hôtel des Invalides, in a giant tomb I have been to on a class trip lead by Mme Cuchon and Mlle Vailland, the history teacher.)

I have a vague idea of where the Panthéon is but let Thomas lead the way.

At the gates of the Luxembourg Gardens, Thomas takes a left, and the Panthéon rises ahead of us, the streets arranged in a circle to accommodate its grand size. A large dome rests atop what would otherwise be just a stately French building.

"It used to be a church," Thomas tells me as he buys us each a student-rate ticket. "But now it is a sanctuary for those . . . departed souls . . ." Thomas struggles for the right English words, "who have given everything to bringing France glory."

I contemplate Thomas carefully. Is he goofing right now? The way he's talking seems very formal, very passionate, and I'm not sure if I'm meant to laugh or to nod my head in solemn agreement. I busy myself looking around the place.

In the middle of the Panthéon is a giant pendulum, swinging back and forth across the atrium. All the visitors stop and stare at it for a long time, including Thomas. It swings this way, and then that way, again and again. After several minutes, Thomas turns to me and gives me a revelatory smile. "Amazing, isn't it?"

I swallow. "Yes, definitely."

After admiring the beautiful marble of the first floor, Thomas takes me to the mausoleums area in the basement, where he points out all the great men of France, telling me what they did and why they are special enough to be celebrated in French history.

When we get to the dark wooden tomb of Voltaire, Thomas places his hands on the smooth side of it and closes his eyes. I am sure we are about to get scolded, but no guards come. Thomas seems to be communing in some way with the giant box of bones. I've never seen anything like it. At one point he even puts his forehead on the surface of the tomb, and whispers something.

When he looks back at me, his eyes are wet with feeling. "I can *feel* him." I figure he's still emotional from yesterday.

I force myself to smile and nod. "Totally."

Thomas's conversation with Voltaire seems to have invigorated him. He visits the rest of the tombs with so much exuberance and pride for the accomplishments of the men buried in them. He's so buoyant in his appreciation that he's being continually shushed not only by docents but also by other visitors and tourists.

"Olivia—this place—it just fills me up. I can't help but want to dance. Like you—I want to fly in the air. I just love this country so much. The beauty of these lives! The risks they took! Their superior minds, all focused on the betterment of French life, French culture! It's too much for me sometimes!"

"I guess so!" I look around, hoping no one who speaks English heard him. He's just so . . . intense.

Thomas and I sit on a bench for a while, and Thomas puts his arm around me. "I wanted to share this with you, Olivia, because you are so special to me. And I know you love France, and I just love to teach you more things about it. I love to be with you. I'm so happy you stayed in Paris. So very, very happy." Thomas buries his head into my neck.

I start to laugh and shush him at the same time. "Thomas! You are too crazy."

Thomas swivels off the bench and pulls me with him. "My dorm is not far from here. Would you like to see it?"

"I would love to," I say quietly, because I do want to see his dorm, finally, but also because this place is starting to creep me out.

When I finally draw back the curtains in Thomas's little student residence on the Rue d'Ulm, it's dark, and I know I need to get back to the apartment in Ternes. Tomorrow is the first day of spring term.

"I've got to go," I whisper. Thomas is dozing with his wire-rim glasses off, his blonde eyelashes long and thick on the tender white of his uncovered face. He responds by pulling my practically naked body back over to him, and I'm tempted to stay under these warm blankets all night.

I wriggle away finally and stoop down to find my jeans. "Oh, Olivia," Thomas moans. "Don't go. You look so beautiful."

"You can't even see me," I tease him. "You don't have your glasses on."

"It doesn't matter," Thomas says. "You are the most gorgeous of anyone."

Hooking the buttons of my coat together, I grab my green Longchamp bag and lean over to kiss him for the last time until tomorrow.

"*Je t'aime,* Olivia," Thomas calls to me just before the door to his room closes behind me.

I don't answer him. For some reason, tonight, those words don't come.

The cold night surrounds me, tickles my ears as I make my way home. The streets are unusually quiet. Suddenly, a question pops into my head: Did I only fall in love with Thomas because it was forbidden and different?

He was so fascinating—*is* so fascinating. But he's also . . . *conflicted*. I thought he was driven, and now I see that he's flailing. He's only just starting to find himself, starting with the realization that being a doctor is not the path he wants to be on. He's not at all sure of his goals. Unlike me. Completely unlike me.

I think of Vince, and how Vince and I wanted all the same things. UCLA, commitment, eventually to have a family together. I know Vince and I had to break up—I simply did not love him anymore—but I miss him. I miss how our dreams once went so well together.

Back at my homestay, I find Mme Rouille has let Jay into the apartment. He's waiting in my room, sitting on the twin bed.

"Have you seen Alex?" he asks as soon as I walk in. His face is stricken.

"No . . ." I'm confused to see Jay here. I thought he was still in Cannes with Alex. I didn't know they'd come back.

"Liv—you might want to . . . um." His voice is shaking and he looks a mess. I suddenly notice his jacket is buttoned lopsided. I've never seen Jay look disheveled like this.

"What is it, Jay?"

"You may want to sit down." He rubs his buzz-cut hair. "I have—"

"You can tell me!" I urge. He's so distressed, my heart starts beating rapidly, afraid of what he's going to say.

"I have . . . bad news. Very bad news. About PJ."

26. ALEX

This Can't Be Happening

*S*unday afternoon, I stop into the Galeries Lafayette and Le Printemps. Department stores usually bring me comfort, but today they seem like they're gagging me with unwanted merchandise on sale for rock-bottom prices, and all the people picking through it look pathetic.

I wander aimlessly along the Grand Boulevards, passing the two famous gates at their eastern end: the Porte Saint Denis and the smaller Porte Saint Martin. At the Place de la République, I see two midwestern girls from my program, drinking café au laits in front of a cheesy chain bistro. They are wrapped up in their coats, mittens, and scarves, talking so animatedly they don't see me. They must have each just gotten back from their trips home for the holidays. I focus my gaze elsewhere so I can pass without having to say hi.

I feel like I'm in purgatory, waiting for my final judgment. I'm surrounded by Paris—beautiful, wonderful Paris, where my life was supposed to change for good. The city that was my refuge, my fresh start, now just seems like the gateway to a fresh hell. Here I just made everything worse. And now I am going to have to go home. Back to Brooklyn. Back to school with Jeremy. Back to my old self.

Most of the Programme Américain students went back to the U.S. to see their families for the holidays, or like Olivia, their families came to visit them. Some, like George and Drew, traveled with their families and *then* went home, too.

Zack has been adamant since the very beginning of fall term that he did not want to go back to Memphis for a suburban Evangelical Christmas. I don't blame him! But I wonder . . . is that maybe why he got so upset at me in Cannes? Was spending his break with me a disappointment?

I know that it was. From the moment I left the gay club to sit with Jay at that bar, just as the New Year was about to be rung in, Zack must have known that I was becoming interested in Jay. Cold, sick guilt pinches my gut. How could I have been so thoughtless? Why do I always want things that get me in so much trouble?

I pat my fur hat to make sure it's still tight on my head. I really, really don't want to lose it. In some ways, it's all I really have to show for my trip.

I pass Paris Store, the gargantuan Chinese grocery store known for selling stunning pottery for next to nothing. They also stock different kinds of produce from all over Asia—papayas and onions and broccoli that you wouldn't even recognize. All of my mom's French friends come to this neighborhood to stock up on things like that—silk shoes to wear around the house, pretty lamps and scarves, cheap, delicious fat-free ramen noodles to eat during a busy week. They love finding out a certain fruit gets rid of wrinkles, so they'll buy a kilo. None of it ever really works, but half the fun is just exploring the city.

I know myself. I know I can figure a way out of having to leave Paris. No one has actually kicked me out of the program yet; as far as I know my mom and my host parents still don't even know that I failed the Final Comp. Mme Cuchon may have sent the letter about the test, but she has to actually remove me from the program, right? And hasn't it always just been a rumor that you get kicked out of the Programme Américain if you fail? Maybe I still have a chance. . .

I pass a Vietnamese restaurant with bright red and orange banners outside of it. Through the windows, I see French couples sipping steaming bowls of soup.

When I told Jay that I am half-Vietnamese, he immediately asked me if I'd tried *banh mi* in Belleville yet. I told him I didn't even know what that is, and Jay was *shocked*. A Vietnamese sandwich of sorts, *banh mi* is supposed to be some of the best fast food in Paris. Go figure!

Jay's homestay is in eastern Paris, a neighborhood called Montreuil that I've never had occasion to visit. Another guy in the Programme Américain also lives out there, and the two of them have explored the immigrant enclaves in the area at length. Jay had directed me toward a certain place, a tiny little storefront on the Boulevard de Belleville crammed in between a travel agency and a laundromat, where I could try my first one.

It's funny, so many people know more about Vietnam and Vietnamese culture than I do. Why would I? My mom hated it there, and when she kicked my dad out, it wasn't like she tried hard to teach me about the place. She only ever went there that one time. If I was anything, it was French-American, not Vietnamese-American, whenever I had to think about my identity.

But isn't it funny how other people's perceptions creep into how you define yourself?

Like when I got to Paris, I knew I loved Olivia and Zack from the get-go. They asked me why I'd come to Paris, and I explained about my dad and my mom living here before I was born. They never said, "So, what are you?" like the Texan twins did, sealing my hatred for them forever. For Olivia and Zack, the fact that I don't look Caucasian, but I don't look totally Asian, either, didn't matter to them. It didn't make them assume anything at all, except maybe that my life was exciting and different from theirs.

But Jay's reaction was totally different from either my friends *or* the ignorant people like Patty and Tina. Instead of ignoring or focusing on the differences between the way I look and the way he looks, he asked me openly about being part Vietnamese. He wanted to hear more about it and, for some reason, that really felt good.

I buy a *banh mi* to go, and I eat it sitting on a bench near the Couronnes station. Then I shuffle through the market that runs down the Boulevard de Belleville and past the Place Ménilmontant, almost all the way to the Père Lachaise Cemetery. The market is full of dark-skinned men and women, taking their time selecting the best produce for the best price. There is boisterous haggling at some stalls, even some outright arguing at others. Kids paw at the Tunisian and Moroccan pastries for sale, hoping for a sample. One little girl, her pink sweat suit dirty with age, stares at me as I walk through the crowd in my black wool coat and my tidy Repetto flats. I smile at her, and her teeth are blindingly white when she smiles back. For some reason, she makes me want to cry.

This neighborhood is so different from Cambronne, where Zack and I have our homestays. Cambronne is middle-class Paris, a scattering of ethnic restaurants catering to a clientele of white-collared office workers and the like. The restaurants here in Belleville aren't like that. They're filled with people speaking foreign tongues: Arabic, Wolof, Chinese. The prices they charge for beer and coffee are ridiculously cheap compared to what Zack and I pay during our breaks and after school in Ternes.

My *banh mi* was pretty good. The chicken was sweet and sour, drenched in a zesty marinade and cooked just right. I think I'll take Zack to try one when he gets back from Amsterdam. I'll take him for lunch, and I'll explain that in a weak moment I developed a crush on Jay, but it wasn't real. I just want us all to be friends.

JUST HAD A BANH MI, I decide to text Jay. THANKS FOR THE REC. HOW R U?

I sit and watch passerbys as I wait for Jay to text me back. When my phone beeps, I suck in my breath in anticipation. I haven't seen him since I took the train back to Paris yesterday. For all I know he is still in Cannes, waiting in the suite for PJ to show up.

MEET ME AT PERE LACHAISE, Jay's text back reads. I AM AT INGRES'S GRAVE.

Well, that answers *that* question. And PJ must be very much still on Jay's mind.

I hustle down the Boulevard de Ménilmontant and climb up the back stairs to the Père Lachaise Cemetery. The last time I was here was when Zack and I came here for Toussaint. That day, among the potted plants and the bouquets people left on the grave of Edith Piaf, I left an old locket on her grave. When Zack asked me what it was, I'd told him it was just something I'd found on the métro. But in truth, I'd been toting that old locket around in my change purse for years, since seventh grade, at least. I'd wanted to leave Edith something special, and that old locket, with its broken clasp and its rusted chain, seemed appropriate. My mom had bought it for me at some crafts fair in Westchester. I'd worn it religiously until it broke a few months later.

I'd left it there kind of on a whim; after all, the locket was junk. But I also liked giving it to Edith because when I remember my parents' divorce, and its aftermath, I remember my mom listening to Edith Piaf records and running a bath every night. She loves Edith. So do I. And I liked giving the dead singer something that had been with me for so long, just like her music has.

Today's one of those days that's so melancholy that a cemetery feels like the right kind of place to spend the afternoon. At the top of the stairs, I scan the map of Père Lachaise. So many luminary figures are buried here: journalists, dictators, poets, actresses, and great artists.

My Gucci sunglasses firmly in place, I walk up the slight hill through the cemetery, trying not to let the late sun get in my eyes. Winter days are so short. I feel like I just woke up, and yet the sun is already making a pointed descent to the west. When the glare dips behind a tree, I gasp to see that I've practically stumbled into a burial. You forget, in a cemetery as grand and as crammed full as the Père Lachaise, that people are still buried here in their family plots or mausoleums all the time.

All in black, a small group of people is gathered around a headstone, murmuring prayers and saying their final good-byes. I watch for a long time, hidden behind a large monument for the deceased members of some French family from earlier this century. My chest feels heavy. By the time the family starts to disperse it has gotten dark, and I'm weeping under my sunglasses, even though I don't know these people and probably never will.

There's been so much sorrow over this winter break.

I start to run, tripping over the crumbling older graves, the rotting chestnuts, and the mounds of icy snow frozen over soggy leaves on the ground. I run uphill, my Repettos slippery on the cobblestones. I just have to get out of here, away from the bustling market, the poverty seeping into the street, the miles of dead people surrounding me in every direction.

Finally, I see Jay. Beautiful, sweet Jay. I want, so badly, to run directly into his strong arms. All I want is to know that things are going to get better.

Since he doesn't step forward for a hug, I keep my distance. Maybe he's afraid to touch me. Maybe, like me, he knows there really was something between us, something that we have to bury.

To keep my hands busy, I light a Gauloise, watching out for cemetery attendants. I'm not sure if this is allowed.

"I just came from Olivia's homestay." He's a bit breathless and his voice sounds frantic. "You haven't heard?" Jay stares at the Gauloise.

"No. I mean, heard about what?" I notice that Jay's eyes are rimmed with red. I'm not sure if I want to know, but I ask him the terrible question anyway. "Jay. What is it?"

When he tells me, my cigarette falls out of my hand. It rolls down the stone path, extinguishing itself in a puddle of melted snow.

"She's dead."

The soggy cigarette floats there. I can't look at Jay. I know the pain in his face will kill me.

"Mme Cuchon emailed everyone enrolled in the program this morning. You didn't get it? They found two backpacks and a joint suicide note. It was PJ and her sister, Annabel. They jumped off a bridge into the freezing Seine. Not in Paris—in Normandy. Near someplace called Rouen."

"*Our* PJ?" She is ours. We loved her, and we looked for her, and we tried to read her thoughts. She belongs to us, to Jay, to Livvy, to Zack, and to me.

"Our PJ. My PJ. She killed herself." Jay shakily lays a bouquet of white roses onto Ingres's grave. His voice sounds hoarse, full of anguish and disbelief. I want to go to him. I hold back because that wouldn't be right, not now, not ever. "This is all I have left of her."

Later that night, back in my bedroom at my homestay I scroll through my texts messages and missed calls, counting how many times my mom has tried to call me in the last couple weeks.

I click on her number, and wait for her to answer in New York.

"Mom," I say when she answers, my voice breaking a little. "I need you. Please come."

27. ZACK

Illusions

An American family gets on the train in Brussels. I can tell they are from Arizona because they are all decked out in Arizona Cardinals gear, from their Starter jackets to their bright red socks to their matching sweatpants. They don't seem to notice how much they stick out, or how odd it is to promote your favorite sports team on a continent where they don't even play.

When they pull bags of food from Burger King out of their carryalls, I can't help but let a tiny guffaw escape. If I wasn't traveling alone tonight, I'd have been a goner. That is just too perfect, too horribly American to handle.

Belgium is where French fries were invented—and this family went to Burger King?

Bobby would have made the best snarky comment right about now, something that would have made me go from quietly giggling in my seat to truly wetting my pants with laughter. The poor family can't help that they are the way they are, but seriously—Bobby would have had them in his clutches from the moment they got on the train.

I'm still grinning thinking of how funny Bobby is. He really was the saving grace during my first few days in Amsterdam. Pierson was so gosh darned *obnoxious* with his starry-eyed devotion to Hannes, and Bobby was the levity that made that bearable.

Maybe Pierson was right, though, earlier today outside the Van Gogh Museum. Maybe Bobby is cooler than I realized. Maybe he and I would have made a cute couple. I don't know for sure if he was trying to kiss me, or hook up with me. It just felt that way at the time, and to be honest, I was still sort of stoned from the hashish we smoked before the Anne Frank House. Something about that memorial made me feel so frightened.

I mean, isn't that kind of understandable?

If you want to hook up with a recently out-of-the-closet guy, don't take him to a place that reminds him how much people have suffered for being different, okay?

I think about that afternoon, with me and Bobby soaking wet on the side of the river, and I can't stop laughing. What a classic picture that would make!

I pull out my camera and click through the couple dozen photos I took this break. There's me and Alex in our slippers at her dad's house in Montauban, eating take-out gyros in front of that huge TV. Then there's me and some of the guys at the club in Toulouse, my new best friends, if only for a night. Me, Alex, and Jay dressed up on the balcony in

Cannes—we had the room-service guy bringing Alex a Coca-Cola Light take our picture before we went downstairs to the hotel bar. Oh, dang, here's the Amsterdam bike tour, that crisp, breezy day we rode around with just sweatshirts on.

I decide to text Bobby.

U KNOW WHAT?

Bobby takes about ten minutes to text back.

WHAT DUDE.

I'M AN IDIOT.

TRUE TRUE. WHAT MAKES U SAY THAT, THO?

A LIL PERSPECTIVE. U KNOW WHAT ELSE?

WHAT?

I'D LOVE IT IF U CAME FOR SPRING BREAK.

REALLY? IT'S NOT 2 WEIRD?

NOT AT ALL. I'D LOVE 2 SEE U AGAIN, SEE WHAT HAPPENS.

THAT WOULD BE V COOL. LET'S PLAN ON IT. JUST DON'T PUSH ME INTO ANY MORE CANALS.

U DO LOOK PRETTY HOT ALL WET LIKE THAT.

PROMISE!

K. I PROMISE.

OK C U IN A COUPLE MONTHS.

I'm snoozing with a slight smile on my face when the train jolts into Rouen station, where I have to make my connection. I dash over to the next platform and hop on the express to Paris Saint-Lazare, hoping there are still some window seats left. There is just one, in the back, and even though I wasn't assigned to it, I sit there anyway. I aim to fall back asleep leaned against the window, instead of on some old

French lady who would find it most unwelcome.

Rouen. I remember the name of the town from *Madame Bovary*. We read it in my World Lit class, and some of the PTA had been up in arms at us reading a book with such tawdry content. That's Memphis for you. Possibly the most exalted of all French novels, and half our town doesn't want their precious kids to be subjected to that kind of devilishly sexual literature. My own parents were among those who wanted our whole high school's reading list to come under a review from their pastor at our church. My dad gave a speech at a school-board meeting and everything.

It was *so* mortifying.

I read the book anyway, while the fight between the teachers (who want to educate their students about the world) and the parents (who want their kids to think everyone grows up to live sexlessly behind a white picket fence) raged on.

I think that Rouen is where Emma Bovary went to meet her lover. I peer out onto the train platform, wondering what other secrets this little town hides. Did Emma leave them a legacy of torrid affairs and senseless deaths and hardships? I let my imagination run away for a minute, picturing the gorgeous scenes as Flaubert described them: Emma dressed in a dark cloak, hiding the spun silk of her dress and the bright satin of her perfect gloves and slippers; the hotel where the couple would meet, decadent and wonderful just like their affair.

I watch two girls hustle down the platform, each of them with long hair to their waists. They have a similar gait to their fast-paced walk, loping and graceful, like gazelles in an *Animal Planet* special. The two girls are tall and most likely beautiful, and one of them, the blond one, wears a scarf in a color that I recognize from somewhere.

The train pulls up its brakes and announces that we're headed straight to Paris Saint-Lazare, with no stops. It moves ahead, at first almost imperceptibly, then faster as it picks up momentum.

As we pass the two girls, I remember where I last saw that color of bluish purple. The periwinkle yarn is particularly striking against the white blond hair of the girl who is wearing it.

Wait a second.

"Lord-a-mercy!" I shout, pounding on the window. "PJ!"

But this train has already left the station.

The End

For their contributions, big and small, to the process of writing and publishing *Wanderlust*:

Molly Friedrich, Lucy Carson, Lexa Hillyer, Ben Schrank, Anne Heltzel, Jessica Kaufman, Jane Smiley, Bill Silag and Barbara Mittleman, Doug Wagner, Jan Wagner, Eva Lange, Conor Callahan, the Alliance Francaise in Paris, and the Katy Geissert Civic Center Library in Torrance, California—

Merci beaucoup!